THE GIZA DEATH STAR RESTORED

By Carl Joseph DeMarco

Cover design by John Neira

Cover illustration by Napoleon Duheme

http://www.lostbreadcomic.com/

ISBN: 9781797497976
Imprint: Independently published

To Joseph P. Farrell, the most important nonfiction writer alive today, who urges us to *own the culture.*

Table of Contents

Everything in this book is true, except for the story.

Foreword

If there is a single kernel of truth in this work of historical fiction, the great wars of the twentieth century were more complex than most of us realize. In our current era of disinformation and "fake news," it's not hard to imagine how easily a narrative could have been controlled in the first half of the twentieth century. Is it possible that the beginnings and even the endings of these global conflicts happened in much different circumstances? Imagine a world in which the seemingly endless armed conflicts of today are sequential to the great wars of the past, with more operators on either side than you ever imagined. Carl Joseph DeMarco delivers a thought-provoking page-turner that may have you turning to Google to fact-check the history you've been taught.

Carl has spent years interviewing hundreds of authors, academics, independent researchers, and heretics of myriad disciplines. *The Giza Death Star Restored* is a remarkable synthesis of the information Carl has gleaned from American writer, theologian, and alternative media personality, Dr. Joseph P. Farrell, that takes on a fantastic thrill ride of possibilities (or, perhaps more accurately, *probabilities).* With a new twist on the familiar narrative of "Cowboys and Indians" of the American past, the novel is a tempest of Nazis, Natives, and Illuminati, all wrapped tightly in an intriguing package of alternative thinking and ancient mystery.

Over the last few years, *The Grimerica Show* has interviewed people and groups similar to those that fascinate

Mr. DeMarco. The various theories and scientific inquiry that we both have gravitated towards are often being recognized and accepted by even the staunchest of critics and skeptics, which invokes a strong curiosity about anything that has been pejoratively described as "fringe" by those indoctrinated by mainstream thinking. It has slowly become clear that many "conspiracy theories" aren't theories at all, in large part due to the broad dissemination of information in the Internet Age. What we are awake to now was only a tickle of curiosity years ago, as many of these subjects were, and occasionally still are, difficult to accept. Under significant scrutiny, however, our denial faded into acceptance.

The history books will be rewritten, as they continually are when new information becomes accessible. We will reevaluate the timeline of human history and the technological prowess of our ancestors. It is my personal hope, ultimately, to experience the full revelation of these mysteries (I am trying to be patient). A single person will not reveal them, but rather a collective, cumulative effort of the many alternative voices who endeavor tirelessly to find what matters most: Truth. Carl Joseph DeMarco, fortunately for us, is one of those voices.

It took me years to realize the importance and prevalence of such truths. Sometimes it seems I've lived in two worlds; the before-and-after feeling that comes with personal revelation. You likely know the feeling if you've pondered these subjects.

This novel seamlessly weaves ancient mysteries with our contemporary mythos of advanced technologies, international intrigue, and shamanic powers. Many of what are now commonly considered "conspiracy theories," may in short time become verifiable fact, and a work of historical fiction can effectively show that possibility. Historical fiction occupies the liminal space between hard fact and creative license. It's the perfect playground to explore and easily digest new ideas.

How else could we better enjoy a story about a race to save the world from power-hungry elites trying to activate suppressed ancient technology? Perhaps after reading this book you'll have, if you don't already, a greater sense of wonder and possibility about the misunderstood machinations of the Powers-That-Be and those that seek to challenge them. Maybe, with a dash of luck, we will soon find ourselves standing on a new foundation of truth that benefits us all. Enjoy.

Darren Grimes and Graham Dunlop

Co-Hosts of *The Grimerica Show*

The Igloo, Alberta, Canada

Chapter 1

The heavy canvas tarpaulin rippled in the wind over their heads as dust blew in and swirled in the pit. It dried their throats and mouths and coated their skin. Yet they seemed nonplussed as they went about their task.

They were speaking German and went about their work with great alacrity. Around them in the pit were ancient remains and artifacts reputed to be Sumerian, but some of the men knew they were much older. It was the subject of a joint German and French expedition invited to Iraq by Saddam Hussein.

However, only a few of the personnel assembled today were archeologists. Most were former Kommando Spezialkräfte, or KSK, Germany's special operations force. The man in charge of the operation began passing out US Government Issue desert camo BDUs. The assembled "troops" began to strip and put them on. This was a page right out of SS Lt. Colonel Otto Skorzeny's playbook.

Skorzeny is perhaps one of the most fascinating and unconquerable personages to emerge from World War II. He had a dueling scar on his left cheek which he wore proudly his entire life. His ingenuity, elusiveness and incredible luck were exceeded only by his evil. His daring and impossible raid to rescue the deposed Benito Mussolini made him a hero of the Waffen SS and a national hero in Germany, although his talent had been recognized long before that. He was hailed as "the most dangerous man in Europe."

In December 1944 during the Battle of the Bulge he dressed his operators in American uniforms, gave them vehicles painted with American insignia to travel around in, and instructed his best, often flawless, English speakers to spread chaos and disinformation among the American lines.

It created such havoc that American GI's had to start testing every Yank they ran into for "American-ness." Even

1

generals were waylaid and diverted by trivia about movies, baseball and state capitols. General Omar Bradley himself was delayed by such a checkpoint.

He gave himself up after the war and was charged with various war crimes that violated the Hague Convention of 1907 for wearing enemy uniforms behind enemy lines. Incredibly, he was acquitted. The most dangerous man in Europe remained in detention, however, awaiting a de-Nazification hearing, but escaped in 1948 with the help of three former SS officers that Skorzeny claims were aided by the Americans themselves.

Skorzeny went on to prosper in the post-war world. He became the quintessential post-war Nazi, devoted to the welfare of former SS members and spreading his skills in wreaking havoc, chaos and violence. Like every "good" Nazi, he went on to associate with wartime associates and help build the Nazi vision around the world, insidiously infecting governments and cultures everywhere they could.

This was all cleverly financed under the evil genius of Martin Bormann and Swiss Banker Francois Genoud, who, incidentally, was also the personal banker to the Bin Laden family (The Germans have a long history of weaponizing Islam). They also worked their own invention, the Bank of International Settlements, or BIS, due to its immunity from Swiss and international law. They made liberal use of BIS diplomatic pouches. DeutscheBank was another favorite institution.

Mainstream historians mistakenly believe that Bormann was killed at the end of the war, but there are three different reports of his death in three different places, all on the same day, and no body, until skeletal remains purported to be his turned up in 1972 at a Berlin construction site. They were coated with Peruvian mud.

Another associate of Skorzeny's was Reinhard Gehlen, a Nazi intelligence officer who ran CIA operations in Europe after that organization's inception and went on to lead West Germany's intelligence service, the BND.

Through the likes of Skorzeny, Gehlen, Genoud, Bormann and others, the Nazis pressed home their vision of world domination from places like San Carlos de Bariloche in Argentina, Madrid, Egypt, and quite possibly Israel. Yes, Israel, where the Mossad hired Skorzeny as a contract hitman and mole.

The history books are wrong. The Nazis were the clear winners in World War II. Germany, Italy and Japan certainly lost. The Allies also won, but only by facilitating the Nazi victory, a nightmarish twist they wouldn't be aware of until the next century.

These epitomes of post-war Nazism, however, did not advance their vision with public demonstrations, ostentatious displays of Nazi colors and insignia, or by displaying photos of Hitler prominently in their living rooms. No. They went about it by insidiously creeping into the worlds of high finance, politics and industry, and taking over Western intelligence agencies like the CIA and the BND.

The captured nations became instruments for advancing their globalist agenda, and even employed "former" Nazi sympathizers like billionaire George Soros and the Mossack-Fonseca law firm, itself co-founded by the son of an NCO in the Waffen SS. Trusting war-weary nations were easy prey, especially amidst Cold War paranoia. Paper Clip scientists weaved their way into the American bureaucracy. Powerful, sympathetic families like the Bushes helped establish financial concerns and connections to the highest levels of government. The process was repeated in Western state after Western state; wash, rinse, repeat.

The prodigious Colonel went on to advise Egyptian president Abdul Nasser and Argentinean dictator Juan Peron, where he is rumored to have had an affair with Peron's wife, Eva. From there he was close to San Carlos de Bariloche, the unofficial central command for post-war Nazis, and from which he could help direct much of the Cold War and social and cultural mayhem that unfolded in the following decades.

He concluded his career by setting up a mercenary

organization called the Paladin Group. They trained guerrilla groups and state security services alike. It was from Paladin that the weather-beaten men in the dig pit came. Although he did not leave any spawn of his own to pollute the earth, these were Skorzeny's spiritual children, and in many cases, the actual grandchildren of dedicated Nazis. Skorzeny was a darkly shining example of what the Nazis accomplished in the naïve, mis- and dis-informed world following World War II.

The mercenaries sprang from the pit. To the casual, or even careful observer, they appeared to be an American transport unit of some kind. Many held lightweight empty crates in pairs, others sported firearms. They were promptly formed up by their commander.

"From here on we speak only English. Any questions?"

There were none. The crates were tossed onto waiting M35s as the teams climbed on board. They shouted back and forth. Someone cursed loudly in German. A tall blonde woman in full battle fatigues appeared suddenly and shot him in the back of the head.

"What we have here is a failure to communicate," one of the men joked to his partner, in reference to the Struther Martin line from Cool Hand Luke.

The blonde stepped up to the pair. "You can crack any jokes you want, as long as they are in English." She turned, shouted instructions, and stormed off to harass someone else.

The men eyed each other with lecherous bemusement and nodded at what they both knew they were thinking, one man shaking his hand as if burned, the other drawing his fist rapidly to his waist. They were the honored grandsons of heroes, and they in their turn were raised to be proud and fearless in service of the 4th Reich, which would soon come to fruition.

Engines growled as the trucks rolled off in an ever increasing cloud of dust towards Baghdad. The mercs in the trucks poured over plans of what appeared to be the interior of a large building while others checked gear, restraining systems, and the crate interiors. Several of them had specially molded padding for the objects they were to hold.

Chapter 2

Before we see the results of our renegades' mission, let's flashback to Feb 5, 2003. Colin Powell is in front of the UN Security Council trying to pull off a "Stevenson" by pitching a war based on Intel and evidence he knows is bullshit. The idea was that Iraq had Weapons of Mass Destruction, or WMDs as they came to be known.

Some sources say that the WMDs were never found. The New York Times printed an article in October 2014 that stated over 5,000 chemical weapons were eventually found. Other sources say that the WMDs the US went in to recover were the ones sold to Iraq by President Bush's father former President George H. W. Bush. Other sources report that the WMDs of interest were not WMDs in the modern sense at all.

To understand this, we must take a fantastic journey back in time and examine impossible, and yet highly probable facts. Let's start with something solid: The Sphinx. Egyptologists tell us it was carved around 2500 B.C. by the Pharaoh Khafre. But was it?

We know from the brilliant work of geologist Robert M. Schoch of Boston University and researcher John Anthony West that the Sphinx shows the effects of water erosion that could not have occurred at the time of the Ancient Egyptians. In fact, it must have been built thousands of years earlier at the very least. It may even have been built before the last Ice Age.

We know from science therefore that at least one element of the Giza complex predates dynastic Egypt. Could other structures at Giza be as old?

Recently, the claim that Khufu built the Great Pyramid fell apart when Scott Creighton proved that the only shred of evidence tying Khufu to its construction was a 19th Century forgery. That shred was an ochre cartouche scrawled on the wall in a sealed chamber and allegedly discovered by Howard Vyse by blasting his way into the chamber with gunpowder in 1837. The authenticity of the discovery has been challenged ever since. Creighton carefully examined the diaries of Howard Vyse and his staff and demonstrated conclusively that the whole thing was a sham, a hoax devised for personal and national glory.

So let us consider what we have so far: A Sphinx that predates Dynastic Egypt by thousands of years, at least, and a pyramid whose provenance is completely unknown. The standard narrative of the Giza complex starts to unravel.

Other outstanding researchers have discovered other anomalies. For example Robert Bauval discovered that the three main pyramids of the Giza Plateau have an uncanny resemblance to the constellation Orion 12,000 years ago. Not only that, but the Sphinx is perfectly positioned to welcome the rising of Leo at the same time. Suddenly, we are in Schoch and West's time frame for the geological dating of the Sphinx.

But what does all this have to do with WMDs and the Iraq war, you ask? We're coming to that. It begins with the work of British Egyptologist Sir William Flinders Petrie. What he discovered in Egypt, among many other important discoveries, were tool marks in Egyptian artifacts that could not have been made by the Ancient Egyptians with any of their known toolkit. Most puzzling of all were drill marks and levels of precision that would have been impossible with anything the Egyptians had to work with. Petrie surmised that either the Egyptians had tools that were not showing up in the archeological record, or someone else had built everything the Egyptians were getting credit for.

Rather than race ahead to solve these mysteries, other Egyptologists ignored him and went on buttressing their outrageous claims and timelines with obfuscations and gobbledygook. You wonder why they would do this when some of the most remarkable evidence for the most remarkable advances in human history were before them. We will soon find out.

Enter Christopher Dunn, a machinist and engineer inspired by Petrie's work. He picked up where Petrie left off and published the summation of his work in *The Giza Power Plant,* which presents a very convincing hypothesis for the Great Pyramid as a giant power generating machine. His case is detailed and rigorous, right down to the chemistry, probable missing parts, construction, and operation. It's as if the thing was a humongous harmonic oscillator.

Do you see where we're going with this?

Just in case, let's summarize: geological and astronomical evidence supports a date for the Giza complex of such great antiquity that it "pre-dates the Flood," as alternative researchers like to put it. Furthermore, we have technical, hardcore engineering evidence, that the Egyptians could not have built the pyramids or made many of the associated artifacts. Could it be that they are a kind of legacy civilization of something much older and much more advanced?

Sounds crazy. But the Nazi scientists and archeologists under Himmler's Ahnenerbe were digging all over the Middle East looking for it. They dug for clay tablets that might reveal secrets of a lost technology. They dug for parts of this lost technology. And back home they dug into physics to make it reality. The secret technology developed by the Nazis is now common knowledge, though many of the debriefings remain classified to this day, and we may have only just scratched the surface. Pushing the limits of quantum and scalar physics, the Nazis produced mind-boggling results.

As a captive state of post-war Nazis and their brainwashed descendants, Germany has been digging for secrets ever since. As have the Americans and the British. It's curious how so many of these digs have had military associations.

And so it is, the CIA and DIA caught wind of an ongoing plundering of the Baghdad Museum that had been going on since the 1980s. Artifacts collected on French and

German digs were assembled in the Baghdad Museum by the thousands and never catalogued: clay tablets, figurines, statues, household items, jewelry, and curious objects of unknown use.

With the assistance of Jaber al-Tikriti and Nawala al-Mutawalli, the two most important figures at the museum, "certain parties" obtained the choicest items for a price, all while Saddam Hussein turned a blind eye. Little by little these artifacts trickled out of the museum. Among the most important were cylinder seals and clay tablets, the contents of which only the archeologists who found them knew. Is it any wonder the museum remained closed for "security reasons" during most of Saddam's reign?

When the CIA and DIA discovered what exactly was trickling and knew that trickles eventually make a flood, they had to move fast. Consulting with Dr. Giuseppe Faro, a professor of both physics and history at South Dakota State University, he put together his "Giza Death Star" hypothesis for them: the Great Pyramid wasn't just a power plant as Chris Dunn suspected. It was a massive, planet busting harmonic oscillator that could emit horrific and colossal death rays. Its initial use was so awesome and catastrophic, it was dismantled by the survivors of the cosmic war it was used to fight. The parts that couldn't be destroyed were hidden, hopefully forever. Afterwards, the civilizations that emerged in Mesopotamia were the keepers of this legacy and wrote about it extensively. They passed on their knowledge to the Egyptians, from whom the Hebrews gleaned most of their knowledge. If the missing parts of the "Giza Death Star" could be recovered or reconstructed, it painted a dim and ominous picture for the Earth and its inhabitants.

Since the best way to hide something is in plain sight, a case was developed for weapons of mass destruction in Iraq. With key Nazi players like George W. Bush and Dick Cheney in charge, it wasn't difficult. Deals had been made with Deep State actors all under the aegis of San Carlos de Bariloche to fabricate evidence of ordinary, everyday WMDs while keeping the real state of affairs hidden from patriotic high level members of the administration like Secretary of State Colin Powell. He was smart enough to know that what he was given was bullshit, but he didn't know why and he didn't know the real story. He performed his duty like the military man he was and then resigned.

Thus, with the US Army on the outskirts of Baghdad on April 10, 2003, Skorzeny's raiders were facing a Hail Mary. It was all now, or nothing ever.

The signal was simple. As the convoy of M35s approached, the leader set off a charge at a specific location on the museum grounds that resembled any bursting shell. The Republican Guard troops guarding the museum knew to stand clear of that spot. As soon as the shell burst, one of the guards whose identity will never be known, opened the museum door, stripped off his uniform along with his comrades, and left wearing the civvies that had been concealed underneath.

Chapter 3

Müller hopped out of the cab of the lead truck and surveyed the grounds. He then waved his hand over his head in a circular motion and the men debarked. The tall blonde woman approached him and stood stolidly face to face. The clanks and clips of men at work made a din around them.

Müller's penetrating blue eyes glared momentarily, giving way to a sly smile. He was all of 6' 4" and broad shouldered.

"Take Red Team to the cellar. Al-Mutawalli will be waiting with the keys to the vault. Dismiss her even before it's opened. Even she doesn't know what's inside. Make sure you count the spheres and that every compartment in the crates is packed before you leave. The cylinder seals and tablets are already together in tackle boxes. Leave the boxes behind since they might be tagged."

"What's a tackle box?"

Müller exhaled. "Tool box. Art supply box."

"I see. Why is it called a tackle box?"

"Edda," he put his hand on her cheek, and stroking it, reached out with his fingers and entwined her golden locks. With the speed of a rattler, he pulled them just hard enough to make his point. "First I will shoot you, then swear in German," He remarked half-jokingly. "This is not the time for English lessons." He released her.

"I will take Green Team to the exhibit galleries where we will take some notable items for the press and the academics to worry about, and to deal with any interruptions." Two operators were just jogging past, one lumbering with a crate because his partner had been left behind for cussing in German, and the other with an M240 machine gun.

Müller stopped them. "Who are you? Rambo? Who brings an M240 to a museum heist?" He snatched the weapon away and motioned for the thug to help the other thug with the crate and jogged off with them towards the museum.

"Why Red and Green? These are not the normal code colors," Edda shouted after him.

Müller stopped and turned, hollering festively, "Poor Edda. You are so rigid in your ways." He raised his arms, M240 and all, "Because today is *Julfest!*" He turned on his heels, snapped them together, and after skipping a few steps, trotted up to his team being careful to sing "O, Tannenbaum" loudly, in English. *Julfest,* of course, was the Nazi re-branding of Christmas.

Chapter 4

A sour-faced Iraqi woman stood impatiently by the vault door when she heard the first heavy steps of the approaching team on the stairs. She stepped out of the vestibule to check. As soon as Edda got to the door, Dr. al-Mutawalli started for the lock with keys in hand. Edda touched her wrist and took the keys herself.

"Thank you. You may go." Edda was dispassionate but careful about her manners.

"But you may-----"

Al-Mutawalli was cut off by the Valkyrie. "You may go! Please. I will not ask again."

Al-Mutawalli looked confused, then scared. She cast pleading looks to the assembly, opened her mouth to speak, but then thought better of it. She turned and dashed up the stairs, past the men wreaking havoc with the exhibits, and out of the museum. Müller eyed her cheerfully as she left.

As the vault door swung open, the thieves outside were bathed in dazzling, blinding supernatural light.

The adjutant, immediately behind Edda and squinting through his fingers, asked, "Can you see anything?"

The light began to diminish, as if it was a gas previously under pressure that was now dissipating. Edda and her adjutant slowly lowered their hands, lifted their heads, and widened their eyes. The adjutant, who was shorter, craned for a look over the taller woman.

"Yes," replied Edda. "Wonderful things!"

She swung to the side and the adjutant stepped into the room making broad fast scooping motions with his hand for the men to hurry. Some men lurched for the tackle boxes which they emptied haphazardly into sacks. Others approached in awe a series of orbs or spheres that sat arrayed on rubber-lined shelves. Still others went for large crystalline objects with odd geometric shapes.

The orbs and crystals were meticulously counted and compared to a checklist on the adjutant's clipboard, and each was put into its appointed compartment in the crates. The spheres came in eight different sizes with the largest being about 36 inches across and the smallest ones about half of that. There appeared to be 27 sets in all.

Somebody tapped one of the orbs with the butt of his knife to gauge what it was made of. It made a sound that was neither plastic nor metallic, nor ceramic, and yet somehow a combination of them all.

"Be careful with those!" barked Edda.

"What the Hell are these balls made of?"

"Do not play with your balls!" she half announced to the entire team and half a direct order to the man in question. "That is for the Doctor to do!"

The men smirked and giggled as they packed up their cargo. In fact, the Doctor was a mysterious physicist named Doctor Richter but Edda's inadvertent double entendre wasn't lost on them.

Several of the crystals were self-luminous, with no apparent power source. Their fanciful light reflected off the shiny spheres. The combined effect of their luminescence produced a dreamlike green glow that was gradually muffled as the crates were sealed. The men eyed one another warily. Edda looked as if she "felt" something, paused her operations momentarily, then came to.

"OK, out! Out! Back to the trucks! Quickly!"

The men responsible for crates hoisted them and made for the stairs, while the men responsible for security mounted their weapons. Prancing up the stairs with the loaded crates one man whispered through the side of his mouth to his partner, "These crates don't feel any heavier than they did empty. In fact, maybe a little lighter."

"You're right. I have a feeling this thing is really big."

"Takes a lot of balls to pull something like this off, right in the middle of a war zone."

"And we got 'em, right here in this crate, brutha."

They broke into a spontaneous but cheerful parody of an old wartime song, fumbling at first, but then picking up the rhyme.

"Hitler, has now got all the balls,
George Bush, will get no balls at all.
None left, after our theft.
Now who's holding who by the balls?"

They sang all the way to the trucks. As the last man from Red Team exited the museum, Green Team defiled behind them.

Müller paused at the museum entrance where he met a man in civilian clothes over which was a flak vest and blue press helmet. He produced a folded paper from one of his pockets and handed it to the reporter, who was from *Deutsche Welle.*

"Here. This is the article we need published. You can take any liberties you want with it but these highlighted details must be in it."

The reporter perused the article. "Baghdad Museum plundered....Appeared to be American forces....thousands of cultural artifacts missing....I see. Yes. It'll be on the wire within the hour. Heil Hitler!"

Müller flashed a scowl at the man, who started with fright. And once again, slowly and gradually, that sly, evil mischievous grin took form upon his face. Then in his best Siegfried from *Get Smart* impression, he quipped, "Zis is ze 4th Reich, Schtarker. Ve don't 'Heil Hitler' here!" and ran off bellowing with laughter.

Chapter 5

"NOTHING! NOT ONE GODDAMNED THING!" He heard as the doors burst open to his Executive Office Building office.

"What are you talking about?" growled Cheney. His beady blue eyes were glaring with the fragile authority of a desperate and cowardly man. This trait only fools other desperate cowards, so to maintain authority; such men surround themselves with even more desperately cowardly men than themselves. Anyone else sees it as desperation given into evil.

The other desperate coward was George Tenet, Director of the CIA. "Task Force 20 got to the museum and the place had already been cleaned out. All they found was this." He tossed a large key ring with a deafening clank onto the Vice President's desk that slid into his lap.

"What the fuck is this?"

"Nawala's keys. She dicked us. Er, sorry, Dick."

"What do you mean she dicked us?"

"She gave it all to someone else. She says they looked American."

"Well, that would explain this then. Sent from Berlin." He tossed a copy of *Deutsche Welle* on the edge of his gargantuan desk so Tenet, who was now standing at the edge, could see it:

BAGHDAD MUSEUM LOOTED BY AMERICAN FORCES

"Shit. What a clusterfuck this turns out to be."

Tenet sat down exasperated and sighed deeply. "She says they were led by a tall blonde woman."

"Who was led by a tall blonde woman?"

"The troops who cleaned out the vault. There was another team in the exhibit hall looting as well and trashing cases."

"Hmmmm. Any ideas?" The VP put his fingertips to his lips with hands together and dropped his chin.

"No." Tenet drummed his fingers on the chair arm. "Should we tell W?"

"Oh fuck him. He's just a stooge anyway." He thought for minute. "Well, what happened?"

"Well, to hear Nawala tell it, she got word, with our codes, that the heist would be the morning of the 10th. She set it up with the guards, who would be signaled of our approach by an exploding charge at a certain spot on the museum grounds from which they should stand clear. After opening the door, they were to depart in civvies so as to avoid capture. Nawala was to meet our guys at the vault door and open it. But they didn't let her open it. They sent her away.

"That afternoon, she gets another message from us with the same codes. So she gets suspicious and alerts al-Tikriti who alerts the Republican Guard who station new troops at the museum. Task Force 20 gets into a vicious firefight and finally takes the museum. Only someone's been there ahead of them."

"If it was already cleaned out, why'd the Guard go back?"

"Damned if I know, but if I had to guess, they probably thought Task Force 20 were the impostors."

Cheney slapped the desk with an open hand. "Goddammit!"

"Easy, Dick. The world's gonna run out of hearts for you."

Suddenly, The VP raised his head in wide-eyed realization and erupted with anger. "YOU MORON! YOU STINKING MORON! How could you let this happen?? Get out! Get the fuck out of my office!"

Tenet looked sheepishly shocked. He stood up, straightened his suit and tie and left. He carefully shut the doors behind him.

Cheney picked up the phone. "Suzy, get me the Secretary of State."

Chapter 6

Secretary Powell picked up the phone. Suzy's voice was on the other end, "I have the Vice President for you, sir."

"Put him on."

"Colin----"

"I'm not helping," interrupted the Secretary of State. "What?"

"I'm not helping. I presented your bullshit story to the UN, and that's it. In nine months I'm out of here."

Dick laughed nervously. "You haven't heard what I'm going to say yet."

Powell swung his chair around and put his feet on the corner of the desk. "I saw the *Deutsche Welle* article, Dick." He paused and then emphasized the final word. "Anyway, sounds like Rummie's mess. Or CIA's."

"True. True enough. But we have another problem." He related what Tenet had told him about al-Mutawali's story.

"Dammit, Dick! I told you that would happen. This is one FUBAR I can't fix for you."

"Well neither Rummie nor Tenet can either."

"What is it they used to say back in the old neighborhood? Oh yeah. 'Well, duuuhhh.'"

"What do you think I should do?"

"I wouldn't disgrace this office by saying it aloud." He slammed the handset into its cradle.

Meanwhile, in Brookings, South Dakota, an odd professor of Physics and History at South Dakota State University was noticing the same article. "Interesting. Very interesting," he mumbled. "I better keep this."

He slid the article into a folder and labeled it "Baghdad Museum Heist" and set it on a shelf.

Chapter 7

Giuseppe Faro was born to Italian parents who came to America just after WWII. He constantly wore an A-2 flight jacket given to his father by a downed American pilot for saving him from German capture. The only time he took it off was for meals and bedtime. He also wore an Australian drover hat, but God only knows why. The outfit was too much for the South Dakota summers, and not enough for the South Dakota winters.

Dr. Faro took full advantage of his new life in America and went on to become one of its most notable men of letters. He graduated from SUNY Stoneybrook with a degree in physics and a minor in history, because he wanted to live at home in the Italian neighborhood in Brooklyn where his family had settled, and he could always get a seat on the train going against rush hour. He went on to get PhDs in both, one from Oxford, the other from Cambridge.

He took up a research position at SDSU where his quirky and Italian mannerisms weren't the only thing that broke the mold. His research was considered quackery by most in both fields in which he was qualified, but no one had been able to debunk any of it. One of his most outrageous claims was that Western physics took a wrong turn down a dead end street with relativity. In fact, he considered Einstein himself to be the real quack. The physicists that followed after him were even worse. He dubbed them the "relativity police."

It was just as well for SDSU, because his numerous publications attracted a steady stream of loyal if off-beat students and under-the-radar government, defense, and industry contracts that helped the small state university remain solvent and competitive. His former students frequently sent him interesting tidbits of information and discovery from around the globe that supported and furthered his research. Most of his work in physics was devoted to the scalar physics first described by Maxwell in 1861, but then later neglected after Maxwell's equations were bowdlerized by Oliver Heaviside. This bowdlerization is what led to the wrong turn down dead end "Relativity Row." It was Faro's work in scalar physics that put Thomas Bearden on the map with DARPA.

Faro liked the quiet small town life but mourned the lack of good Italian food that kept him forever cooking, as much a hobby as it was a necessity. But being in the upper Midwest, Brookings had some of the best steaks anywhere.

But why would an odd professor of physics and history at a small Midwestern state university be filing away an obscure article from a German newspaper about a museum heist that occurred in the midst of the Iraq war? Because he knows something most people do not. In fact, he knows things most people never even imagine. In fact, he knows things that most people try fervently to forget once they do know them.

When a scholar is competent in more than one field, he is able to put together pieces that specialists miss. We saw in Chapter 2 that such is the case with the Giza Plateau in Egypt.

But that was not always the case. One thing that scientists of every field do is research prior literature to see what work has already been done that may be relevant to theirs. They also scour it for previous work that has gone unnoticed or neglected. Often this research will take them back to the very earliest ponderings of ancient peoples. It's common for scientists of the 21st Century to revisit and even test the work or observations of the Greeks, or the Babylonians, or even older civilizations.

In exploring the works of Newton, Faro came became intrigued by Newton's obsession with measuring the Great Pyramid in order to get an accurate measurement of the earth's circumference so that he could further develop his theory of gravity. This struck Faro as strange: what would measuring the pyramid have to do with the circumference of the earth?

As it turns out, John Greaves and Tito Burattini did measure the Great Pyramid in 1639 and Burattini and Newton both used those measurements to derive the circumference of the earth. This led Faro down a spectacular rabbit hole and into all kinds of scientific and historical discoveries, most not his own but those that had been neglected or suppressed. Others, already mentioned, were doing the same thing. Faro just took the work to its farthest extent.

As part of his research, Faro also discovered that the mythologies and legends of ancient people were not so much religion or superstitious mental wanderings, but the encoded science of a "paleo-ancient" civilization, as he put it, indicating that it was far older than the most ancient civilizations already known to historians. Most of his work in this regard was based on the *Hermetica,* which he was able to determine was as much a treatise on the scalar nature of the Universe as it was on human nature. Thus, the alchemical wedding of his interest in physics and his interest in history was accomplished.

There are literally hundreds of significant mathematical formulae and relationships encoded in the Great Pyramid, from Planck's constant to the speed of light, to the mass of the Earth, to the value of Pi. But even more so, they are all only close approximations thereof, so that the Great Pyramid as rather like a "well-tempered clavier:" it had multiple harmonics built in. And that was the key to unraveling the "Giza Death Star," as it came to be called. This realization enabled Faro to take the leap that Dunn landed short of.

The possibility of the Giza Death Star was horrifying enough that Faro was forced to think the unthinkable: The darn thing was sitting right there in the desert. What if someone were to start it up again?

Then on April 20th, 2003, just 10 days after the museum theft, Dr. Faro noticed another headline in the news: JU-390 TO FLY FROM MUNICH TO BUENOS

AIRES FOR AIR SHOW

"In its first flight in almost 60 years, the world's only Ju-390 begins a flight of over 11,000 km today from Munich to Buenos Aires for the 2003 Buenos Aires Air Show, which opens in June. Only two of the historic aircraft were ever built, one of them being lost in the chaos of WWII. The plane was originally built as a long range cargo aircraft and strategic bomber for Germany. In one flight during the war it flew round trip from Germany to New York City on a reconnaissance mission without refueling, but never fulfilled its role as a bomber during the war. It is one of the highlights of this year's show."

"Huh," remarked the professor to himself. "Right on Hitler's birthday. And from Munich no less. And there's that number 11 again too." He stuffed it into his "Baghdad Museum Heist" folder.

Chapter 8

Slowly the deep steady undulating din of six giant propeller engines grew louder and louder over Buenos Aires. People came out of their homes and places of business with binoculars to see the giant plane pass overhead. It roared low over the suburbs so spectators could have a good close look, then landed at Morón Airport just outside the city.

It immediately taxied into a purpose-built hangar where it was parked next to its twin, flown to Argentina in May of 1945 by Hans Kammler after making a deal with the Allies. Also in the hangar were another convoy of trucks and serious looking men in expensive but "ruggedly" fashioned clothes who tried to be inconspicuous. They were approached by Müller and Edda who were the first two off the plane. All the discussion was in German.

"Is that everything?"

"Everything," answered Müller.

"How did you make the flight with all that cargo? The plane was never tested with so much weight."

"In fact the cargo is practically weightless," explained Edda.

"The only objects with weight were the cylinder seals and tablets. Everything else weighs nothing for some reason."

The mysterious men nodded in approval. "You have done well, and will be rewarded when we get to Bariloche."

"It was honor enough to be a part of it," stated Müller.

"Still, good work, when it is so difficult, should not go unrecognized."

Another gray-haired man stepped forward. "But you and your team must be exhausted. We have made accommodations for you here in Buenos Aires tonight. You will follow us to Bariloche in the morning. Mr. Silva will see to your needs." He gestured to a waiting bus.

A broad-shouldered, bow-legged man sporting a sand-colored tropical Luftwaffe flight jacket tipped his Greek fisherman's cap and smiled wryly. He stood sideways, puffed out his chest, and extending his arm, and thus presented his bus.

"Thank you so much."

The bus proceeded to the city. Mr. Silva's first destination was the Alvear Palace Hotel in the La Recoleta.

The airbrakes hissed and Mr. Silva got up from the driver's seat. He reached up to the overhead rack and produced a pair of his and her tan leather satchels and a suit bag. He then approached Müller and Edda who occupied the first pair of seats. He was both cheerful and formal in a dark sort of way.

"Excuse me, my friends. This is your stop. Herr Bormann has sent these for your convenience. Evening wear for tonight," he said raising the suit bag. "Travel wear for tomorrow and daily essentials," raising the satchels. "You'll be in the presidential suite. I shall pick you up at nine tomorrow morning for the trip to Bariloche."

"Thank you, Mr., uh, Silva."

"The pleasure is mine." He grinned broadly.

As soon as Müller and Edda had debarked, he addressed the remainder of the team on the bus. "We have special plans for the rest of you. Argentinean barbecue on the Pampas! I'm sure you will find it irresistible."

The men cheered with approval.

The bus choked and roared to life. Mr. Silva wound his way through the city and began the southbound journey. As they entered the marshy Pampas south of the city, Silva turned off onto a dirt road that led to a large campsite with cabins and lean tos. Some gauchos were working a massive barbecue. A large pile of carelessly stacked wood lay next to it. Two other gauchos cheerfully strummed guitars.

"Excuse me, gentlemen. I have to check on our arrangements."

Silva reached for the lever and swung the door open.

He walked over to the gauchos who shook his hand familiarly. Silva bent over close to the grill and inhaled the intoxicating aroma of barbecued steak. He pierced one with a long-handled fork and lifted it to inspect it. A small group of slim, scantily clad model type girls exited one of the cabins and strolled toward the gauchos and their grill.

WHOOSH!

The entire interior of the bus was consumed in flames and men screamed. Then a loud explosion lifted the bus about a foot into the air. A rattle like buck shot on a steel roof accompanied the explosion. The bus came to rest again almost exactly where it had stopped, its roof pimpled by shrapnel.

The gauchos doused the cook fire, got into cars along with the girls and Mr. Silva and drove off. Mr. Silva, in the passenger seat of one of the cars still had his steak on the fork and held his hand under it catch the dripping fat. He took a healthy bite and remarked with his mouth full, "Mmmm. I love a good barbecue," and bit it again.

Chapter 9

Frank and Melissa Shorley were both former students of Dr. Faro's. After graduating from SDSU, they tied the knot and bought a large tract of land in the Nevada desert with an inheritance. There they intended to develop Tesla technology for industrial and consumer use. The wide-open spaces in the Nevada desert not only afforded them a measure of privacy, if not secrecy, for their work, it allowed for plenty of margin for error in case any energy experiments got out of hand. They didn't want to go around killing livestock or people if they screwed up.

They were out in the desert playing with a large impulse magnifying transformer one bright summer day when such a screw up occurred. An impulse magnifying transformer is a device that shocks local systems into non-equilibrium with huge electrical discharges. It was discovered by accident, as so many things are, during World War II at a humongous arc welding facility built by the Navy.

In fact, this is one of the strangest events in the history of science ever recorded, and yet largely unknown. With the war in full swing the Navy was under enormous pressure to produce ships. They built a huge facility for arc welding armor-plated hulls. It was powered by huge capacitor banks that were so powerful, workers could not be in the capacitor room while the welders were active. When the welds were sparked, the incredibly high voltage released a storm of X-rays. But that wasn't all.

Strange and inexplicable phenomena occurred. During the electrical blast from the welders, an "optical blackout" occurred. At first this was attributed to retinal bleaching, a natural biological response to sudden flashes of intense light. This explanation fell apart when the Navy's investigators realized it would also show up on film.

But it didn't stop there. Workers reported that tools

left in the capacitor room would disappear without a trace during the blackouts. They would go into retrieve the tools once it was safe, and the tools would be gone! The Navy, having little tolerance for woo-woo, set out to test these reports. Investigators deliberately placed objects in the room and filmed what happened. Lo, and behold, the objects vanished in the blackouts! At first they thought the objects were being vaporized by the X-rays, only no trace gases from their vaporization remained in the room either.

The Navy called in Thomas Townsend Brown, who the Navy apparently considered more of an expert in weird, freaky space-time warp phenomena than Einstein. Brown himself had had a very interesting career at Caltech and Kenyon College and went on to perform incredible sorts of scalar research in gravity for the Navy before the war.

Dr. Brown carefully observed the arcs created by the welders. What he surmised is that the explosive force of the plasma arcs drove all atmospheric gases out of the arc, creating a momentary vacuum that hindered the complete discharge of the capacitor bank. The tsunami of plasma discharging across vacuum space caused space-time to warp in an electrogravitic interaction. Around the explosive electrical impulse, local space was collapsing. The blackout was caused by light being sucked into the collapsing space, and if strong enough, unable to escape the collapsing space, the blackout would spread as more and more light was sucked in in the vicinity. When the effect was intense enough and slow enough, it could actually modify matter, which could literally blow apart in fierce, redoubtable explosions of sparks. The matter would be ripped apart at the atomic level and even the trace gases would be drawn into the void, leaving nothing in the room to detect.

These vacuum arc effects had been described decades earlier by Nicola Tesla while working on his impulse magnifying transformer. However, he had never gotten to the stage of disintegrating chunks of the local matter.

Wisely, the Shorleys decided to do their research

with this in the middle of nowhere in the Nevada desert. On this particular day, they were upping the ante. They had added considerably to their capacitor bank and wanted to see what kind of blackout effect they could get. Using a remote control in the control room, they threw the switch, and an area the size of a football field went dark all around them. "When the lights came back on," their machine was gone and a deep, black hole 30 feet across stood in its place.

Frank stepped out of the control room with Melissa on his shirt tail and her finger in his rear belt loop. The Shorleys were seized with bewilderment, jaws agape. That wasn't supposed to happen.

They squinted towards the hole as if it were a desert mirage. They beheld one another's amazement. Melissa reached out and lifted Frank's jaw back into the closed position. They turned again in unison to behold the hole, this time wincing at what they'd done.

Twisting his body, but not his head, Frank reached back and grabbed a stick by the control room door they kept handy for rattlesnakes. The Shorleys approached the hole slowly, poking the ground ahead of them as they advanced. Upon reaching the rim, they peered over and down. Black.

Melissa bent over and picked up a stone. She dropped it in the hole. They listened. Five seconds. 10 seconds. 30 seconds. Nothing.

"Maybe it was too small to hear," offered Frank tremulously. He bent over and picked up a bigger stone the size of a football and heaved it over the lip. They listened. Five seconds. 10 seconds. 30 seconds. Nothing.

"Well try a bigger one!" opined Melissa as much out of fear as scientific curiosity.

Frank looked around for the biggest rock within easy reach. He found a regular boulder he could hardly pick up and carry. He dropped it at the edge of the abyss.

"1, 2, 3, HEAVE!" He and Melissa pushed it over the edge together.

They listened. Five seconds. 10 seconds. 30 seconds.

Nothing.

"Did you hear anything?"

"I'm not sure."

"I don't think I did."

"We better call Dr. Faro."

Chapter 10

"GEORGEANN! GEORGEANN!" The professor was practically choking as he absent-mindedly flung things from his desk fumbling with the phone.

"What? What?" Georgeann leapt to the doorway fearing the old man was having a heart attack.

Faro sprung from his chair and rounded his desk all in one move. "Pack your bags! We're going to Vegas, Baby!"

"What? Vegas? What for?"

"I'll give you what for."

Georgeann chuckled. "OK, let's have it, you crazy old man."

"Do you like to gamble?"

"Not in Las Vegas, no."

"Oh, that's child's play for mafia wimps," he answered as he waved his hand dismissively through the air. He clutched her shoulders and stared her right in the eyes. "We're going to gamble with the Universe."

The secretary chortled mischievously with childlike delight. "Oh, ho ho ho. I love when we have an adventure."

Chapter 11

Frank and Melissa were waiting at the airport in a Land Rover 109 Series IIA with two jump seats added to the bed. They liked it because it didn't have any electronics to tamper with, was easy to work on, and could go anywhere they needed it to on their vast property. Unfortunately, it lacked air conditioning, so they'd removed the top.

Faro and Georgeann giddily greeted them with hugs all around and tossed their bags and gear in the back. It was a long drive through the hot Nevada desert from Vegas, but the chatter never stopped. The Shorleys stood, quite literally, at the threshold of something stupendous that dominated the conversation. But there was catching up and small talk to do as well.

When they'd arrived, they unloaded the gear from the back. Frank reached over the side panel and clutched a bag in each hand, but paused to take in Prof. Faro who was standing at the rear. Faro looked puzzled. "What?"

"Aren't you hot with that jacket on?"

At that very moment the professor had removed a handkerchief from his pocket and began to mop his brow. He stopped, looked at the hanky in his hand, looked at Frank, and then guffawed. "Oh never mind that. Let's have lunch. I'm starving."

The Shorleys cooked up some delicious pronghorn whose meat was flavored by the sage on which it fed. The meat was accompanied by potatoes and a special salad with fresh vegetables from the Shorleys' greenhouse. Faro filled them in on the Baghdad Museum theft as they munched.

"So why do you think it's significant?" asked Melissa.

"Think about it. You have a convoy of trucks roll up and clean out the museum in the midst of a battle. And then ten days later, on Hitler's birthday," he started chortling ironically as he finished, "the only Ju-390 in the world is flying to Argentina 'for an air show.' Who's buying that?"

Some bits of flying salad punctuated his laugh. He laughed harder as Frank dodged to the right. Still heaving he put a napkin to his mouth, "Excuse me."

"One thing's for sure," added Georgeann. "The Nazis loooove anniversaries."

"And symbols."

"Which is the Ju-390," Melissa chimed in.

"Precisely!" the professor continued. "If I'm correct, and this is just high octane speculation here, Nazis dressed in American uniforms (how hard are they to get?), were looting the museum of thousands of uncatalogued artifacts that are either parts of the Giza Death Star, or tablets and seals containing information about them. They'll be all the easier to move because nobody knows what they are. They're uncatalogued"

"Holy jumpin' catfish!" exclaimed Frank. "So what do you think they got?"

"I have no idea. But it'll take years, perhaps decades for them to assemble everything, so we have time to find out."

"And," noted Georgeann, "it was a German newspaper, *Deutsche Welle*, which first broke the story. On the same day. How suspicious is that?"

They finished their meal in pensive silence.

"First rate meal, Shorleys," remarked the professor.

"Yes," continued Georgeann. "Absolutely first class. I'd never eaten pronghorn before."

"They're all over the range here," explained Frank. "Beautiful animals. And free eats," he added with a wink and a smile.

"Why don't you guys get settled and changed before we go out?" offered Melissa. "I'll show Georgeann to her room and Frank can help Dr. Faro."

"Dr. Faro. Dr. Faro." Georgeann knocked repeatedly on his door.

"Coming." He opened the door and stood presenting

himself in what appeared to be a complete authentic WWII British Desert Rats uniform. Georgeann burst into hilarious laughter.

"You like it?"

It took a few moments, but his secretary finally composed herself. Still chuckling she had to ask, "Where did you get that get up?"

"Bought it on Toppots.net! Couple of months ago." His pride was somewhat satirical. "I've been waiting for just the right opportunity to wear it."

"Well, this is it. My God. You got me." She continued laughing.

It wasn't unusual for the two of them to set up jokes for each other. But then, when a guy wears an A2 flight jacket and a drover hat everywhere, and he's getting ready to explore the desert and appears wearing this outfit, one can't be sure.

"C'mon, Georgeann. You have to get into it. I believe in going all in."

"Oh I can see that!" It was all she could do to control herself.

He took a dramatic step forward and cocked his head boyishly, "They've even got an old Land Rover to drive around in."

"Well, it's too bad it doesn't have a machine gun mounted in back or you guys could play *Rat Patrol* all day."

Faro threw back his head slapped his knee in glee. "Hahahaha! I suspect we practically will be."

When they got downstairs, Melissa reacted just like Georgeann had. Melissa put her arm around him affectionately and said, "Glad to see you haven't changed over the years, Doc."

Outside, Frank was throwing the last of the gear into the Rover. He heard the crunching gravel from their approaching footsteps and looked up. He motioned the trio to get in, then hopped in the driver's seat next to the professor. He turned to the doc, looked up and down, then remarked, "Huh. No jacket?"

Frank turned the key and off they drove.

Chapter 12

Vaporous mirages marked the horizon. The sun roasted everyone's thighs. Faro regretted wearing shorts, and everyone else regretted wearing long pants. The open car didn't help. Instead of a cooling breeze, they were hit with the constant blast of a giant hairdryer set on "hi." They were relieved to reach their destination.

They piled out of the vehicle, which was parked about 10 yards from the hole. Faro walked over to a new addition to the scene and beheld it with his hands on his hips.

"What's all this?"

Dr. Faro was referring to a trailer of junk that included everything but the, wait a minute, it did in fact include the kitchen sink--one of those big old cast iron sinks with the white ceramic coating.

"I put that together while we were waiting for you guys. If we're going to test the depth of this hole, we might as well have fun doing it. Saving the car for last."

"Well, OK," laughed the professor.

"How do you get into this stuff, Giuseppe?" asked Georgeann. "This is one I'm glad I didn't miss."

Before the fun started, our intrepid crew of explorers wanted to conduct some more scientific type experiments. Frank had rigged up a 10 million candle power spot light to sit directly over the abyss. It was suspended from four poles pounded into the ground around the giant hole and connected to a portable power source.

"Oh my God!" Faro mockingly clutched his heart. "You actually got over that thing to rig that up?"

"Not exactly," said Melissa. We pounded in the stakes, then wired it up and adjusted the cables until it was centered."

"Dear God. I'd've been afraid just to pound the stakes this close to that thing."

"I've got this mirror on a pole. We'll hold this over the hole and see if the spotlight picks up anything down there."

Frank handed it to the professor who passed it to Georgeann like a hot potato. "Here. You handle it."

Frank switched on the light that blazed even in the midday sun. The hole lit up like daylight, but no bottom could be seen. It was just spotlight beam as far as the eye could see.

"See anything, Georgeann?"

"Yeah. A whole lot of light. Get it? A 'hole' lot...."

"We get it. We get it." Faro thought for a minute. "What about a 'laser?'" he said with air quotes impersonating Dr. Evil from the Austin Powers films.

"Brought one."

"Well let's rig that up and see what happens. You have a rangefinder to time the return?"

"Of course."

Frank and Melissa maneuvered the spotlight and detached it from the rigging. They had designed their own laser rangefinder. When the laser was turned on, it started a timer, which then recorded the time when the reflection of the laser hit a sensor on the device. They attached it to the same rigging as the spot, having had planned it into their designs.

"Let her rip."

Frank switched on the laser and the gang waited for the beep on the rangefinder. The numbers raced away on the timer like a stopwatch. They stared in amazement as it raced over 10 seconds. Now the speed of light, as you probably know, is approximately 186,282 miles per second, which means the laser beam in the hole had so far traveled over 1,862,820 miles, or over five times the distance to the moon, yet this hole was directed toward the center of the Earth! Frank switched off the rangefinder.

"Who else knows about this?" Faro asked lifting his hat to scratch his pate.

"No one but you two, as far as we know."

Melissa walked over to the vehicle and came back with a Geiger counter. She switched it on and it clicked like a chorus of katydids that were all out of sync.

"It's well above background radiation but it has subsided since the first day."

Frank tried a Gauss meter. "Gee-hose-a-phat! 2000 MilliGausses!"

"It's a wonder we're not dead already! Or gone mad."

"Well, what's with the junk trailer anyway?"

"I figure we toss it down the hole one item at a time from smallest to biggest."

"What's that supposed to prove?"

"Nothing really. We won't hear it hit bottom, but we might find irregularities in the hole if anything gets jammed up or bounces off. Then we can try the laser again where we think the irregularity is."

"Fair enough."

"At least it'll be fun."

They started with a microwave oven. Frank and Melissa started singing "Money for Nothing" by Dire Straits. "We gotta install microwave ovens....we gotta move these refrigerators....we gotta move these color TVs..."

And so, according to the song they worked their way through the discarded merchandise and each time heard nothing.

Finally, they got to the car. It was a 1971 Buick Estate wagon.

It still had a tattered interior and the 455 engine, but the exterior color had long rusted away. They shifted it into neutral and carefully rolled it off the trailer and stopped it with a couple of rocks for wheel chocks.

"Everyone ready?" asked Frank.

Everyone nodded and took positions around the car.

"Any message for the Devil?" quipped Faro.

Frank kicked the makeshift chocks away and shouted, "Look out below!" as the quartet shoved the behemoth of a car into the abyss.

They listened. Five seconds. 10 seconds. 30 seconds. Nothing.

Chapter 13

In a secret meeting room not far away at Area 51, some men in blue uniforms with lots of stars and ribbons were meeting with other men in green uniforms with lots of stars and ribbons, and a few other men in short sleeve dress shirts with pocket protectors.

It was a nice room but not too fancy. The walls were covered with various nicely matted and framed photos with military or aerospace themes. It had a long pressed wood conference table with a cherry veneer and black leather chairs that matched. An overhead projector hung over the table at one end and a screen covered the far wall. Neither was in use.

The men were gathered at one end of the table.

"We detected the anomaly here," one of the pocket protectors whose name tag said "Smith" said pointing at a satellite map of Nevada.

"So what kind of anomaly was it?"

"The bad kind."

"Define 'bad'," requested one of the generals, also apparently named Smith.

"Space-time warp of an unknown cause. It almost sucked in one of our experimental craft that happened to be passing by at the time, General...er, Smith."

The conversation continued, alternating between the men according to their interests and specialties. Most of the explaining came from the civilian scientists who monitor these things from their underground laboratory and commute in and out of Area 51 on Janet Airlines every day. Most live in and around Las Vegas, and their wives hate them because they never talk about their work.

"Experimental craft?"

"I suppose if you were supposed to know that, Smith, you would."

"Right. Well, how serious is it?"

"We're still getting readings. We've sent probes out over the last three days and don't see much of a change. One of our satellites took this picture."

He slid a color photo across the table so everyone could see it.

"What the hell is that black spot in the photo?"

"That's the anomaly."

"It looks like a big...hole...in the ground."

"It is. A really frikkin' deep hole."

"How deep?"

"Can't tell. Bottomless?"

"A bottomless hole?"

"I thought only we could do stuff like this. Who or what made that hole, Mr. Smith?"

"Beats me. There are rumors of some couple who bought land up there a few years ago so they could do their own science experiments. Inventors. Entrepreneurs. You know."

"Could they have done that?"

One of the men in short sleeves blew air threw puffed cheeks and stroked his head. "Ppfffhhhoooo. Not unless they can build the stuff we got here."

"Let's say they did do it. Why'd they want a...'bottomless' hole? Smith, what about you?" As it turns out, everyone was named "Smith" for security purposes.

"Damned if I know."

"Sure would be useful for 'waste disposal'," joked Smith. "A lot of, uh, Eye-talians, in Vegas."

Smith shrugged his shoulders. "Could it be an accident?"

"An accident??" asked one of the Gen. Smiths incredulously.

"Well bottomless holes just don't open up on their own accord." Then he continued to ensure he was technically correct, "Typically."

Smith was making thoughtful motions with his coffee cup. "Were they testing something? And it went awry?"

"Well, that would fit Smith's data."

Finally, General Smith addressed them, "OK, OK, OK. Just find out who it is and take care of it. General Smith, We can't just have anybody in control of that space, but people with that kind of money and brains can't just disappear, so handle it accordingly. And we may need them later if they're as smart as they seem. Just get a hold of that hole! So to speak!"

"What are you going to do, General Smith?"

"I'm going back to Washington, where nobody calls me 'Smith!'"

Chapter 14

None of them saw the splendor of the desert sky at night. Although they dined on the patio, they munched pensively and passed serving bowls around without looking up. They played with the food on their plates as much as ate it. The jackrabbit was delicious, fried in garlic, butter and lemon, but it wasn't enough to keep their minds off the gravity of the situation.

Gravity. Get it? There was little of the usual jocularity. Occasionally one of the somber diners would look up and start to speak, only to think better of it, and go back to the food. The only talk going on was among the coyotes, whose yelps and howls provided a playfully haunting dinner serenade.

After the meal, and the dishes were washed, they retired to the living room to ruminate further. Faro drummed the arm of an old upholstered wing-backed chair while Georgeann leaned with her rump on an end table leafing through a Nexus Magazine, perhaps hoping something would jar her mind. Frank stood at the mantle puffing on a colonial style clay pipe. Melissa stood by the large front window peering into the night.

"Hey! Hey! Look!" She shouted turning towards the room.

They turned towards her, and behind her through the window they saw the ghostly brightness of tungsten lights growing brighter in the distance, exactly in the direction of the hole!

"What's happening?" asked Faro as he sprang from his seat and rushed to the window.

"Oh my God!" wondered Georgeann. "Is the hole reversing?"

Frank chimed in, "Not a chance. That looks like human activity to me."

"You told us no one knew about this."

"That's what I thought."

Frank dashed back to the mantle and grabbed a Winchester Model 94 .30-.30 that hung above it. Melissa snatched a Model 1100 20-gauge from a cabinet by the front door. Frank was about to toss a 10/22 across the room to Faro when he saw him produce a matte black M1911 .45 semi-automatic from his jacket, so he tossed it to Georgeann instead.

"I believe in going all in," stated Faro, brandishing the weapon. "Quick! To the bat mobile!" he exclaimed thrusting his finger high in the air without a shred of humor and bolted for the back door, outside of which was the Land Rover.

The four of them raced for the back door shoving aside the kitchen furniture in every direction.

They literally leapt into the vehicle and sped off as fast as the rough terrain and the desert blackness would allow them. The dim headlights of the old Series IIA cast such a kaleidoscope of shadows from the low brush and stony rubble that it was almost as hard to track as if it'd been pitch black. Jackrabbits and kangaroo rats darted and dodged every which way in the approaching lights.

Faro held his hat on with one hand while using his .45 to brace himself on the dashboard. Above the din of bouncing he hollered over to Frank, "You know Georgeann told me earlier it's too bad this thing doesn't have a machine gun mounted in back!"

"I'll keep that option in mind next time I'm at Landrover Ranch!"

Chapter 15

As the hole drew closer, they were abruptly confronted by a military cordon being erected. Frank slammed on the brakes. Troops were running to and fro engaged in the business of cordoning while the stuttering thunder of choppers roared overhead. The army had swept in from the opposite end of the property from the house and had gone unnoticed until the lights came on.

The group's firearms were suddenly impotent. They were outmanned and outgunned. They debarked from the Rover and approached the cordon where they were stopped by an MP. He spoke into his headset.

Shortly, a tall gray-haired but wiry and solid looking colonel appeared and accosted them.

"Who are Francis J. and Melissa Shorley?"

They looked at each other and raised their hands somewhat tentatively.

"You have precisely two choices," bellowed the colonel over the din. "You can either move to Australia and accept an annuity of $250,000 a year, or you can go to jail on trumped up drug charges."

Faro flashed a gesture that involved wiggling his fingers in front of his breast but was too fast to really see, and then tilted his hat forward. "They'd like 10 years up front," he stated.

The colonel beheld the professor quizzically surprised. He adjusted his hat, tugged at his uniform, and gesticulated in the manner of a third base coach, eyeing Faro suspiciously as he finished. He then addressed Georgeann.

"And who are you?"

Faro sidled up to her and said, "She's with me."

The colonel raised his hand to his shoulder gesturing to the man behind while simultaneously forming the gesture of benediction. Another officer stepped forward. "Captain, write these people a check for two and half million dollars."

The captain opened a binder, wrote the check, tore it loose, and handed it to Frank, who couldn't believe any of this was happening. Melissa slid up close, and pinching one corner of the check, tilted it up so she could see. Her jaw dropped. Frank, using his extended index finger under her chin, pushed it closed.

"You have 12 hours to vacate the property after which time you shall never return. Is that clear?"

The Shorleys nodded.

The colonel turned to leave, then stopped. He looked back over his shoulder at the quirky professor in the A2 jacket and Australian drover hat still dangling his .45 at his side. He winced and puzzled momentarily, shook his head, and receded into the blinding light inhabited by bustling silhouettes of men.

Chapter 16

"What the Hell was that?" huffed Frank back at the house?

"Looks like someone found out about that hole."

"Well, that's obvious!" he railed. "I mean that thing with your hand." Frank imitated the gesture poorly.

Faro shrugged his shoulders. "You pick these things up."

Melissa chuckled ironically. "Where can I get one?"

"I have to keep his Rolodex locked up in a safe," Georgeann chimed in. "The Doc 'knows people.' It goes with the territory."

"I wish you'd teach us that."

"Officially, I have no idea what you're talking about. Unofficially, it got you two and half million dollars instead. I suggest we make haste."

"Yeah, I suppose we should thank you for that," Melissa stated sincerely.

"Thank me for what? Your property is gone. Your work is ruined. You'll never get all of your belongings out of here in time, and you'll have to start completely new lives. You might as well thank a rattlesnake for biting."

"Yes," said Melissa thoughtfully, "but we still have almost 12 hours. I suggest instead of rushing, we look carefully at what we have and take the most important items."

"But let's not get too sentimental," added Frank. "We need to be practical above all else."

"I agree. You'll never get back to the control room though. It was inside the cordon. Focus on what's in the house."

"Fortunately we brought the trailer back from the hole, so we don't have to be too stingy about what we take."

The four friends spent the next several hours packing, rummaging through old boxes and closets, combing the basement and the attic for the most important items of personal and practical importance, and making last minute phone calls.

The sun was just coming up as the loaded vehicle and trailer rolled through the gate for the last time.

"Our first stop should be Las Vegas where we can cash that check. And I mean cash it. That's something you don't want to take any chances with."

"Right."

"Georgeann, you can make arrangements with my usual guy to handle the Shorleys' new financial windfall. I've got some other arrangements to make for them."

In fact, Dr. Faro was not a wealthy man, he thought having too much money would make him soft, so any lump sums that came in were immediately poured into his research, his students' research, carving out a fiefdom in the university that was free from the usual academic bullshit, and, of course, his favorite charities. However, he did have connections. You'd be amazed at the array of wealthy financiers, industrialists, and kooks wanting to invest in the professor's unique abilities. Elon Musk? Richard Branson? Pshaw! Child's play.

"We need a place to stay and a trip to plan. We can't get home and we have to get crackin' on our relocation."

"Nonsense!" interjected Dr. Faro. "I've already got a place for you to stay; you're not moving to Australia."

"Yeah, but the colonel said..."

"Look. You've got 2.5 million dollars to work with. Don't you think we can arrange a work around? I know a brilliant, and believe it or not, honest, lawyer named Farquelle in Anchorage. We'll arrange a perfectly legal and legitimate name change through him. Meanwhile you go where I've arranged. When you emerge you'll be new people. Quite literally."

"But first Las Vegas," Georgeann reminded him.

"Yes. You think we can catch *Crazy Girls* at the Riv?"

Chapter 17

"Pull up here. A valet'll park this for you."

"The Luxor? You want me to just pull up to the Luxor in this jalopy and us reeking like three day old fish."

"They know me here."

Frank shook his head. "Doc, you get more interesting by the minute."

"What? I used to work here."

Frank and Melissa stared incredulously.

"OK. OK. I can't stand academia, so I quit for a while and took a job here as a floor manager until the SDSU gig came along. They were people I could work with."

"The Luxor. A giant pyramid. Well that just figures. I would've thought Circus Circus was more your vintage."

Faro frowned at him. "Anyone have a better idea?"

"Why not just some cheap, seedy motel?"

"We'll have better privacy and security here for what we have to do. They're expecting me. I called before we left."

"Oh that's great. A call I'm sure was tapped. Privacy? They'll know exactly where we've come."

"Which is more or less what they'd expect with a couple million burning a hole in your pocket. Had you gone to a seedy motel, now that would have been suspicious."

The valets looked perplexed as Frank piloted the old heap and its trailer under the canopy. Just then a rotund middle-aged man named Provenzano stepped out.

"Mr. Provenzano!" exclaimed Faro embracing the man warmly.

"Hey, hey, Paisan!" he joked, slapping his back affectionately. "Call me Rico. I'm not your boss anymore." He referred to a shortening of his first name, Enrico.

"OK. Rico." The professor chuckled. "It seems so strange."

The valets by now were catching on.

"Put my friends', uh, 'SUV' here in the special parking garage." He tipped the valet himself, and as Faro reached into his own pocket, Rico made a dismissive gesture that stopped him. Faro shrugged his shoulders.

"I've got two adjoining suites arranged for you, but don't worry, there's three bedrooms between them."

"You are too kind, Mr. P. I mean, Rico."

"Not at all. Not at all. We've missed you around here. Frankly, truly impeccably honest floor managers are hard to come by these days."

"I would think that goes with the territory," said Melissa.

Rico threw back his head and laughed. "Unfortunately, Mrs. er...."

"Shorley. Melissa Shorley."

"I'm Frank."

"Nice to meet both of you. And like I was saying, unfortunately, you're right. It does."

He placed his hand gently in the small of her back as she entered, followed by Georgeann and then the men.

"Why don't you guys check in and get cleaned up before lunch. You smell like a bad Taleggio," he added playfully.

"Hahaha! That's putting it mildly."

Chapter 18

Lunch was at the Peppermill, a Las Vegas institution that had changed little over the years while hotels and casinos had come and gone. At the time of our story, it was celebrating its 30th anniversary. It was famous for its pop culture kitsch and giant portions of food. The crew was famished, having not eaten since dinner the night before, and the Peppermill was the perfect place to cure a famished crew.

Dr. Faro had the club sandwich which was an old favorite of his for its simplicity. Frank dove into the famous steak and eggs to make up for missing breakfast, while Melissa tried the eggs Benedict. Georgeann just had to try "The Sinatra," a sandwich comprised of grilled tomato-basil chicken sausage, double-smoked bacon, mozzarella, lettuce and tomato on grilled Parmesan sourdough bread. Rico, who was an old pro on the strip, had the chicken parmesan.

Enthusiastic "ooohs," "aaaahs," and "mmmmmms" accompanied the meal. In between they found a little time for chit chat. Rico, an honest businessman, was famous on the strip for his fairness and integrity. Nevertheless, he knew all the dirt on the strip and entertained his guests with some of the juiciest gossip he knew. He'd become the General Manager at the Luxor since the professor had left and was well-connected. The name Provenzano was a hefty one in a mob town like Vegas, though Rico was only distantly related to the infamous mobster and had never met him. That didn't matter to anyone else. He *could* be family. Rico just let people think what they wanted.

Then it was time to get down to business. Faro told the Shorleys' tale of the last few days being careful to reveal only enough to get the help they needed.

"So the first order of business I guess is to get this check cashed. Once we do that, Georgeann has a guy who will help secure that."

"Do you have the check with you?"

Frank produced the check for Rico to examine.

"Well it's drawn on an HSBC account, and you know what that means."

"Oh God!" Faro laughed, his hands resting on his stuffed belly. He raised one of his palms to Rico, "I do not wanna know where that money came from."

"Well whatever else HSBC does, there are two things they esteem in business: privacy and completing transactions."

"Well, that's good news. I guess."

"It shouldn't be a problem to cash this at the casino. That'll give you an extra layer of privacy and another day before it's deposited."

"We can't thank you enough," Melissa said earnestly.

"Don't mention it."

The professor continued, "Then we're expecting a man named Farquelle to arrive at some point today, a genius lawyer and one of the few honest ones. We have some affairs to settle with him with a bit of that cash so the Shorleys can be spared a move to Australia. If you could let him up to our rooms we'd very much appreciate it."

"Of course."

Frank broke in. "Look, I really don't know what to say to the two of you. Our lives were just about crapped out yesterday and you two mugs have really come through. My faith in humanity has been restored about as suddenly as it died last night."

"Yin and yang, my good man," explained Rico. "The Universe is never out of balance. Whatever evil there is, there is good to balance it."

Chapter 19

A large man in a sport coat, shorts and flip flops burst into the room. Frank and Melissa looked startled. Georgeann rushed in from the adjoining room to check out the ruckus.

"Where is that crazy old wop?" asked Farquelle with a fiendishly playful grin spreading across his face.

Faro appeared in the doorway. "You better watch who you call a wop in this town, Mister." The two men stared menacingly at each other momentarily, then burst into laughter and embraced.

"They probably like me more around this town than you," laughed Farquelle. "I actually spend money here."

"Indeed you do. And we intend to facilitate your vices tonight."

"Great. Let's get started."

The company seated themselves around the suite and got down to business. Farquelle checked some documents the Shorleys made certain to secure before their flight from home and questioned them on events. They could open up a lot more with the lawyer owing to attorney-client privilege.

"This'll be easy. You guys will return to Anchorage with me. We'll get you settled in a place and establish state residency immediately. Then we'll go through a legal name change, get new social security numbers, passports, the whole deal. At that point you'll be sufficiently under the radar and can chill out. Just don't come back to Nevada."

"Can't we do all that here?" asked Melissa.

"Yes, but this is the first place they'd look. Alaska is one of the last places they'd look."

"I see."

"Then it's settled. Let's celebrate."

"Georgeann, pay the man for his services."

Georgeann produced a wad of cash more than sufficient to provide a night of fun in Vegas.

"Dinner's on me," proclaimed Farquelle. "And the show!"

After dinner and the show, the Shorleys, Dr. Faro, and Georgeann were far too exhausted for a night in the casinos. But Farquelle, who could easily have awaited the Shorleys in Anchorage, never needed much of an excuse to hit Vegas. He also never had a problem pulling an all-nighter when the right kind of fun was afoot, which Vegas had plenty of.

Our intrepid crew had other plans. They rented a car and drove out to the desert just beyond the city. There they parked the car and watched one of Las Vegas' best nighttime spectacles: the Luxor Sky Beam. At 42.3 billion lumen, it is the most powerful man-made beam of light in the world. It's comprised of thirty-nine 7,000-watt bulbs that send a blue beam of light straight up into the air that is visible for 275 miles around. It's even been designated by the FAA as an aviation navigational landmark.

The quartet leaned against their car in the crisp clear desert air and beheld with marvel the intense blue beam that reminded them of a cosmic death ray.

Chapter 20

In 2005 a book came out called *Thieves of Baghdad* by Matthew Bogdanos chronicling the investigation into the Baghdad Museum looting and subsequent recovery of thousands of artifacts. No one was more qualified to write the book since Bogdanos led the investigation. Since he was a Marine Corps Colonel, some say that, despite the books truthful account and insights, it was released, at least in part, as a distraction from the real issue: the disappearance of thousands of uncatalogued items and why they were left uncatalogued in the first place. And what were French-German archaeological teams doing digging up Iraq mostly in secret in the first place?

About the same time, tales of an Iraqi stargate began to emerge. The story goes that an ancient stargate used by the Sumerians was discovered in the 1920s at Ur. In the 1980s, Saddam Hussein began restorations of the Great Ziggurat at Ur, not only to preserve the Ziggurat and develop the tourism, but to protect and study the stargate within. Apparently he got it working at some point, and that became the point of contention that led to the 2003 Iraq War. The US wanted to prevent him from revealing whatever he found by using it, and take control of the stargate for itself, hence the Imam Ali Airbase only a few miles away in Nasiriyah and constant military presence.

The Powers That Be knew that no professional journalists would investigate the museum theft on their own, or even the causes for the war for that matter. The mainstream media had been bought, sold, and packaged years before. But independent researchers are a tireless and dogged lot who would never give up the search for the real motivations behind world events. So, the story of the Iraqi stargate was planted in conspiracy theory circles as another distraction for them.

Unfortunately for the elites who try to manage world events, ludicrous stories like Iraqi stargates only fool the idiot fringe. One of their more recent efforts to discredit independent researchers is their "flat earth" ploy. This was intended to be picked up and promoted by prominent so-called conspiracy theorists and the alt-media, but everybody immediately spotted the scam. The only ones who did pick up were the worst sort of clickbait junkies.

The hardened, serious researchers, of which there are enough to get the truth out, stuck to serious research and didn't fall for the Iraqi stargate con or the flat earth ploy. Thus, we know about the cargo of goods that flew to Argentina on a Ju-390, ostensibly to attend an air show in Buenos Aires. It's little tidbits like that that show up in the mainstream press, innocently enough, that lead to the high octane speculations, that eventually lead to complete pictures of connected dots.

Also in 2005, at a secret laboratory high in the Andes, but within easy reach of San Carlos de Bariloche, the Ju-390 cargo had been unpacked and catalogued, and analysis had just gotten underway, all under the supervision of Dr. Hans Richter, grandson of Nazi physicist Ronald Richter.

The elder Richter is largely dismissed as a quack by today's mainstream scientific community, but if he was a quack, he had some awfully illustrious supporters. To begin with, aeronautical genius Kurt Tank recommended him to Juan Peron himself after the war. Tank designed highly successful and state-of-the-art aircraft for Nazi Germany including the Fw-190, the Ta-152, and Fw-200. Tank went on to design aircraft for Argentina and India in the post-war years and finished his career as a consultant for Messerschmitt.

Nazi spy August Siebrecht, who ran the macabre, filthy and chillingly efficient Chilean operation for the Nazi International at Colonia Dignidad, greeted Richter personally at the airport in Buenos Aires. Little is known about Siebrecht, which probably means he was very good at what he did, but his excellent work for Rudel's *Kameradenwerk* in assisting Nazis to escape justice after the war is well-documented.

Furthermore, in the 1950s, the US Air Force and Intelligence communities took a very keen interest in this "quack" and secretly funded his work, even referring to him as a "mad genius." We may never know what came of it. Perhaps President Dwight D. Eisenhower's visit to San Carlos de Bariloche in 1960 had something to do with this.

Thinking beyond the vicissitudes of politics and election cycles, the Nazi International set up for the long haul. Children and grandchildren were carefully groomed to replace their predecessors. They were raised with certain ideals and attended special schools. Marriages, while not arranged, were always encouraged within certain circles. Business and financial empires were forged and fortified to survive political change and economic crises. And, most importantly, one's Nazism was never displayed publicly.

So, building on his grandfather's and father's work, Hans Richter was well-prepared for the current work, work which his people believed would actually enable the Fourth Reich to take hold of the world and have its coming out party. Some will say it already had its coming out party on September 11, 2001, but that is for another discussion.

Chapter 21

The same group of stern gray-haired men that greeted Müller and Edda at the airport now entered Richter's lab. The conversation was in German.

"Ah, Herr Richter. We would like to introduce two new members of our circle. This is Herr Müller and Fraulein Siebrecht. Perhaps you have heard of them." They both wore modest lapel pins that upon close examination revealed them to be Knight's Crosses of the Iron Cross with oak leaves. They also came with new bank accounts. The award was also given posthumously to Müller and Siebrecht's unfortunate comrades.

"I have. Fine work getting this cargo to our humble lab."

"Our pleasure."

"It's a pity about your companions. A most unfortunate accident." He paused thoughtfully here, peering over his glasses at Edda. "Siebrecht. I know that name. I used to hear it from my grandfather."

"I'm not surprised," Edda replied. "My grandfather was also a significant figure in the 3rd Reich. And after."

"Well, it appears I'm in good company."

"Hahahaha! The best. I hope." Müller was a complex character, always so cheerful for a man of his ilk, rather like George H. W. Bush: so likable, and yet so dark and despicable.

"Enough pleasantries. How are things progressing, Herr Richter? And where do we go from here?"

"I'm glad you asked. I've just finished working on a presentation. You know how our corporate stooges love PowerPoints. Let's go to the conference room for a preview."

The group all seated themselves in plush, high-back leather chairs around a richly gleaming ebony conference table with the symbol of the Black Sun inlaid with onyx into a milky white polished marble circle. To the rank and file of the SS, to the population at large, and to academic historians, SS stood simply for *Schutzstaffel.* But to the present company, all of which were initiated into the occult circle, SS stood, and still stands, for *die Schwartze Sonne,* or, in English, the Black Sun!

Richter pushed a button on a remote to lower a projection screen and pushed another button on another remote to switch on the projector.

An old color photograph of an enormous factory appeared on the screen.

Richter began his presentation: "If there's one thing we Germans have always been good at, it's concealing research. One of the most masterful examples of this was the gargantuan synthetic rubber factory built by I.G. Farben at Auschwitz. It consumed more electricity than the entire city of Berlin and cost over $2 Billion in today's terms. Over 300,000 inmates from Auschwitz were impressed to work on its construction and approximately 25,000 of them died from exhaustion.

"As it came out in the Nuremberg Trials though, not one ounce of synthetic rubber was ever produced there. So after using all that energy, after gobbling up so much in material, money, and life, the synthetic rubber plant never did what it was ostensibly doing. So what was it up to?"

He paused here. No one in the group indicated any knowledge of this, and some looked quizzically at one another.

Richter switched to another old color photo of human migration during the war.

"It didn't stop there. Tens of thousands of local residents were relocated from their homes to provide accommodations for tens of thousands of our top scientists, technicians and workers. Clearly the plant had a function..."

He looked questioningly at the group again. The older men were characteristically inscrutable. The others were calmly expectant.

He clicked through a series of slides to match the explanation that follows.

"We were obviously up to something else. The most conventional alternative explanation would be that it was a uranium enrichment plant. Few other wartime endeavors would consume that kind of electrical power, space, and labor. There is also speculation that secret SS research was going on related to Black Sun energy, antigravity propulsion, and death rays.

Whatever the case may be, it was not a synthetic rubber factory, and some kind of secret research was going on there. While it may be known to some, it is not talked about. Fortunately Herr Kammler's father left Europe and brought all of his knowledge here with him." He nodded graciously to Herr Kammler who replied in turn.

He then switched to a slide of the Colossus of Rhodes labeled "I. G. Farben" with various body parts emblazoned with the names of companies.

"This wasn't the only place. I.G. Farben was a colossus, a conglomerate of companies drawn together by being made offers they couldn't refuse. It created layers within layers that could conceal secret objectives while making and selling products for public consumption. Projects could be overfunded, and then money could be skimmed and applied to secret research done undercover of some public, or even other secret, projects."

He switched to a series of slides that appeared to be legal documents.

"I.G. Farben created such a monstrous, tangled web of relations that since it was broken up after the war, the liquidation has been impossible to complete even to this day."

He changed the slide again to a smiling jack-o-lantern.

"Our target for completion is Halloween 2012. An auspicious date."

Again he clicked to a new slide, this one showing a vast array of links between various media, entertainment, drug, chemical, food, and agricultural corporations.

"This strategy continues to work today. The fascist business model has been applied again and again to create media and entertainment giants, Big Pharma, and that menace we love to hate most of all, the Military-Intelligence-Industrial Complex that Dwight D. Eisenhower made so sure to warn the American people about. Did he see that on his own, or did someone here inform him?"

Smirky laughter broke out around the conference table and then faded.

He now flipped through an apropos series of concentration camp photos and WWII Nazi propaganda posters.

"Of course nowadays we can't afford the public relations nightmare of concentration camps, slave labor, and gas ovens to achieve our goals. No. No public anywhere would ever fall for that and it'd be too hard to keep secret. No people anywhere would ever be duped again by ideologies based on racial superiority or the global menace posed by this or that ethnic group."

Two fresh slides followed.

"Nowadays we must go about it differently. We medicate nations to death with their Big Pharmas and Big Pharma lobbies. We brainwash them in schools with "progressive" education. Hahaha! It's 'progressive,'" he added with air quotes and a sly grin.

Another round of chuckles around the conference table.

Again he clicked through slides of famous brand chemicals, a jet releasing chemtrails, and media logos and personalities.

"We can poison water and food supplies with carcinogenic pesticides and industrial chemicals. We can poison the air with 'geoengineering' to counteract 'global warming.' We can control the information people access through giant media conglomerates that are made up of brands that used to be independent companies that had to actually compete with each other. We can invent global environmental crises that justify the loss of sovereignty. Global warming, for example, came out of our friends in the Club of Rome."

He now added print ads and short clips of TV commercials.

"We sell this agenda using warmly domestic advertisements shot in soft focus with soft lighting featuring puppies and parents in pastel-colored crew-necked sweaters coddling their children. It's all done under the guise of caring for and about the masses."

Now he showed a series of prominent independent researchers who had been labeled as conspiracy theorists, nut jobs, libeled and shamed, and concluded with a few who had met untimely ends like Gary Webb and Dorothy Kilgallen.

"And when someone comes along who tells the truth, we muster our conglomerates' virtually unlimited resources and focus them on branding dissenters as fake news, as 'conspiracy theorists,' a term invented by the CIA itself, with our help, to discredit skeptics of official stories. We even pay for 'professional skeptics' to be skeptical of everything *except* the narratives we push. Some dissenters even meet unfortunate ends. And the best part of it is, we get the idiots to fund their own demise. We have gotten very good at our game while the rest of the world has gotten worse at theirs."

Excited and enthusiastic muttering erupted around the table. Then one of the gray-haired men spoke.

"Herr Richter, what does all this have to do with the work in question?"

"I'm coming to that."

"And what does it have to do with Germany?" asked Edda.

A contemptuous scoff was heard from one of the oldest gray-haired men. "It was never about *Germany*, Fraulein Siebrecht." He scoffed again and drew approving smirks from the others. He turned back to the scientist. Edda appeared puzzled, though not surprised.

Richter continued his slide show.

"We have four critical tasks at hand:

1. Figure out what parts we have, how they work, and where they fit.

2. Figure out what's missing and how to recreate it.

3. Make necessary repairs to the structure to ensure it functions properly

4. Restore the casing stones."

The group began to nod at one another approvingly.

"I would like to discuss items 3 and 4 first because they are the simplest. These will be funded through Rockefeller and Soros foundations with heroin money that has become available in the wake of the Afghan war. We have a long and prosperous history of cooperation with them, and even now plans are being laid for 'preservation' and 'restoration' of the pyramids. We are meeting some opposition from the legitimate academic archaeologists, but this will not be a serious problem."

He shows some slides of quarry work, shipping, and stone working.

"The casing stones are already under production so that if there are any delays in politics or administration we will have a jump on the work. Our goal is to finish this by 2014."

Edda broke in, "Won't people get suspicious when all these casing stones suddenly appear for the restoration project?"

"Yes. That is why we will simultaneously conduct very public quarrying activities concurrent with the project. Very few will notice that the stones are going up too quickly. After all, they actually believe the Ancient Egyptians quarried and placed over two million blocks, *with their mortar*, in only 22years with stone hammers and copper chisels."

Müller roared momentarily with laughter, then collected himself.

"We will also be repairing the damage to the King's Chamber caused by Vyse's 1837 expedition. This will be necessary to ensure the proper functioning of the resonance chamber and interferometer, which is what the King's

Chamber really is. A special polymer has already been developed and tested to exactly match the granite and repair the stones in place. This was developed at one of our BASF plants, a former member of the I.G. Farben cartel as you know."

Müller laughed again. "We don't make the granite blocks, we make them better," referring to the old BASF commercial. The group chuckled at this.

He switched to a picture of Zahi Hawass.

"Dr. Hawass is causing delays because he loves showing off Vyse's forged cartouche to every press lackey that comes along and every female intern he fancies too much. Plans have been drawn up to remove him if necessary."

Then with a subdued laugh he added, "It's also quite hilarious how he and Erich von Däniken, who hate each other so passionately, have grown to so closely resemble and sound like one another."

Müller interrupted with a wisecrack and a question. "Excuse me Herr Doctor, remind me to do my Zahi Hawass for you some time. It sounds just like my Erich von Däniken," he chortled. "But how is it that such a busy scientist such as yourself has time to plan all this intrigue?"

"An excellent question. I cannot take credit for it. That is the genius of Herr Kammler and Herr Bormann whose fathers accomplished the same things for the 3rd Reich, even in our darkest hours. Bormann handled financing and Kammler organized construction, research and production. That is how we are here today."

The two men nodded graciously again. Richter acknowledged. He paused, scanning the assembly for inquisitive looks. There were none.

Richter presented a slide enumerating the steps he now described.

"Items 1 and 2 will take more time. We must compare the inventories in the tablets and seals to what we have recovered from Iraq as well as other places in the Middle East, and indeed, around the world. Then we must match up the items and determine what is missing. Before any of this can be done, we need to translate or decode all the tablets and seals, which will take some years to complete."

"How many years?"

"Under current conditions, about six and half years, but as more translators are acquired and trained, that figure will be reduced. But the inventory will begin immediately with the first relevant translation.

"Testing has already begun on some of the objects. The spheres, for example, we already know are made of high temperature baked ORMEs."

"Which are......"

"Orbitally Rearranged Monotomic Elements. Most of them are from the Platinum Series of metals. We suspect some of the crystals have this property as well."

"Fantastic! Truly fantastic!"

"We also know, quite obviously that we are without this..."

Richter now clicked to a slide of a glowing white pyramidal crystal emitting bright blue rays....

"The pyramid capstone! This of course is an artist's reproduction of what we need to find or recreate."

He then clicked through a series of pictures representing corporate and university logos as well as headquarter buildings, production plants and campuses.

"Many of the parts we have now will be studied and analyzed by our corporate allies or in university laboratories that we fund. Some of this will be done in secrecy couched within other secret research currently going on or planned with these partners."

"What about the parts that aren't recoverable?" a gray-haired man asked.

"Another excellent question. You obviously know that according to the ancient texts, some of the parts were deliberately destroyed in the remote past after the Second Pyramid War. These will be developed in a manner similar to the process I just mentioned using corporate and academic partners. This may require the development of new processes, systems of production, and materials.

"Like I said, these items are much more complex and time-consuming. They will also require vast sums of money to accomplish in the shortest time possible. Fortunately, the Americans, and Bill Clinton in particular, have obliged us by repealing Glass-Steagall. American banks can now generate enormous quantities of wealth quite easily."

Someone raised a hand and spoke, "How are you sure the casing stones will fit properly, and work once they do?"

"Excellent. Excellent. We actually managed to find buildings in Cairo that contained the original casing stones and take measurements. We were able to extrapolate the rest. It doesn't really matter if they match the originals exactly, as long as we can fit them precisely enough to reproduce the concave, collective properties of the original surface."

"And how will that be accomplished?"

"With this." Richter fumbled through a few slides until he found the one he was looking for. It was of the great pyramid, but appeared to be indoors.

"This is a mock-up of the Great Pyramid which was created using precise laser scans of the structure at Giza, and then reconstructed under two miles of ice in Antarctica, only the outer surface of course. As each stone is produced it is added to the structure to ensure a tight, secure and functional fit. The effects become more and more curious as more and more stones are added."

"What do you mean 'curious'?"

"That it works."

Edda raised an important question: "Who do you intend to see this presentation? It would be dangerous if the wrong people got their hands on it, others would find it outrageous or even ridiculous."

"You are quite correct, Fraulein. The latter we d   ﹁t have to worry about, for they will dismiss it as quackery. sure our employees at Skeptical Questioner will have a day with it. It is only for the highest level partners who we have already cultivated and vetted over the years. Their job will be to assign the proper work tasks down the chain using whatever plausible pretenses suffice. It is, of course, all tightly compartmentalized."

"What about Faro? It is clear from his publications that he is onto this. And our contacts at CIA say the agency did consult him on the matter."

One of the gray-haired men spoke up. "He has a firm grasp of the general concept, I'll admit. We need to keep an eye on Faro. But the project is so vast and so compartmentalized, even he won't know what's going on, even if one our tasks were a part of his own research. And even if he did, who would believe him? What was it Fraulein Siebrecht just said? 'It would sound outrageous, or even ridiculous.' No government or organization with any resources would ever take it seriously."

Chapter 22

No one could see them. No one could hear them. No one could track them. No one knew they were there. They had been trained in the tradition of Geronimo and Cochise. They were not even phantoms or illusions. They simply didn't exist.

The first thing they learned was how to track. To learn to track men, they learned to track mice. To learn to track mice, they learned to track ants. But in the Apache tradition, tracking was more than just reading footprints. It was reading the Universe.

On a practical level this means reading the concentric rings in nature. Birdsong and animal behavior tells you everything that's going on around you. If the birds behave one way, then everything's normal or peaceful in the forest. If they behave another way, you know a predator has appeared. You can even tell exactly what kind of predator is near by the bird behavior—absolute silence means one thing, flight to the treetops means another, loud alarm calls from the same spot mean something else again, and birds flying up into the trees every which way like popcorn is yet another signal, and a "bird plow" is a sign that noisy, obtrusive humans are about 2 minutes away. This is also true for the behavior of mice, or the behavior of deer, and so on.

These responses are most intense at the locus of disturbance and spread out through the wilderness like concentric rings on a pond, gradually dissipating in intensity. The Apache tracker, or those taught in the same methods, learns to read these rings like a newswire that is constantly and continuously updating all the wild inhabitants of a place. Or a human who knows how to read the interference patterns.

This is why 5000 troops of the US Army could never catch Geronimo. 5000 men on foot and horseback with wagons and artillery throw some gargantuan concentric rings.

It was easy for Geronimo and his 27 warriors to keep three days ahead because they always knew where the army was, even three days away. The best Apache scouts who had turned against their people and worked for the army couldn't even track Geronimo and his 27 men. That is because they were not true scouts in the Apache sense, or they wouldn't have been working for the army to begin with.

Besides, the master tracker is also skillful at counter tracking. He can make it look like he's going one way when he's really going another. He can lay false tracks that lead his pursuers into traps. He can appear to be in one place when he is really in another. He can even leave no tracks at all.

This level of skill is reserved for the true Scouts, a secret society of highly trained individuals whose own spouses don't even know they are members. Even the chief and elders of the tribe don't know who the Scouts are. They move in the shadows between darkness and light. They travel in the places people never look, the "dead space." They devise new ways of walking and running to conceal their tracks and hide their intentions. They are masters of camouflage and invisibility. Thus, instead of confronting their enemies directly, they defeat them instead through psychological warfare, which usually means confounding them so badly it scares the bejeezus out of them such that they turn on each other.

The day may come when your teacher tells you, "If you understand the concentric rings deeply enough, couldn't you reproduce the concentric rings yourself? And if you can reproduce the concentric rings of a fox, wouldn't you, therefore, be perceived as a fox? If you can reproduce the concentric rings of a coyote, wouldn't you therefore be perceived as a coyote? Thus, you stand at the threshold of shapeshifting."

A certain pair of coyotes was well-known to the soldiers at the hole. Familiar members of the local fauna, they emerged daily from their den to forage, hunt and rest among the sage. But they were not coyotes. They were men.

Chapter 23

These "coyote-men" had been contacted, indirectly, by Dr. Faro. Another man he knew well had been trained from his youth in the ways of the coyote. He, in turn, trained others, who trained more.

The men in question had come from Utah. No, not the infamous Skinwalker Ranch introduced to the popular consciousness in George Knapp and Colm Kelleher's chillingly compelling book *Hunt for the Skinwalker*. These men came from an organization so elite, few know of its existence: Point Man. To those familiar with military tactics, the name's meaning is obvious: the man most important who goes in front of a patrol as a lookout, to be the patrol's eyes and ears and subsequently bearing the highest pucker factor.

The second most important man is the tail. He brings up the rear and has to look two ways at once. Hence, he has the second highest pucker factor to deal with. In a tracking formation the tail is called the diamond. The other two men in a tracking formation are called wings and fan out to the sides. But company names have to be simple, and "Point Man" was obvious to its clientele which almost exclusively came from America's elite forces and some of its allies'. The few remaining were not exactly clientele, but hand-picked members selected by the company's owner Kelvin Greaves. Greaves referred to them jokingly as "Kelly's Heroes."

Kelly's Heroes were recruited from various tracking clubs, primitive survival schools and prepper communities mostly in America, but people came from all over the world to the States to participate in such events as the Falling Leaves Rendezvous or MAPS Meet or Tracker School because the US had the most active communities. No one's really sure if these people were paid or not, there were certainly no records of it, but then they didn't seem to have any other occupations either.

Greaves and the professor were well-acquainted. When the military showed up and chased the Shorleys off their property with a 2.5 million dollar check in hand, Faro had a hunch the situation needed to be watched closely, and he only knew of one kind of person that could do that in the semi-barren scrubland of Nevada—an Apache scout. He didn't know any Apache scouts personally, but he knew one guy who'd been trained like them and that he knew others.

Kelvin, or Kelly to his friends, dispatched two guys at a time who worked in 3-month shifts in a kind of on-the-job training. When operating, they went only by their "Indian names," monikers which were customarily given after ironic or embarrassing circumstances as a kind of homage to the Native lineage of knowledge. The two at the hole today were known as Thorny and One Flare. Thorny got his nickname because he was a total prick, especially to cultural Marxists who he liked to offend or insult at every opportunity. One Flare got his when he failed to light a fire one rainy day despite consuming one entire road flare in an effort to ignite his soggy tinder bundle.

They were well-matched. One was a former bike messenger and the other a former pro-skater. We say former only because once a guy joins Kelly's Heroes, whatever kind of livelihood he may have had, seemingly evaporates. Thorny had a masterful knowledge of plants, while One Flare was a master tracker and hunter. They combined their talents for daily meat and vegetables and stole water from the camp when needed. They'd been on the scene now for two months having relieved the previous team.

Suddenly, the bird life exploded, then fell suddenly and hauntingly silent. Even snakes and lizards were darting for shelter. They'd never seen anything like it and thought an earthquake was about to hit, since they'd heard stories of animals anticipating natural disasters.

They inched into a clump of sagebrush and lay next to each other to take in the goings on. The sun was just setting. As it dipped below the horizon, a dim white glow began to gather at the top of the hole, which grew gradually brighter as darkness descended on the desert.

Thorny and One Flare looked at each other in wonderment. Thorny began to get up but One Flare stopped him and pointed. A man scribbling on a clip board and another with a handheld video camera approached the hole. Men started shouting as engines roared awake. Eventually, a blazing pillar of white light shot up into the sky as far as they could see.

Thorny whispered over to One Flare, "That'd be pretty cool on a couple o' tabs, huh?"

One Flare suppressed his laughter. "Why'd'ya always have to say shit like that at times like this?"

"Can't help it. I'm incorrigible."

"You're somethin'."

"We have to get that clipboard and camera."

"I know."

Just then, something solid seemed to rise up out of the hole. A giant, white pyramidal crystal rose peak first until it was fully visible, floating above the chasm it had emerged from.

"Jeeee-zuss! What th----"

"Whoa! Dude! That must be what we're looking for."

Their coyote appearance faded as they talked, which changed the concentric rings, but they still had camo comprised of mud, sand, charcoal and plant debris coating them from head to toe with nothing on but a pair of buckskin shorts and thin moccasins each, that they'd made themselves. Thin-soled mocs leave much less conspicuous tracks than bare feet, and to lessen their impact even more, they never took the same route up to the camp. This avoided any trails from forming other than the ones already utilized by the local wildlife.

The aggressive colonel we met earlier swung open the flap of his tent and came out. He stared momentarily in bovine amazement at the object. "Captain!" he barked. "Get Jorgensen over here! Tell him to bring his radio. We need a secure channel to SCB."

"Yessir!"

The giant flood lights came on one by one around the fortified camp. Most of the guards were suddenly ineffectual as their awe for the risen crystal distracted them from the perimeter. Giant equipment whirred to life and moved in on the object as the salvage operation commenced.

Now for anyone who has ever played around a campfire, you know that the blazing light destroys your night vision, and that things just beyond the immediate fire light are completely invisible in the blackness. It is so much more so under the glare of humongous, powerful floodlights, especially when they are all turned inwards. Thorny and One Flare certainly knew this and silently inched up to the edge of light.

The two men with the clipboard and camera had moved out of the glaring spots to the edge of camp so that they might better view the camera footage. They sat on a large rectangular crate just outside the mess tent.

The man with the clipboard set it absently on the crate next to him and leaned in to the other man to watch the video. Slowly, silently, imperceptibly, a dust covered hand briefly penetrated the world of light and ever so slowly and silently receded again into the shadows with a clipboard.

Again absently, the clipboard man reached over for his clipboard with his eyes still on the video, perhaps to compare his notes with what was on the display. His hand danced around on its fingertips feeling for the pad, but couldn't find it. Puzzled, he turned his head to where he'd laid the clipboard. He leaned over the end of the crate expecting it to have fallen off. Nope. He spread his knees and looked down between his feet. Nothing. Now he began spinning and agitating.

"Hey, what'd you do with my clipboard?"

"Nothin', man. Where'd you put it?"

"Right here. But now it's not there!"

The cameraman laid down his camera on the crate as the two men stood up. They did the "turn and look shuffle." You know that dance you do when you drop your keys? Your feet shuffle left and right as your body rotates back and forth with your head down scanning the ground.

While they did this, another dust and charcoal shaded hand slowly and steadily rose to the top of the crate and withdrew the camera into the world of shadows.

"Maybe you left it back at the hole. Let's go look."

"I'm sure I brought with us. It must be here."

"Well, it's clearly not. Let me just grab the cam----. Hey! Where's the camera?"

"How should I know? I haven't touched your camera."

"Ya did so!" He shoved clipboard man in the chest. "Ya took it cuz ya thought I took your clipboard!"

Being innocent, clipboard man raised his hands over his head. "See for yourself."

Camera man patted the outsides of his pockets but came up bupkis.

"Well where the Hell's our shit, man?"

Just then they heard the Colonel shouting above the din of the salvage equipment. "Bueller! Grossman! Bring me that camera footage!"

They ran over to the colonel and snapped to attention. "Ah, sir?"

"What's the problem, Bueller?"

"Ahhhh. The camera and the notes are gone, Sir."

"Gone?"

"Yes, Sir. Gone, Sir."

"What do you mean, 'gone?'"

Bueller and Grossman gave a breathless account of what had just happened, being sure to interrupt and blame each other frequently.

"Damn, you two!" the colonel exploded. "Sound the alarm! We've been compromised!"

A loud siren broke the desert silence for miles around and spots were spun outward to pan the rocks and scrub for bandits. Using the tumult for cover in a maneuver the two misfits had practiced many times as boys fleeing security guards and police, Thorny and One Flare bolted, the ruckus drowning out any sound their footfalls might have made, as well as their gleefully mischievous laughter.

The powerful lights swept the ridges and ravines casting precisely the kinds of shadows Thorny and One Flare designed their camo to be most effective in. But it didn't matter. They were neither on the ridges nor in the ravines. They were darting through the dead space, in between.

Chapter 24

Now Thorny and One Flare had a choice. The typical Apache tactic would be to keep moving nonstop, without rest or sleep, for three continuous days. Back in the day, this tactic worked marvelously since their enemies would usually break for meals and a night's sleep. By the end of the flight there would be two days distance between the Apaches and their pursuers. But back in the day there were no such thing as helicopters.

The other choice was to dive into their scout pit until next morning. The scout pit was an underground shelter with at least 3 feet of dirt on top. The door was a basket filled with soil that plugged the entrance snugly enough to be unnoticeable. The whole thing was landscaped so as to appear natural. In said pit, they'd be invisible to FLIR through any night searches. They could gamble that the search would be called off the next morning and that they could resume their getaway.

They dove into the scout pit to palaver. Thorny lit a candle and One Flare plopped the lid in place. They whispered.

"Dude, what do you wanna do?"

"I don't know, man. If they call in a chopper with FLIR we're busted."

"They don't even have a chopper. We haven't seen one in two months."

"I know they don't have a chopper. Notice I said 'call in'."

"OK. Can they do that?"

"I dunno. That's what these people do. They 'call in' things. You know what Tom said: don't move at night. You'll have better invisibility in daytime with all the night vision shit they have nowadays."

"So you wanna hang here till tomorrow?"

"I say we let those doofuses drive their jeeps and fly their helicopters all night looking for us and break out tomorrow."

"Welp, joke's on them I reckon. I doubt these lunkheads can track from a moving vehicle anyway, especially at night."

"These asshats couldn't track a dinosaur in peanut butter."

"C'mon. No one's that bad. Let's hunker down."

Just then Thorny heard a sucking sound and smelled something sweet yet smoky, something intoxicating and seductive.

"Dude, djoo just light a doob?"

"A-yeah."

"Well give me a hit."

One Flare passed the doob to Thorny.

"You hear that?"

"A-yeah. Sounds like they drove right over us."

"Yeah it does."

They started giggling, then composed themselves and lay still, passing the joint back and forth.

"Whoa! You hear that? Another one."

"Hey, let's check out that video."

"Good idea."

They switched on the camera and fumbled with the buttons until the video started playing on the display. In the dim blue glow of the screen their jaws dropped in amazement at what they beheld.

They shared the joint until there was nothing left. Holding in his final hit as he spoke, Thorny remarked, "Low tech beats high tech every time."

"Yep."

They blew out the candle and went to sleep.

Chapter 25

The salvage operation continued amidst the alarm, while the colonel dispatched search teams to catch the perpetrators.

"All right, teams, we're looking for the folks who stole a vidcam and a clipboard. Both contain valuable information that must be returned to HQ with this thing we just pulled out of the ground. Recover the camera and clipboard by any means necessary. Am I clear?"

"Yessir!"

"Any questions?"

"Yes, sir. How many people are we looking for?"

"We don't know. Whoever it is, or they are, they must have gear and water for survival in the desert. The gear will weigh them down. A vehicle will make a dust cloud. Boots should leave obvious footprints. There should be a campsite. They may have lights for navigation at night. Look for any clue that will lead you to them."

He scanned the search teams for any other questions. There were none. "OK, Hammer and Thor teams, go out the perimeter where the theft occurred and look. Huginn and Muninn teams search the other three sides. All of you are to coordinate with the chopper when it arrives."

Men in SUVs lumbered into the desert spraying clouds of dust from under their wheels.

This was the "bigger hammer" more so than the "Thor's hammer" approach to search and destroy. If you can't track, you send out a whole lot of people to look in every nook and cranny or perhaps to "flush your game" and hope for results. Even for people wanting to be found, the method often fails. But all this gang had were hammers, and the colonel sent out the biggest one he could.

Neither their headlights nor the door-mounted spots could find any trace of the boys. They scared up a lot of rodents, flattened a few snakes, and chased off the odd fox here and there. The clipboard and camera thieves could not be found. When a black, unmarked helicopter joined the chase, it didn't help. Everything the FLIR picked up that wasn't in an SUV had four legs.

As dawn broke, the search teams returned to camp and the helicopter was out of fuel.

"No sign of them, Sir."

"Damn!"

Teams in hazmat suits with specially contrived poles maneuvered the crystal away from the hole and secured it, still levitated, to a hastily constructed rack. The rack hung, suspended a few inches above the ground from the base of the crystal. Using the rack, the men guided the large glowing crystal over the hike back to the house. There a flatbed tractor-trailer had been parked for years waiting for its cargo.

The rack was secured to the bed while another team carefully constructed an 8x8x8 wooden crate to fit over the crystal. The size of the crate was as much to disguise the size and the shape of the object as for safety. Room was needed for the walls to be lined with a layer of thick rubber mats over another layer of special lead-based ceramic tiles. It was only just now being constructed because nobody knew exactly what would come out of the hole or how big it would be. In the meantime, a tarp was thrown over it.

The rubber mats and ceramic tiles were a lesson learned from the German physicists that worked on *Die Glocke*, otherwise known as The Nazi Bell, under Hans Kammler's SS secret weapons program. It was an experimental device shaped like a bell (*glocke* in German) designed to test concepts in torsion energy and anti-gravity propulsion, and it emitted strange forces when operating. The first group of scientists to power it up died sudden, painful and agonizing deaths. Subsequent experiments revealed that the Bell had strange effects on living tissue from crystallization to decomposition into disgusting black goo. In their evil twisted wisdom, the Nazis only permitted slave laborers from the neighborhood concentration camp to enter the room where the device was tested. The rubber mats and ceramic tiles protected the scientists who remained outside.

Now having retrieved a self-luminous giant crystal from a bottomless hole, the group at the hole didn't really know what to expect or what effect it would have. They surmised that what worked to contain the strange emissions from the Bell might work for this thing as well.

After the laborious process of building the crate. It was lowered over the object and fastened to the rack. The remaining space was filled with soil before fastening on the lid. The weight of the soil alone would help conceal that the cargo was in fact weightless. It rolled out of the gate just as Thorny and One Flare emerged from their scout pit. They raced up to a higher ridge and perched themselves where they watched until it was out of site.

Chapter 26

Back in the Colonel's tent, he was seething. The recovery of the mysterious object had gone well. But a thorough search for the perpetrators of the theft turned up squat, as did an in-camp search for the camera and clipboard, which meant he would fail to deliver them. The Colonel didn't like failure, and now it was his duty to report it.

Jorgensen sat with a headset on operating his radio as the Colonel stood beside him, also wearing a headset, speaking German into the mic. "The pyramidion is on its way....my congratulations to Herr Richter, his speculation was right on target....no, Sir....I'm afraid they're missing.....probably not lost, stolen.......yes, Sir.......Jawohl.....Jawohl!"

Just then a sergeant came in. "Sir, we have some more activity at the hole. We think you should have a look."

"Thank you, Sergeant. Have Bueller and Grossman meet me there."

Bueller and Grossman were quickly found in the mess tent just having breakfast. The sergeant instructed them to abandon their meals and proceed immediately to the aforementioned meeting place.

They hiked over with the sergeant and arrived to a great commotion. A geologist was bent over frantically sweating over a seismograph. Other men, some scientists, some technicians, tapped on dials and gauges as if they were malfunctioning. One guy was waving a Geiger counter while another had is head buried in casing and wiring. Another called off readings from a device I'm sure you've never heard of: a torsion field detector. This device detected changes in local space-time due to changes in the torsion fields in the ether. When these changes become detectable, something big is about to happen.

In fact these changes are occurring constantly and

continually around us, but within ordinary limits we can call baseline. These ordinary states can be altered when scientists start messing around with certain kinds of geometric forms, motion, and powerful electromagnetic or electrogravitic fields. That is because certain geometric forms, especially tetrahedrons and pyramids, and electromagnetic forces, even with null vectors, can have scalar effects on the ether. The torsion field detector interprets these changes and translates them into a meaningful scalar value using Maxwell's quaternion equations.

The Colonel stood about 6 feet from the great chasm consulting with his scientific staff when the two men reached him. Touching one man on the shoulder he guided them into position between himself and the hole. Shoulder to shoulder, they snapped to attention and he responded with the "at ease" command.

He stood proudly and confidently erect with his hands comfortably set in the small of his back. Silently he positioned himself exactly in the center in front of the pair. He cast his glare back and forth from one to the other only inches from their faces. They began to fret.

The Colonel did a quarter turn so that now he was perpendicular to the men and looked off into the distance thoughtfully.

"Gentlemen, if there's one thing I can't stand more than incompetence, it is betrayal."

They looked askance at each other not knowing what the Colonel was talking about.

"What do you mean, Colonel?"

The Colonel turned to face them again and continued with stern and measured speech. "We have conducted a thorough search of this site, and of the desert surrounding it. There is no trace of the camera or the clipboard, nor of any alleged perpetrators. Not a track, not a trail, not an abandoned campsite, not a tire track, not a sign of a single human being who doesn't belong. That leaves me with only one conclusion."

Their eyes widened. "Wait a minute, Sir. It's not like that."

"Isn't it?"

"No, Sir. There must be some mistake."

"Well, then, why don't we do this the easy way? Just tell me where the articles are so they can be retrieved and sent to their rightful owners."

"We told you yesterday, Sir. They were stolen. We don't know where they are. We need to look harder for the jokers who took them."

"Gentlemen, do you love the Reich? Do you love serving the Reich?"

"Of course, Sir." They threw terrified sideways glances at each other.

The Colonel looked at his feet and sighed. "Let me make this easier then."

Immediately he shoved Grossman into the hole. His screams were heard until they faded into oblivion. Bueller turned left and right then tried to flee, but he was stopped by a couple of MPs.

"Bueller?"

There was no response, just terror.

"Bueller?"

His mouth was open, his jaw twitched, but only a desperate silence came forth.

The Colonel repeated, "Bueller?"

His eyes shifted left and right at the MPs restraining him as he struggled to free himself. The Colonel gave a dismissal flick of his hand and the MPs hurled him into the hole to follow his partner.

"Check their quarters. Shred every goddamned thing in there if you have to. Find that camera and clipboard!"

The MPs marched off. One slapped the other playfully on the chest with the back of his hand. "Bueller, Bueller, Bueller? Hahahaha!" He joked referring the 1986 movie Ferris Bueller's Day Off.

"Hahahaha. Ja. You can't make that sort of thing up!"

Just then, the world around the MPs changed. It changed for everyone on site. A slow motion, muted, dreamlike quality infused the place. A sudden flash blinded everyone present as if the hole had disgorged in one great belch all the light it ingested when the Shorleys ran their fateful experiment.

When the men came to, the hole was gone. In a gruesome act of poetic justice, it had partially claimed the colonel. Parts of him stuck up out of the earth in a Hellish arrangement that was physically impossible. A foot stuck out here, a leg there. A forearm dangled limply from its elbow. His head protruded from a boulder that had been at the periphery of the hole. It was silently screaming.

Chapter 27

Jay and Chloe Seeling had a nice place in Fallon. It was a homey little ranch house with a big yard. Jay built a kind of pole barn blacksmith's forge in the backyard where he practiced his hobby of, you guessed it, blacksmithing, with scrap metal he found around old wrecks in the desert. His favorite pastime was turning leaf springs into knife blades that he mounted in handles of horn, bone, or wood. He made an informal business of it selling them off to friends and family or doing occasional commissions for them.

He was thus engaged when two visitors appeared under the roof of his forge. They said nothing but stood there quietly watching him work. The noise of the bellows, the roar of the forge, and his ardent absorption in the iron prevented him from noticing their arrival. Thorny and One Flare stood there "acting naturally."

Jay then turned from the forge with the red hot iron gripped firmly in his tongs towards the anvil when he spotted the two intruders. He was so badly startled he dropped the iron and danced a jig to avoid the burning hazard. His fright immediately turned to joy when he saw who they were.

"Hahahaha! You know I have to get you back for that."

"Do your worst."

The trio embraced like the old friends they were.

Jay picked the iron with his tongs and placed it on the anvil. "How are you guys and what the Hell are you doing here?"

"We need a ride."

"That's it? No 'How are you, Jay, and how's Chloe? And by the way we'd like to buy a couple of knives.'"

"How are you, Jay?"

"And how's Chloe?"

"Sorry, we don't have any money with us."

"That figures. I'm fine. Chloe's at work. C'mon in."

They entered through the back door.

"It's a good thing we have a mud room," quipped Jay, "because you guys are covered with it."

"A yeah. Maybe we should shower."

"Now that you mention it, there's a garden hose next to the door. Use it. You got clothes?"

Thorny and One Flare each held up a handmade deerskin musette bag they'd retrieved from a cache along the way.

"I should have known," Jay chuckled. "I'll get some towels."

Thorny went first gently spraying himself with the ice cold water. Then adjusting the nozzle, he set it for full blast and sprayed One Flare.

"Ow! Dude! Whattaya doing? Gimme that!"

A good-natured wrestling match ensued over the nozzle as the two boys got wetter and wetter and their camo ran down into their shorts and soaked their moccasins.

"Oh God! Right in my eyes!"

"You deserved it!"

"Damn."

"Shit."

Jay appeared with the towels. "I'm not giving you Chloe's nice clean towels until that's all off."

"OK....OK. Stop!.....Stop! Time to help Jay."

"Alright. You go first."

One Flare finished rinsing himself thoroughly scrubbing parts of himself occasionally with his hands.

"Here. You're turn."

Thorny finished up. They dried themselves and put on their street clothes. Thorny had a Sex Pistols T-shirt depicting the *Never Mind the Bollocks* album cover with the sleeves torn off, cargo shorts and chucks topped off with a dew rag. One Flare somehow managed to conjure up a Bad Brains T to wear with his cut off 'somethings' and Adidas skate shoes. Just to round out the picture, Jay was a Carhartt man.

Thorny looked at One Flare's feet in bewilderment. "Adidas makes skate shoes?" There was a slight tone of indictment for wearing a brand that belonged to "The Man."

One Flare emphasized the reason he wore them, "They were free. Aren't the Sex Pistols a bit, uh, passé?"

"Oh, and the Bad Brains aren't?"

"They're not *as* passé," joked One Flare with mock superiority.

"Change of topic. Do I wanna know what all this is about?" Jay asked circling his finger.

"No."

"Where are we going?"

"Utah."

"Sounds like Kelvin's."

"Can't say, but it's in the same town."

"Why'd you tell him, man?"

"He's driving us there. He's gonna know anyway. Gyawd!"

Jay laughed. "Lunch first?"

"We're in kind of a hurry."

"I'll have to call Chloe first."

"Sure."

"You see that? That right there. That's why I'm not married. Can you imagine doing this with a wife?"

"Oh yeah? I can think of a LOT of reasons why you're not married."

"You know, maybe we should call Kel and tell him we're on the way."

"I already sent him like a gazillion bubbles."

One Flare referred to a technique they'd learned to form a "bubble of intent." You create, in your mind with all your passion, thoughts and feelings, then put them in a bubble and send them to the person you want to effect, or leave it somewhere where you want it to be found. The bubble then has the desired effect on the individual or individuals. It was great fun to practice this in airports and shopping malls and see if you could make someone scratch their nose or change direction.

"Oh, good thinking. But why a gazillion?"

"I'm never sure if they work."

"Then he didn't know they came from you, cuz I keep getting bubbles that say 'take it easy' and 'enough with the bubbles already!' Couldn't figure out why."

One Flare tilted his head back and looked curiously along his nose at Thorny. "Ahhh, so they did work."

"Why'd he think I sent 'em?"

"Cuz yer the wise ass."

"Or you set me up with yer frikkin bubbles."

Just then Jay came back. "Aiight, let's roll. Chloe sends her love and wishes you could stay for chili."

"If she's making her famous chili, we wish we could too."

"Let's hit a 7-11 for a burrito on the way."

"Dude, that's nasty."

"Not as nasty as what comes after."

Jay threw his head back and laughed heartily. "I can't believe I'm gonna spend 10 hours in a car with you guys, especially after burritos."

"You just offered us chili."

Jay pulled out of the driveway and entered the highway.

"Oh wow. Route 50. If we stay on this long enough we'll end up in Ocean City."

"Should've brought our boards," added One Flare shaking his head. "Did I ever tell you guys about the time we stole this big fiberglass gorilla from an OC miniature golf?"

"Not this week."

Chapter 28

Lucky for Jay they didn't hit 7-11 or have any burritos. He forbade it. Instead they hit the Sonic on 50 before heading east.

There is a lot of nothing between Fallon and Moab. It's a very bright and hot nothing in the daytime, and pitch black nothing at night with an increased risk of roadkill. Furthermore, the two scouts slept most of the time having had been awake for two and half days while Jay's only company was his radio and CD collection. We therefore jump to our friends' arrival.

Thorny and One Flare directed Jay to the inconspicuous entrance to the Point Man office which was hard to find in the middle of the night. It was on a large property just outside town. The entrance road was padlocked but Thorny handily picked it with the lock picks given to him by the property owner himself as a gift.

Two similar looking older men came out to greet them. They were both burly confident men who swaggered slightly. One wore his customary A2 jacket and drover hat, the other wore a similarly styled King of the Mountain bowman jacket and a matching felt fedora.

Kelly chuckled as he approached the trio. "Thorny and One Flare. What could go wrong?"

The boys had originally caught Kelvin's interest when they revealed to him that they'd been living in a hogan, they'd built themselves, out of sticks and leaves just outside Washington, DC, completely undetected, for over a year. When he asked how they managed that, they described how they'd carefully chosen the location, were cautious to only enter or leave the park at certain times, and never, ever took the same route twice.

"Why do they look like they're up to something?" commented the professor.

"Because we're always up to something."

"Jay, it's good to see you. Been a very long time. Thanks for giving these two jokers a lift. They'd probably be lost without you."

Jay laughed. "You're probably right. I thought I'd be away from trouble out in Nevada."

"You're never safe from these two. They could show up anywhere, anytime."

"Unfortunately."

"How's the knife making going?"

"Not bad. In fact, they interrupted my current project when they showed up." Jay related how they'd startled him with their stealthy arrival to everyone's amusement.

"I still have that knife you sold me years back."

"I happen to have some with me if you want another. I've gotten better."

"We'll look at those later. Right now, meet Dr. Faro. He's the reason you guys were out there."

Introductions were made all around.

"Thorny, you really gotta take it easy with those thought bubbles."

"It wasn't me! It was One Flare! And I didn't cut Eddie's piss bottle either."

Everyone had a good laugh except Faro who was confused by the inside humor. "I don't think I want to hear about that piss bottle," he remarked.

"Oh you do, but another time, perhaps." Kelvin turned to One Flare. "You're getting good at those bubbles. Not only did I know to get the Doc here, you made me think it was Thorny."

"A yeah. The fun never stops."

"Let's go inside."

They sat down to a midnight snack. "Here, got these because I knew you guys were coming." He handed each of them a pint of Ben & Jerry's.

"Word," said One Flare.

"Nice! Banana Split," added Thorny.

After snacks, Kelvin turned to Jay. "Jay, Can you let us talk a while? Just make yourself at home. Watch TV, get online, tons of books on tracking, skills, woodcraft, Apaches."

"Copy."

After Jay was out of the room the men began in earnest.

"Whattaya got?" Kelvin opened.

Thorny produced the camera and notes from one of his pockets and placed them in the center of the table. Doctor Faro reached over and slid them in front of himself. He unfolded the notes and scanned them intently occasionally going "hmmm" or "ah." Then he reached for the camera and turned it over and around.

"How's this thing work?"

"Here." One Flare reached over and the Doc surrendered the camera to the more tech-acquainted younger man. One Flare flipped the screen and pressed the play button, then turned the camera back over to Faro.

Faro watched thoughtfully for a few minutes and then said, "How long is this?"

"About 30 minutes. Here's what we saw a few nights ago." One Flare fast forwarded to the pyramidion emerging from the hole and then gave it back to the professor.

"Holy cow! And you saw this in person?"

"Yep."

"What else did you see?"

"We saw a flatbed semi roll out with that thing loaded on it. Headed off south before we lost sight of it."

"Tell 'em about the good part."

"You tell 'em. You're better at stories."

Thorny then related the earthquake and the closing of the hole.

"Gee-hose-a-phat! Got a map?"

"Yeah."

Greaves came back with a road atlas and opened it up to Nevada.

"OK. The Shorleys' place is about here, off 379."

"Well south of there you got Vegas and....Area 51?"

"You're correct, Kel." Said Faro. "But Nellis Air Force Range, of which Area 51 is a part, would be too dangerous. Too many regular military personnel around. My high octane speculation has them going somewhere else that is completely compromised and free of any possible honest government intervention, some place so black and so mysterious, there isn't even any visible security. The place I'm thinking of is so rogue, that when the government finally did try to take it down with Delta Force under Carter, they were repulsed and never went back."

"Jesus, Mary and Joseph! And that's right here in America?"

"Where is that?"

"Archuleta Mesa in Dulce, New Mexico."

"That's Jicarilla country."

"That's right. And they have their own contemporary accounts of the strange goings on."

"So wait a minute," said One Flare while supporting an elbow with one hand while holding his chin with the other. "What is this place and how is it compromised?"

"You seem like nice boys," (Kelvin interrupted with a mock cough) "and you've truly done men's work, so I'm going to let you in on something," the professor began.

"This is gonna be good, guys. Pay attention. This is almost as good as what Tom teaches."

"Yes." Faro threw a confused glance at Kelvin, but it was clear everyone but him understood the remark so he went on. "To continue: It's a long and sordid tale but I'll keep it as brief as possible."

"Wait a minute," interrupted Kelvin. "Jay should hear this too. Hey, Jay! C'mere. The Doc has something you should hear."

"Be right there!" Jay entered the kitchen and joined the group around the table.

Faro threw another furtive glance at Kelvin. "To continue. Our government has been compromised, at least since the end of World War II, by its own doing. You boys may have heard of Operation Paperclip under which numerous Nazis were brought to the US and given gainful employment, usually in government or government contract jobs. Gradually they ensconced themselves in the bureaucracy and big corporate contractors and hired more and more of their ilk until they'd wheedled their way into every government agency and corporation they could.

"What you may not know is that in 1946, Admiral Byrd..." Thorny began to interrupt with a gesture, "Yes, that Admiral Byrd, led a military expedition to Antarctica called Operation Highjump. It was ostensibly a scientific expedition, but then why did they need 4000 ground troops and an aircraft carrier?

"What's more likely is that they went to mop up the vestiges of the Nazi base in Neuschwabenland, founded in 1938 under the aegis of Rudolph Hess and Hermann Göring. If so, they failed, and the expedition, which was scheduled to last six months, was canceled after only 8 weeks with the loss of aircraft and men. On his way home, Admiral Byrd told the Chilean newspaper *El Mercurio* that in the future, we would have to face enemies that 'could fly from pole to pole at incredible speeds.' He never spoke about it again publicly and the ship's logs and Byrd's personal journal of the expedition remain classified to this day.

"Clearly the party encountered in Antarctica had some kind of superior technology and was able to finance operations there after the war was over. Then in July 1947 you had the Roswell UFO incident, to which the Army summoned the best Paperclip scientists to investigate thinking the craft was probably German! You put two and two together.

"Let's jump ahead to April 1961 when Kennedy gave his famous speech on secret societies. Most fringe conspiracy theorists will tell you he was talking about the Free Masons and the Illuminati. Utter nonsense. He was referring to the Deep State that was fast taking over the US government and running it in secret. The same can be said for Eisenhower's Farewell Address in which he warned of the Military Industrial Complex. It was an obvious clue to where this rogue element centered its power and financing.

"This rogue element, nowadays more or less referred to as the Deep State, grew in power over the following decades financing themselves through drug and human trafficking, semi-legitimate financial activity and big government projects. At every opportunity, they got more and more public officials under their collective thumb by bribing them with fame and fortune, and when that failed by finagling them into blackmailable situations, or with threats and coercion.

"If you want to know how this works, the 1980s is a clear example. Bush lost the Republican candidacy to Reagan in 1980, much to the dismay of the Deep State who wanted the son of loyal Nazi sympathizer Prescott Bush in office. They couldn't corrupt Reagan so less than three months into his Presidency they had him shot by known Bush family friend John Hinckley, Jr. They then told Reagan next time they wouldn't miss if Bush couldn't implement certain important parts of their agenda.

"Bill Clinton had far less moral fiber than Reagan, if he had any at all, and was easily bought with a profitable drug running operation into his home state of Arkansas. Anyone who tells you Clinton didn't know about the 100 million dollars a month in cocaine moving through Mena every month is dangerously naïve, at best. And that's 100 million in 1980s dollars. It would be far more today. Bush was rewarded in 1988 with the Presidency, and Clinton got his reward in 1992. Two of his final acts as President were to repeal Glass-Steagall and permanently enslave America's young people with student loan debt, even reinstating debt that had expired under the statute of limitations! Both acts legitimized further wealth accrual for hidden operations.

"The coup d'état came on September 11, 2001. The rogue government whose public face was Dick Cheney needed a Middle East war. So they launched the attacks of 9-11 to justify an invasion. What they didn't know, is that the rogue element itself had been compromised by a deeper rogue element who hijacked the operation. Bad as he is, Dick Cheney would never idly slaughter thousands of American civilians in a false flag attack. The idea was to have a plane hit a tower, kill a few dozen people, and then launch his Middle East war.

"What happened instead was far more grisly. On the morning of the attacks, an anonymous caller to the White House revealed knowledge of secret codes used by various branches of government in various emergencies. No one person EVER knows all of these codes. It's too dangerous. Among them were codes used by the DEA, the FBI, FEMA, and even the launch codes for America's nuclear arsenal that, if used, would surely start a nuclear exchange with whomever those weapons were launched at. This rogue element within the rogue element was so entrenched in our intelligence, defense, and security agencies, they had access to virtually every emergency code the government used. They then hit the towers with a second plane, and the Pentagon! The towers were then brought down with a high energy resonance weapon employing scalar technology first developed by the Nazis during the war and perfected in the decades that followed.

"The stooges in the Bush administration and their Deep State masters knew they were screwed. Afterwards we got the so-called Patriot Act which basically wiped out the Constitution. Americans were so unsettled by the 9-11 attack they actually fell for it, hook, line and sinker.

"When we went into Iraq to confiscate weapons of mass destruction, there were weapons of mass destruction all right, but not what you think. The Deep State within the Deep State was after something far more sinister than chemical and biological weapons, or even thermonuclear weapons for that matter. They were after planet-busting weapons of cosmic terror.

"I consulted with the administration on this. As much as I despised them, I knew it was better for Darth Cheney and friends to have them than the rogue group that was racing to acquire them. The only problem was, against my and Colin Powell's advice, Dick and Donny included the CIA in the group specifically set up to seize said weapons of mass destruction: Task Force 20. We knew the CIA was completely compromised by covert Nazi operators and would spill the beans to their own overlords in Argentina. Cheney and Dumbfeld should have known based on the events of 9-11, but they were poisoned long ago by their hubris and wouldn't listen.

"The result was that a group of Paladin Group-trained commandos disguised as Task Force 20 beat us to the punch. Using our own codes, as they did on 9-11, they beat the real Task Force 20 to the Baghdad Museum and got away with the goods."

"Wait a minute," interrupted One Flare. "WMDs in a museum? What?"

"That's right. These were 'archaeological artifacts,'" the professor explained with air quotes, "that were actually components of a terrifying weapon built by a paleo-ancient civilization, that even now that group is trying to reconstruct for their ungodly purposes. That pyramidion you saw emerge from the hole in Nevada is actually the capstone to the Great Pyramid and a key component in the weapon system the pyramid was originally designed as in humanity's dim and forgotten past."

Thorny and One Flare were about to protest the preposterousness of the professor's tale, but considering what they had witnessed, decided better of it.

"So then who were those guys at the hole?"

"They showed up looking like normal military, a special operations force perhaps, but there were not. They were another Paladin force dispatched to take control of whatever was happening there. The reason I know that is because I had a run-in with these Nazis during research on one of my books. Apparently I was going to deep and getting too close to something and they wanted me to back off, or else. Fortunately, I have a dead man's trigger which I informed them about.

We came to an agreement: I would back off if they would give me something that would always get me out of trouble should I have any more run-ins. They taught me a secret hand sign, which I used with the commanding officer at the hole. He immediately understood it and seemed baffled that I knew it. Furthermore, the check they coughed up as compensation for seizing my friends' property was not a US Government check but drawn on a private account, which, by the way, turned out to be good for the amount."

"Whoaaaaaaaa! Dude! No way!"

"Way, my friends. Way. And to get back to my original point, these people built and operate an underground base at Archuleta Mesa in Dulce, New Mexico. It started out as an actual black project, but it was so deep and so black, they were able to usurp it and operate almost completely unnoticed for quite some time. When the government finally realized what was going on with their own black project, they couldn't very well complain to Congress, so they sent Delta Force to try and oust them from it in 1979, and failed miserably.

"Now, the idiot fringe will try and tell you that it is some kind of joint alien-human secret base that does biological experiments and creates human-alien hybrids in perverse genetic experiments. That's all hogwash and a legend that is in fact encouraged by the base's true operators, the post-war Nazi International. They have worked there to perfect rediscovered ancient technology and flying craft."

"Anything else you wanna add to ruin our evening?"

"Well, if you insist I add insult to injury: all the precious democratic institutions we hold so dear are, at this point, nothing more than a charade."

Thorny slapped One Flare on the shoulder with the back of his hand to indicate he was about to recite a movie line, "That figures! That fuckin' figures!"

One Flare looked at Thorny snapping his fingers in recognition, then pointed decisively. "*Apocalypse Now*!"

Chapter 29

"So after all that, we still don't know how or why the pyramid thing got into a hole in Nevada," observed One Flare.

"Ah, sorry, Jay. I think we're done with the part you can hear."

"Hahahaha! I don't want anything to do with what you guys are up to. I'm going back to your book collection now."

"The answer to that is simple," stated Faro. "The Templars brought it there."

"What? The Knights Templars?"

"Correct."

"The gay guys, in white suits," added One Flare.

"Wait a minute," interjected Thorny. "Practically the first thing they did after their formation was dig up everything under Solomon's Temple. Are you saying they actually found this thing there and then shipped it off to America? Or the New World, I guess. America hadn't been named America yet....."

"How do you know this shit?" asked One Flare. "You always know about shit like that."

"You're friend is more or less correct, One Flare," the Doc continued. "Although there is no actual evidence they were gay, the Templars did in fact find something while digging under the Temple, and they went about it so quickly and with such priority, they must have known something was there. Whatever it was it made them fabulously wealthy.

"While it has never been definitively proven what they found, it had to be something of immense importance, something that gave them power over the Church and all the kings and princes of Europe at the time. They were finally driven into hiding by Philip the Fair of France who attacked the order and tortured and executed practically every member he could get his hands on. He went to the Templar port of La Rochelle to seize the ships, but the fleet had already sailed, most likely loaded with the secret treasure they'd found in the Holy Land. There is evidence to indicate they came here, and there is even evidence they were in what is now the Southwestern US. It doesn't take my particular brand of high octane speculation to put two and two together in this case."

"What makes you think it's the pyramidion, specifically, that they found?"

"It is known from ancient tablets that the important parts of the Giza Death Star were scattered or destroyed. Some of those parts were kept to be used for other purposes, other parts were destroyed, and what could not be destroyed or repurposed was hidden. It's my supposition that Moses, who was initiated into the Egyptian priesthood and a close associate of the pharaoh, would have been familiar with those articles. When the Hebrews fled Egypt, he would have tried to take what he could with them.

"Now imagine, you're the king of Egypt, thousands of Hebrews are leaving your country and you find out they are absconding with your most treasured and powerful items, which they may share with your enemies or even use against you themselves. Thus you have the perfect motivation for sending your army after them the minute you find out."

"Well slap my ass and call me Sally! You've just rewritten the entire history of the world and religion....'n' just frikkin' everything."

"It's just tracking, guys," added Kelvin. "He's just following the tracks and asking, 'What are the tracks telling me?'"

"Yeah, yeah. Just like tracks tell you where someone's been, they also tell you where they're going before they get there and what they're going to do before they do it. So our guys are going to Dulce to unload and possibly transport a weird ass glowing mini-pyramid to somewhere else."

"Very good, Thorny. I can see listening to the Sex Pistols hasn't caused too much brain damage," observed Faro.

Then he added thoughtfully, "Although I have to admit, Johnny Lydon had it right when he wrote "God Save the Queen" and called out Jimmy Savile for his despicable crimes. He earns my respect at least for that." Faro threw back his head and laughed, "Leave it to an Irish Catholic boy to speak the ugly truth!"

Kelvin spoke up, "Like I said before, that's Jicarilla country. I know a guy out there I can call. You guys ever meet Daryl?" asked Kelvin turning to Thorny and One Flare.

"'s he the guy we met at Scout class?"

"Yeah. On his 12th birthday his grandfather took him horseback riding out in the desert. Then he took his horse and said, 'Wait for me here till I get back.'"

A year later, on his 13th birthday, his grandfather came back with the same horse and said, 'Congratulations, Grandson. Now you are a man.' That guy?"

"That's him. Also did a stint in the Army Rangers."

"Man, that is one dude I would not wanna mess with."

Chapter 30

The choppers circled briefly and then swooped down in a spiral. Their arrival at the Shorleys' property was expected. We call it the Shorleys' place now instead of "The Hole" because the hole is gone. The choppers sat, rotors still turning ready for a hasty departure, like a scene from *M*A*S*H.*

Our old friends Müller and Edda were among the first to debark. They were met by the captain who was now the officer in charge.

"Very sparse camp for this kind of operation," stated Edda.

The captain responded, "I took the liberty of anticipating a rapid departure and loaded everything except the bare essentials."

"Excellent," commented Müller. After the company stood together awkwardly for a moment he added, "Well? Where is it?"

"Over here."

He led them to the spot where the hole used to be. They beheld the grisly sight of arms and legs protruding from the ground, and the colonel's head, by now, had been mercifully smashed to put it out of its misery.

Müller smiled approvingly. "Now here is a man who understood sacrifice. Talk about giving an arm and a leg, eh, Captain?" He gave the Captain a hearty slap on the back. Then he turned to Edda. "All yours."

"All right," she shouted, "break everything down. You there, clean up this mess," she added indicating the colonel's remains. "You will move out within two hours and return to your previous assignments. Anyone who is not gone within two hours will join the colonel! None of this ever happened, none of you were ever here!"

The men responded with great alacrity. Furniture folded, tents collapsed, and anything remaining from water to food to blankets was tossed on waiting vehicles. Müller and Edda and their team boarded their choppers and took off. Shortly after that, the convoy of trucks left the Shorleys' place for the last time. They looked like a National Guard unit out on maneuvers.

To be sure, the helicopters that carried our villains returned in two hours on the dot, this time with door guns mounted, locked and loaded. But there was nothing but a couple of prancing coyotes and some sage.

Chapter 31

Back in Bariloche, Müller and Edda entered the hall Kammler, Bormann, and the other gray old men had prepared. Red, black and white streamers hung from the chandeliers, the walls were draped with rich matching tapestries, and a long banquet table was laid with a luxurious white tablecloth and the finest tableware. A large banner hung over the door proclaimed, "*Alles Gute zum 100. Geburtstag!!*" Happy 100th Birthday in German.

Müller issued a great belly laugh upon seeing the sign. "May I live so long! I think someone has made a mistake with their math!" He kept laughing.

Kammler and Bormann broke away from the old men mingling inside and came to the door to greet them. "Herr Müller! Fraulein Siebrecht! You made it! It's so good to see you both safely back in Bariloche! Our little sign no doubt has amused you."

"No doubt," echoed Müller. "But whenever I see something this out of place, I can't help thinking you devils are up to something," he laughed while wagging a finger at them.

Kammler and Bormann shared his laughter. "Indeed. We have a surprise for you. But first, let's eat. Surely you must be famished from such a long journey."

Müller was given the place of honor with Edda to his right and Kammler and Bormann flanking them. The other 50-odd guests sat around the table, and it was a veritable who's who of Nazis in South America, and a few from elsewhere. They were served a magnificent feast of venison, wild boar, and salmon. This of course was topped off with birthday cake and a round of "Happy Birthday" and "For He's a Jolly Good Fellow" as well as an assortment of old German songs, including of course "Die Wacht am Rhein," which readers may recall from the scene in Rick's in the movie *Casablanca*.

At the appointed moment, Herr Bormann called out, "Achtung! Achtung!" and gathered everyone's attention. "And now, we have a special presentation in honor of our birthday boy. If everyone would please direct their attention to the screen that is now being lowered."

As the film opened, heroic music swelled within the room and a deep-voiced, passionate male narrator began the story to old and rare family photos that faded in and out as the camera panned over them.

"This future hero of the Third Reich was born on June 12, 1908. If he were alive he would be turning 100 years old today...."

Müller dropped his jaw in astonishment. He immediately knew who they were talking about for he had studied his favorite hero carefully and with a perverse affection and endearment that can only be fathomed by the dark hearts that harbor it.

The film went on to recite with movies and stills the life of the abominably great Otto Skorzeny, which was already rehearsed at the beginning of this book. It even contained secret closely-guarded home movies of his postwar life which included some, shall we say, very warmly affectionate footage of Skorzeny with Eva Peron at a garden party, and again on Christmas, and on a beach trip, that weren't quite scandalous.

The narrator went on, now more seriously, "What is not well known is that 'The Long Jumper' and Her Excellency had a son, in secret. Due to the nature of the relationship and their public standing, it was necessary that the child be raised in secret as well. He was given to a family of German émigrés in Osorno, Chile to raise as their own.

"They named him Otto, after his father and gave him an excellent upbringing." At this point Müller bolted upright in his chair and became utterly fixated on the film. It continued on in an effusively wholesome and nauseatingly innocent version of *This Is Your Life* of the born and bred Nazis of Patagonia.

"With a little assistance from the *Deutscher Verein*, Otto Müller was able to obtain the best education and attend the best universities. He became a successful businessman and prominent member of the German diaspora in South America.

"In 1975 he married Heidi Schnellenkamp, and on June 12, 1976, the loving couple gave birth to a son they named Reinhardt." The music swelled with emotion as Müller burst into tears of joy, and in one of the few genuine shows of affection in her life, Edda put her hand on his shoulder.

The narration continued, "Reinhardt was given a modest and humble upbringing but his grandfather's spirit impregnated and saturated his being. Despite his modest childhood, he dominated his peers and rose through their ranks to show that he was every ounce the man his grandfather, Otto Skorzeny, was." A heroic image of Skorzeny froze on the screen and the music slowly crescendoed.

"Rise, Reinhardt Müller. It is on this occasion, we reveal and mystically reunite you with, your sacred heritage."

Müller rose, and his figure, illuminated by the projector, merged with the image of Skorzeny on the projector screen. Kammler and Bormann rose ceremoniously to which the assembled company responded in kind. One of the old men produced a vial of thick red liquid with a miniature tag tied around the lip that read "Skorzeny." He removed the cap and lifted a goblet of wine into which he dripped a few drops of the precious fluid. Holding his hand under the foot, he carefully made his way to Müller and formally offered it with both hands.

Müller, somewhat in awe and somewhat confounded, took the vessel in both hands. While gingerly holding the glass, he soaked in the assembly as if it were an intoxicating aroma, the warm glow of a fire, a spirit that rushed in. Then with a determined breath, he imbibed the liquid. He put down the glass and stood to accept their approval, with the film's image indistinguishably intermingled with his own visage, and the shadows of the Nazi leadership behind him.

The gray old men and their minions applauded and cheered what they betook for a true transfiguration, and Müller believed it too.

Chapter 32

Kammler had been entrusted with Skorzeny's SS belt, ring, and dagger after he passed away, in anticipation of this day. Now he was presiding over this ritual disguised as a birthday party. He motioned to an attendant who wheeled over a cart with a black leather case on top. He opened it. It was lined with red satin, and carefully set into its compartments were the belt, dagger, and ring that had belonged to Col. Skorzeny in life.

First he produced the belt and dagger which he placed around Müller's waste. Then he lifted Müller's hand and placed the ring on his finger. His eyes sparkled with madness as he examined and stroked it with his fingers. Then his countenance changed to one possessed of infinite confidence, and he straightened his arm and held out his fist for all to see his grandfather's ring. Or was it his own from another incarnation?

Talismans of power are also talismans of seduction. When a man's esteem among his peers increases, his lover's affection for him grows in direct proportion, if not in excess of it. Thus, Edda, whose affection for anyone was never much more than basic biology, was now taken over by a passion for Müller she couldn't fathom in that moment, because it was formerly reserved only for killing. She soaked up his sinister and tenebrous glory and gazed transfixed at the newly anointed man of power, seized by the profound comprehension that his glory was also hers.

Chapter 33

Meanwhile, in Dulce, Greaves was getting a report from his Jicarilla friend, Daryl.

"Yeah, that truck you describe, we saw it come in. About 3 days ago."

"Where'd it go?"

"It was pretty late at night and dark. Hard to say. But, you know, a lot of weird stuff goes in and out of here."

"Surely, somebody must see this stuff come and go."

"It's not as easy as all that."

"What do you mean?"

"You know, sometimes things come in here and just disappear. Sometimes they leave like they came out of nowhere. A lot of strange flying things. They go into the mesa."

"Archuleta Mesa?"

"Yeah."

"My friends and I really need to know what happened to that truck."

"That mesa, it's not a good place. We don't mess with them and they don't mess with us."

"What if we wanted to get inside and have a look?"

"No one here would go with you, even if it's possible. You know, we don't even know where the real entrance to that place is. We go up there to the top, we hunt all around here, go camping, we've never seen any kind of entrance. It's like all of a sudden you see a jeep, or a truck, and you don't know where it came from. Other times it comes in and you don't know where it went."

"Weren't you ever curious, Daryl? I mean, *you*, you've been in the scariest and most secret stuff a guy can face."

Daryl laughed modestly and then held up his finger to make a point, "That scary stuff was all scary stuff I understood. This stuff is weird," he added shaking his head. "I don't know, maybe some of the elders or medicine people know."

"What if I was to bring Thorny and One Flare up here?"

"Oh, them? How they doin'?"

"Guess."

Daryl threw back his head and laughed. "Like that, huh?"

"Well?"

"I helped train those boys," he answered with affection. And concern.

"I did too."

"You know, this isn't normal stuff. Even our medicine men are wary of that shit. It's not like normal medicine. It is dark, and dark, not even normal darkness. But, hey, it's from your world. Maybe you get it. But no Indian from around here is gonna go in there with you."

"So?"

"I better talk to the elders. It could create a problem for our people if anyone goes in there. You know, Delta Force tried to take that place in '79. That caused problems for us and we had nothing to do with it."

"They stormed it. We'd be invisible."

Daryl chortled. "I'm sure you would be...."

Chapter 34

The locals thought they'd rib Thorny and One Flare a bit, as men are inclined to do with newcomers.

"Hey, man, why you guys got Mohawks? We're all Indians here and we don't have Mohawks."

"Well, you're not Mohawks, are you?"

They laughed light-heartedly. "Good point. But we're still closer to Mohawks than you two."

"Well why's he wearin' a cowboy hat? He's not a cowboy," said One Flare indicating a man working the fire.

"Yeah," added Thorny. "Seen a lotta Indians around here today wearin' cowboy hats. What's with that?"

A big Apache looked at them both and blinked once as he remarked flatly, "Looks like the Indians wanna be cowboys, and the cowboys wanna be Indians." And they all shared an ironic laugh.

"Actually we're both half Italian, half Polish and half Southern," joked Thorny.

"That sounds bad. But not as bad as your math."

"They're confused," chimed in the medicine man. "They're three halves different things, and have haircuts like Indians. Maybe after tonight they'll be less confused."

A loud explosive pop startled a guy who was standing too close to the fire. He was wrapped in a towel and barefoot.

"Whoa!" he exclaimed as he danced clumsily away from it.

"Watch out, man. Don't burn your dick."

It wasn't uncommon to crack all manner of manly jokes while waiting for a lodge to start. At signal or word from the medicine man that could be instinctively recognized, the men would immediately shift into sanctity.

"You hear that?" asked the medicine man. "That's strong medicine."

The lodge was constructed in the Navajo fashion with

logs stacked up in a cone and the floor below ground level. Dirt was piled up on the logs for insulation and blankets were rolled up over the A-frame entrance. They would be unrolled to seal the door when the lodge started.

Greaves had returned with Thorny and One Flare to ask for permission to "do their thing." This violated the normal scout rule of "It's often better to ask for forgiveness later than ask for permission first," but there were too many people possibly affected to be cavalier about it. The elders were very specific that all involved would have to be purified in the sweat should the spirits decide that it was OK to infiltrate the facility.

Now, I know what you're thinking. How could they infiltrate that place? You've seen drawings on the Internet of all the subterranean levels that get progressively worse and increasingly horrific as one descends to Nightmare Hall, and you've seen a YouTube video of Tom Costello's testimony, and so forth.

Certainly Nazis are no slouches when it comes to creating nightmares and horrors, but as the good Dr. Faro has already pointed out, it's all hogwash. None of that has ever been proven. Anyone can claim anything, especially when it's unverifiable one way or another. And the existence of extraterrestrials has never been proven if there is any evidence at all. Produce any type specimen of an intelligent EBE, and I'll rewrite this paragraph in the next edition.

So, back to our infil. Kelvin and the boys had to join the sweat so that their spirits could be tested and purified. Even if they were, it didn't mean the mission was a go, but at least all would benefit from the ceremony.

The medicine man in charge of this ceremony spread the coals of the fire to get to the hot rocks within. As he spread them, he observed the omens revealed in the burning embers and ash while singing Apache songs. He carefully selected the rocks he wanted with a pitchfork and put them in the lodge's fire pit.

The men entered the sweat wrapped in their towels.

Most removed them as they sat down. It was held that one must enter the sweat to meet one's Creator as He made them—naked. Owing to the presence of three white guys in the lodge, nobody split hairs over "sitting on" vs. "sitting on while still wrapped."

The medicine man began in English, "We're going to do three rounds in this sweat. I suggest you leave the lodge between rounds and drink some water. If it gets too hot, just lay down, except you three. You have to sit up like warriors today no matter how hot it gets and how much it hurts, and show the spirits you're ready for the task at hand. It's not out of pride you sit up, but out of a willingness to suffer so that others won't have to."

He then sprinkled tobacco on the glowing red rocks that glistened like stars being born and then resorbed as black dots by a great nebula and continued in his native tongue. In fact, this "tobacco" was not strictly the smoking plant, but a mixture of local herbs that burned aromatically. As he did this, he shouted to the door, and an attendant, most likely his apprentice, passed in a spackling bucket full of water with a gourd ladle and the same tobacco floating on top, then rolled the door shut.

The interior of the lodge was now pitch black except for the throbbing fiery heart in the pit. The lodge quickly filled with aromatic smoke as the medicine man sang his shamanic songs of power. He touched a stick to the rocks which instantly flamed up and used it to light the pipe. This wasn't one of the long wooden pipes with soapstone bowl of the plains Indians. This was a handmade clay pipe of the desert southwest. What it lacked in feathers and pizzazz it made up for in medicine in the hands of the shaman.

He passed the pipe around the circle and each puffed in turn until it came back to the shaman. Then he started pouring water on the rocks while still praying in song. The three white guys fidgeted a bit, but everyone was silent as the lodge filled with warm and invigorating steam. They immediately began to perspire.

This first round lasted about 30 minutes and got steamier and steamier as generous portions of water were ladled over the stones, the perfect intermingling of yin and yang, to cleanse the flesh and purify the spirit. The old shaman shouted in Apache towards the door again and the apprentice rolled it open. The cool night air rushed in and refreshed the participants. Slowly they raised themselves out of their cross-legged positions and crawled outside and stood up. There was another spackling bucket of spring water for all to drink.

They stood around more quietly this time, occasionally lifting a foot to brush pebbles or sand from the sole with a hand or by rubbing it on the opposite calf. They drank copiously because the pure spring water would push toxins and impurities through their pores. The perspiration was usually wiped off with their hands and cast into the fire where the sin sizzled as it was incinerated. Coyotes howled nearby.

Meanwhile the apprentice spread the fire out again as the shaman read its portents with rapt attention. The apprentice moved nine more rocks to the center of the lodge. The stack of hot rocks was now just below the lip of the pit.

The old shaman called out in Apache again, and the men moved toward the lodge with Kelvin, Thorny, and One Flare following their lead. They crept in on hands and knees and took up their previous positions. It was noticeably hotter, like an oven. The old shaman began sprinkling tobacco and the apprentice unfurled the door into its closed position.

The medicine man immediately began pouring. The water hissed and the rocks popped as the lodge filled with a thick stifling cloud of steam. The men took deep breaths to relax into the discomfort, all the while wiping streams of sweat from their heads, faces, and bodies and flicking the torrents into the rocks.

Their eyes became heavy. Greaves, Thorny and One Flare shifted position repeatedly to relieve one over-heated part of the body or another or to find a more relaxing position. Colored lights swirled in the lodge and the herbal steam became intoxicating. The shaman sang louder and shook his rattle. The colored lights coalesced into ancient animals made of iridescent crystals that grazed and trotted through the steam. Then they'd turn and face the trio with fire in their eyes and go back again to circling the blackness.

The Indians in the lodge with them sat serenely, eyes closed, heads cocked back, listening to the songs, softly rocking, and silently moving their mouths.

This went on for another half hour before respite came and the door was flung open. It was as if they couldn't get out fast enough. The fresh, cool dry air contrasted sharply with the burning humidity inside. A vast cloud of steam gushed out of the lodge and rose heavenward until it was invisible. The shaman watched intently. Everyone drank a lot of water.

The old shaman went over to the other Apaches participating in the lodge and spoke in hushed tones with their native tongue. They nodded in agreement. They reached for towels hanging around the sweat lodge area and began drying off and shifting back into "social mode."

The shaman then approached our three friends and explained that only they would do the third round, the others were finished.

The apprentice began forking the rocks into the lodge. He spread the fire wide to uncover every last rock that was there and added all of them to the pit inside.

The pile now bulged over the rim of the pit like a blazing red sun. Inside was like a blast furnace with the temperature still rising. The old shaman took his place by the door and the three seekers took up their positions. The door was immediately shut and they sat there baking while the shaman sprinkled tobacco into the crimson hemisphere before them.

A hot wind began to circulate the orbit of the lodge. The shaman splashed the water wholesale into the fiery center. The steam, caught up by the hot wind, swirled around and encircled the inside of the lodge like the Milky Way and scorched the faces of our trio while the shaman barely broke a sweat. Creatures leapt from the fire with intense expressions, then vanished.

Kelvin and the boys began to swoon. They tried to lean against the wall to stay erect, but it was too hot. They tried kneeling, sitting on one leg, sitting cross-legged, then fidgeted some more to stay upright.

The shaman was pouring faster now. The ring of steam circulated faster and became a ceaseless blast of searing torment. Mysterious figures appeared like transparent holograms, and the men began panting as it became insufferable. Their sweat ran like rivers no matter how assiduously they wiped themselves.

POW! POW! POP! The rocks exploded and chips blasted through the lodge. The shaman rocked serenely and continued to sing and pour. The trio could feel themselves being touched and jostled by invisible beings as the tortuous blasts of steam intensified. They winced, and sniffled.

Crying children appeared in a sunlit meadow where death rained down all around them blackening the place, and demons danced menacingly. They found themselves together wanting to get to these children but were withheld by mysterious means. Their faces felt like they were submerged in a deep fryer and they began to scream. Still the children cried. They beheld each other's scorched and reddened faces and could see the lymph begin to ooze from their burns.

Still the children cried. The shaman let out a deep, deafening "HO!," and the mysterious force holding them back vanished. They rushed forward gritting through the tears that streamed down their cheeks and rushed the demons like madmen in mortal desperation. When they were right up on them, the demons scowled and slurped with narrowed eyes of death and braced themselves. The men flung themselves upon them, but instead of the slap and thud of colliding bodies, the meadow again was calm and sunny.

Birdsong filled the air. The children stood before

them with arms outstretched as if welcoming a hug, but then each suddenly transformed into the most colorful and powerful bird you have ever seen. The men approached the birds but were plucked up and swallowed. Each bird took on the characteristics of the one they swallowed, like a bird version of each, and then spread their wings and soared to a mountain top where they perched and drank from a refreshing icy pool. They could see past the farthest horizon, deep into the firmament and beyond the edge of creation to the primordial scission of the nothing that gave rise to everything.

Chapter 35

"Hey! Hey!" they heard.

Opening their eyes they stared through the open lodge door and beheld all the stars and Milky Way like they had never seen them before. They were exceedingly vibrant, yet so tranquil, pulsing with life they hadn't noticed before, dancing in their stillness.

The men outside were fully dressed and cooking meat, corn and stew on the fire. They turned to meet the crew as they emerged from the steaming womb of logs and earth.

"D'you get a sunburn in there, man?" asked one of the men with reassuring laughter.

"Feels like it."

They looked at each other. "Oh, man, you should see your face."

"If it looks like yours, I'd rather not."

Greaves exhaled mightily and stretched his arms, "Man, that was good! I've never been cooked alive before."

"Now you know how lobsters feel."

"Except they get eaten."

"Maybe that's what he means," quipped the old shaman as he threw a glance and a wink towards the three.

They stood around the drinking bucket gulping water from plastic party cups and looking like they'd just finished an Ironman.

The old shaman came over to talk to them.

"You fellas alright?"

Deep sighs and nods answered affirmatively, "Pretty cooked, but otherwise yeah." "Sure." "I reckon."

"Then I'm gonna tell this to you, and only to you," he went on in a hushed tone. "You can't ever talk about it around here. I saw the Thunderbirds swallow you and take you to the mountain."

The three men, who were lifting their cups to their

lips, stopped and returned their cups to the "rest position" at their wastes. They gave the old shaman their rapt attention. Because of their training, instead of being shocked or surprised, they understood the reality they'd just passed through with the old man and that they were about to receive important words.

"That's big medicine. Because you respected us and our culture the spirits liked it. My advice is before you go in that place, you rest up for a day. You still don't know what happened to you. Eat. Have some stew and Apache corn. Tomorrow you'll feel different."

"OK, thank you, Grandfather." "Thank you, Grandfather, for everything." "You're the boss, Grandfather."

"And besides," he added pointing to their faces with a crooked finger, "you look like shit."

They all laughed with relief. "C'mon, now, let's go eat. And sing."

They dove vigorously into the feast prepared for everyone. A group of drummers set up their drum and beat out powerful, soaring, and ineffable songs, to which some of the locals sang along. Gradually some of the women made their way out, some fat and gray beaming with wisdom, others young and soft with long sumptuous raven locks, high dark cheekbones, and beaming with mischievous coyness.

Thorny and One Flare were immediately taken and leaned their heads together to comment in private. Unbeknownst to them, the old shaman was right behind them. He was beaming with smiles.

"Sometimes it's nice just to have them around, just to appreciate. Even when you're too cooked to do anything."

The boys laughed.

"When you're my age you'll appreciate it more. Now go appreciate it."

The boys took seats on logs amongst the women, and much to their own surprise, sat there like gentlemen appreciating the good company, sharing a few laughs and appreciating the fine music.

Chapter 36

They woke up under their tarp which they'd rigged over a bed of pine needles. The air was crisp and clear, the worst sort of weather for the kind of operation they were about to run.

One Flare pinched his eyes with thumb and forefinger to wipe the sand out, leaned up on an elbow and saw Thorny and Kelvin just waking up too. "Damn! I have to wake up with you two instead of one of those Apache girls," he joked.

They started getting up and shaking out their bed rolls and getting their outerwear on.

"I think you're trying to appreciate them *too much*," observed Greaves, the elder of the trio.

"There are no limits to my appreciation."

"Yeah, I've seen how limited it is," added Thorny. "In fact it was hard to see at all."

Greaves snickered, "Is *everything* a double entendre with you guys?"

The pair looked at each other. "Pretty much." "Yep."

Just then the old shaman and his apprentice approached their camp. He was carrying something.

"Morning!"

"Morning! How you fellas this morning?"

"Great."

"Never slept so well in my life."

"I made something for you guys. These are medicine pouches." He placed a small pouch of some kind of animal skin hung on string of the same material around their necks. "Make sure you keep them on."

They lifted them in their hands to inspect them and asked, "What's in them?"

"Medicine. That's why we call them medicine pouches."

"Of course."

"Do we *wanna* know what's in them?"

"I don't know what you want. But if I wanted you to know, I would have told you by now."

"Fair enough."

"Go to the mountain you went to last night. You'll find what you're looking for there."

They looked around. "That mountain?"

"Is that the one you went to last night?"

"Yeah, it sure looks like it."

"If you know that then, why are you asking me? As soon as I gave you those pouches my job finished."

"Aiight then."

The old shaman and his apprentice started heading back down the hill when they stopped. They old man turned around but was only visible from the waste up.

"Dinner's at my niece's house," he hollered. "7 o'clock." Then he disappeared down the hill.

"Where's his niece's house?"

"Beats me."

Chapter 37

Greaves was a big John Goodman-esque sort of guy, but he was nearly as agile as the two younger men, and in equally good condition. They started towards the mountain in a scout run, which is a method of minimizing their tracks and conserving energy. As they altered their concentric rings, they appeared to shapeshift into a 3-pack of coyotes for the remainder of their run.

The top of the mountain was shaped exactly as it had been in their sweat lodge vision. A cool mountain pond and some scrub covered the summit. Aside from that, they couldn't see anything that they might be looking for, presumably a way into the facility they wanted to scope out.

"Alright, so now what do we do?"

"What do the tracks tell you?"

"There weren't any after about a 1/3 of the way up. Not even human."

"That means all the wildlife and all the locals avoid this place like the plague. Not one damn bird or rodent up here."

"Animals aren't the only ones who leave tracks," began Thorny pensively. "Take a look at that."

"What?"

"Those bushes there."

"What about 'em?"

Thorny went into mock David Attenborough mode. "I'm standing here on the top of a Mountain in Southwestern North America. Here, in the alpine forests, we find a very, very unusual plant indeed. It appears that while Nazis excel at physics and are obsessively thorough about secrecy and security, they are indeed, rather poor botanists."

One Flare widened his eyes as he does when his friend is onto something and said what he always does, "Huh? Just looks kinda like poison ivy."

"Western poison ivy, *Toxicodendron rydbergii*, to be precise."

"I guess if I wanted to plant something that would keep people out, that would be it," surmised Greaves.

"And it's a little out of place here, and there isn't any more of it around here. Haven't seen any since we got here. And considering the complete lack of wildlife up here, I'd say the chances of having its seeds dropped by a bird or some other browser are pre-tay slim."

"Oh, dude! We're all gonna get poison ivy goin' through that."

"You two might, but I won't," Thorny clarified. "I don't get it."

"You mean you don't get *any*," One Flare snickered.

"Hyuck hyuck hyuck. Very funny."

"C'mon, guys. Focus."

"Did I ever tell you about the time my friend Ian and his girlfriend did it in a poison ivy patch? Oh, dude! They got rashes all...."

"We don't wanna know."

"Just wash off with soap right away and you'll be OK."

"Anybody bring *soap*?" asked One Flare sardonically, emphasizing "soap" and holding his hands open while thrusting his hips forward.

"The...thunderbird...is...protecting...us, *doofus!*" Thorny enunciated each word like Adam West as Batman until doofus which he strongly ejaculated. He then turned and leaned over to inspect the ivy.

"OK, well since you don't get it, you go in first to make sure it's worth it. I promise I won't poke your ass."

Thorny poked his head through the poison ivy on his hands and knees slapping once at his behind just to make sure One Flare was keeping his promise. They heard him exclaim ever so quietly, "Whoaaaaa.."

"What'd you see?" asked Greaves. He found it difficult to keep his composure around these two because they were forever yucking it up, but hey, it worked.

He extricated himself and turned to face them. "A tunnel. Or a ventilation duct, or something."

"Yeah, I got somethin' for your tunnel right here."

"OK!" announced Greaves giving a faux noogie to One Flare, "shit just got real. Hand signals and bubbles only from here on out."

Chapter 38

Our scouts had trained many days and countless hours to master crawling absolutely silently on leaf litter in the forest, so crawling silently and invisibly down a concrete shaft was no problem. They made their way a long distance, through a large fan that was currently powered off, and then came to the grate at the end of the shaft where they could peer inside the underground lair.

Lucky for them it was exactly where they needed to be. The crystal-like pyramidion was on a stand in the center of a giant room. Rather than bore you with a detailed description, just imagine any supervillain lair full of laboratory equipment and stainless steel appointments. The people inside however were not wearing orange jumpsuits.

They just wore regular street clothes. Most of them sported short-sleeved white shirts with black ties and black slacks. The women wore navy blue suits with skirts and blouses.

Hovering above the crystal was a large lenticular disc 30 or so feet in diameter. On the underside was the image of the Black Sun. As they reconnoitered, the center of the sun opened up to reveal the interior of the disc, but was not in a clear line of sight for the trio. The scientists and technicians carefully monitored the ascent of the crystal into the center of the craft whereupon the porthole closed again.

At that moment, the workers near the disc stepped back behind what looked a lot like glass walls, but not quite like glass walls, on either side of the disc and donned protective goggles and jackets. When they were all ready, one of the workers signaled a man at a control panel high up in the rafters of the facility. A red light started flashing and a noticeable but unobtrusive alarm sounded. The man threw switches into place, and then connected a massive circuit that discharged on the disc from every direction.

The disc hummed metallically, emitted a bluish-green aura, and suddenly shot straight up in the air and disappeared. The scouts were stunned and almost gave themselves away. They had seen every sort of mysterious and occulted art on a primitive and natural level, but had never seen technology perform such feats. Their minds were blown.

Chapter 39

Their thought bubbles popped all over themselves in such cacophony, if we can use that word, that nobody knew which ones were whose. Greaves signaled with his hand to return to the surface.

When they got back, they carefully checked the poison ivy to make sure there was no trace of their penetration. This time they ran around the mountain, down the other side and through a canyon to get back to camp. It was a lot longer, but they knew better than to return the same way they came.

The sun was now only three fingers over the horizon. They carefully packed up their camp and removed every trace that they were ever there. They toted their small quantity of gear down the hill towards their vehicle. Daryl was waiting for them buy the car carving a stick.

"About time you got here."

"What are you doing here?"

"Figured you'd need help finding the old man's niece's house."

"Now that you mention it, we're starving."

"Yeah, let's go."

They heaved their gear into the back and got in the vehicle.

In a short while they arrived at the house which was much nicer than they were expecting based on their stereotypes of the plight of the American Indian.

"Wow. Nice digs."

"She works for ANC."

"What's that?"

"Apache Nugget Corporation. They run the casinos."

They entered the house and were immediately taken by the savory fragrances from the cooking. A man in an A2 flight jacket and Australian drover hat stood up from the sofa and chortled as he greeted them.

"Well if it isn't my old friend Kelly Greaves and the dynamic dudes."

Thorny turned to One Flare. "It's amazing how people just show up around here..."

"Well look who else just showed up," added Faro. "My secretary Georgeann. I don't believe you've met."

"Nice to meet you." "A pleasure." "Likewise."

"Dr. Faro told me about you guys. He always finds the most interesting characters."

"That's us alright," commented One Flare somewhat sardonically.

"I thought it expedient to meet you gentlemen here..." he paused for a beat to question if this actually applied to Thorny and One Flare while looking askance at them with his mouth open in mid-sentence. He continued, "since what you have to relate is best done discreetly."

"Awfully crowded in here," remarked Thorny as he spied what he took for the Old Shaman's gorgeous niece and her friends from work. "Then again, maybe that's not such a bad thing."

Tapping One Flare on the shoulder, they went and joined the group of young ladies.

After a delicious dinner of wild game, corn, beans and fry bread, they sat around a campfire in the backyard. Alcohol was forbidden but tobacco was OK. They smoked hand-rolled American Spirits and sipped coffee, two of the finest of life's simple pleasures.

The old shaman had the recognizable place of honor around the fire even though it wasn't formally established. Everyone could just tell. Next to him sat his wife. In fact everyone seemed paired up boy-girl, an arrangement that alternated by sex around the fire, even though the pairings weren't necessarily romantic, though Thorny and One Flare's were rapidly progressing in that direction.

On either side of the shaman were Faro and Greaves. The shaman and his apprentice quietly poked at the fire while the folks present chatted in small groups or pairs. Thorny and One Flare, as it turns out, had something in common with the girls they met since they were originally from The Big Rez, the Navajo Nation, where they had played in a "rezzed out" latter day punk band.

The chatter gradually faded until everyone was staring at the fire in peace and contentment. The shaman, squatting and poking, looked up expectantly at Faro, who picked up on the signal.

"So, you gentlemen had quite an adventure to the supervillain lair."

"Are we being discreet?" asked Thorny looking around at all the people.

"Hahahaha! Nobody beats our Indian friends when it comes to discretion, for very obvious reasons I might add. Certainly Hillbillies are a close rival. Yessir, if there're any people in this world you can trust to be discreet, it's Indians and Hillbillies. When you've been as unjustly maligned and persecuted as they have, you learn to keep your business your business and only your business."

Those present nodded in agreement.

"So what did you see?"

"It was like out of a frikkin' James Bond movie or something."

"Yeah, I didn't think it was possible to blow my mind anymore with all the shit I've been through, but that sure did."

"OK, I believe you, but you haven't given me any useful information yet."

"Tell 'em what we saw guys," added Greaves by way of encouragement.

One Flare related what had happened at the "lair," particularly the crystal rising into the disc-shaped craft and then disappearing.

"I'm surprised they didn't have a grating with sensors over that entrance," Faro commented. "But I guess anyone can get lazy or complacent."

"It's pretty hard to get to, if you even know it's there.

And even then it's not easy to find."

"Well, the origin of the craft you describe is San Carlos de Bariloche in Argentina. That's where the Nazis continued their wunderwaffe development in secret and under the protection of the Peron regime after the war."

"How do you even know that?"

"The way you men research the natural world and spend time in nature, I spend in the world of technology, black ops, and hidden history."

Greaves spoke up, "My team reports that the thugs that were at the Shorleys' abandoned the place. What are you going to do about that?"

Georgeann answered, "I'm going to the courthouse to see if that property ever switched hands. I suspect it didn't, but it's best to make sure. If so, the Shorleys may be able to go home, two million dollars richer."

"Hardly worth the trouble and fright they've been through," added Faro.

"So what's next?"

"Good question. It's now an absolute certainty that the Nazi International is trying to restart the Giza Death Star. They have got to be stopped. The question is: how?"

One of the rezzed out girls spoke up, "I've got an idea how to shut down that facility under the mesa."

Daryl began snickering delightfully. Then the niece and her other friend joined in. The newcomers cast puzzled glances between them.

"Oh when she gets an idea, watch out!"

Chapter 40

The girl with the dangerous idea was Carrie Tsosie. She was slim and dark with long black hair with blue streaks dyed in, and a mischievous glint in her eyes that never faded.

She spent weeks at the top of the mountain watching the patch of poison ivy Kelvin, Thorny, and One Flare had crawled through. All the while her idea gestated in her mind. When she noticed the leaves moving towards her, she watched more carefully, got up and listened, and put out her hand to feel the air, sniffed. When the leaves seemed to recede, she got up, listened carefully, and put up her hand to feel the air, sniffed. Occasionally, Daryl or her friend Mary would join her. Sometimes Thorny or One Flare would go too. When she understood what was going on, she left.

A few days later, our new crew of misfits returned to the mountaintop to wreak their unique brand of havoc on the evil inhabitants within.

They carried big bundles of poison ivy vines they had gathered from all over and dried in the sun. They placed them at the base of the patch guarding the ventilation shaft. They'd also toted large sheets of cardboard.

"Now there's no real pattern to this," began Carrie. "It seems like they suck in fresh air whenever they need to, and blow out stale air whenever that's necessary. We'll just have to wait until the right moment."

"I can hardly wait for the fun to begin," giggled Daryl.

They heard a faint rustle. Carrie indicated the subtle movement of leaves and explained how they indicated the base was blowing out stale air. Thorny was getting excited that a chick with blue streaks in her hair was as interested in poison ivy as he was.

"When will it suck again?"

"I got something for ya ta suck right here."

"Do men ever not talk about their penises?" asked

Mary with mock shock.

"Not really."

"Well, look, we may be a couple of cool punk Native chicks to you, but here on the Rez we still like to keep our dignity. Keep it for your men's circle."

"Alright, alright. You're right. We're sorry. We'll keep it for our men's circle." Their apology was reluctant but genuine.

"It might 'suck' again," stated Carrie with a mischievous glance at the boys, "anywhere from 20 minutes to a couple of hours from now. Based on smell, I'd say this is a 20-minute suck." She eyed Thorny.

"A 20-minute suck, she says."

"OK!"

"Sounds good to me."

The girls eyed each other superciliously in response to the boys' obviously ironic tone. Women are subtle in their ways of relationships, and therefore more often victorious, and women from more traditional cultures are far more masterful at it than so-called modern women.

They sat on their haunches carefully watching and listening to the poison ivy. Finally the leaves rustled ever so faintly and bent ever so slightly towards the shaft.

"Now!" Carrie jumped up.

Daryl sprang forward with a kind of miniature homemade blowtorch and torched the dry bundles. The others fanned the flames with the sheets of cardboard. The flames quickly engulfed the live green poison ivy and hardly a wisp escaped. A thick choking cloud of urushiol-laden smoke engulfed the denizens of the secret lair.

Inside, panic ensued. The fire control systems came on initiating the alarm and sprinkler system. Hunched coughing workers scrambled to find the source of the smoke. People shouted at one another and raced for gas masks. But it was already too late.

The urushiols had gotten into their lungs and been identified by the Langerhans cells. These in turn raced to the lymph nodes to alert each and everyone's T-lymphocytes to the chemical invasion. The T-lymphocytes raced in turn to the point of contact and began producing cascades of cytokines. In layman's terms, the allergic reaction had already begun, and in the worst place possible--the lungs and eyes.

"What the Hell is happening?"

"It's coming from ventilation shaft 9! There must be a brush fire we missed!"

"You idiots! You're supposed to watch for that!"

"Instrumentation didn't pick anything up until a few seconds ago."

"Get out there and extinguish it, you morons!"

A burly guard donned a gas mask and headed up the shaft with a fire extinguisher.

Meanwhile, on the mountaintop, Thorny and One Flare had just high-fived.

"Low tech beats high tech every time!"

Daryl took a break from heaving laughter to say, "We better get out of here. Now."

The group shot down the slope at full speed, galloping like the local antelopes and struggling to keep their footing. It was then that Carrie tripped on a stone and tumbled. She lay there momentarily stunned and catching her breath. At that moment, the huge hulking Nazi in the gas mask emerged through the smoldering vines just in time to glimpse the arsonists. He jogged over to Carrie and stood over her like some kind of google-eyed monster about to devour his quarry.

"Wait! Stop! Look!"

"Shit! C'mon! Help Carrie!"

"We'll never make it!"

One Flare reached in his cargo short pocket and pulled out something that looked like deerskin cordage. He reached in his pocket again and pulled out a pebble the size of .75 caliber musket ball that was almost perfectly round.

"Dude, can you hit him from here?"

"I sure hope so!"

The gas mask Nazi was lifting the fire-extinguisher over his head as if to finish Carrie off. Thorny and Daryl sprinted up the hill toward them as if in defiance of the laws of gravity, arms pumping like the rods of a steam locomotive, and panting like its powerful expulsions of steam.

Carrie blinked drowsily in the sunlight and groggily beheld the sinister giant looming above her.

One Flare swung his sling once around and released. SPRINK!

Carrie saw the giant swoon, and then collapse. The extinguisher just missed her head as it fell. One Flare connected with just enough thump to break a lens in the gas mask and knock the villain unconscious.

Mary looked at One Flare and cocked her head flirtatiously. "Hmph. Low tech does beat high tech."

"Every time," he nodded as he viewed his handiwork in the distance.

Daryl bent over the giant and felt his pulse. Then with his knife, he slit his throat. Thorny winced as the blood pooled around his head and trickled down hill in small rivulets.

"You white men were always such pussies," teased Daryl.

Thorny did a face palm, then gesticulated in circular motions with his hand to indicate they should hurry.

Two more guards just coming out of the tube through the smoldering brush saw the futility of the situation and skulked back into their lair.

They got Carrie on her feet and ran all the way home.

"Oh my God!" heaved Mary. "That was way too fucking close!"

"It's never too close if you're still alive," quipped Daryl.

Carrie pulled a couple of ice packs out of the freezer and put one on her knee and one on her head. "Just closer than we would've liked."

"Why'd you kill that guy?"

"Are you crazy? Why would I let him live? A) He's a vicious Nazi, and 2) He can identify us."

"A and 2, huh?"

"Uh-huh."

The next day, the Albuquerque Journal ran the following headline:

MYSTERIOUS RASH OF GERMANS AT AREA HOSPITALS

Chapter 41

Georgeann came out of her room to see what all the laughter was all about. Faro sat in front of his laptop with a hand-rolled smoke between his fingers mightily guffawing trying not to spill the coffee in the other hand.

"What's so funny?"

Faro could barely contain himself. "Look at this, Georgeann. The *Albuquerque Journal.*" He set down the coffee and turned the computer so his secretary could see it. "Mysterious Rash of Germans at Area Hospitals. HAHAHAHA! They actually did it! I thought it was hilarious when she first told us about it, but now they've actually gone and done it! My Lord!"

"Oh dear." Georgeann couldn't contain herself either. She barely got out through the laughter, "Those poor people. I've had poison ivy, Giuseppe. I wouldn't wish it on my worst enemy." They laughed harder.

"And yet...." She made a pregnant hand gesture.

"Those rascals!"

They heaved and sighed thoughtfully for a while as Faro sat finishing his morning smoke and coffee.

"What's the world coming to when even ruthlessly meticulous Nazis start getting careless? Seems like this dumbing down is affecting everyone."

"Don't I know it!"

"So, you have the Shorleys all sorted out. I mean the Barstows."

"Yes. They arrive tomorrow and we'll meet them at the airport. Then we'll start them on assuming ownership of their place under their new names. They'll just buy it from themselves, so to speak, using the trust Farquelle set up for them," she laughed. "It will help conceal the 'new' owners since they kept the same first names."

"A shortcoming in their plan, for sure, but after

you've been to school with, and then been married to the same person for years, how can you ever call them by a new name? I'll never get used to 'the Barstows' though."

"You have to, Giuseppe. Their lives depend on it."

"I know. I know. What's that paper you've got with you?"

"Something the Barstows sent me. They want you to look at it."

"Well what is it?"

"Your finance guy sent it to Farquelle to look at. You know he's not only a lawyer, but a competent coder from his time in computer games."

"Well what is it already?" said Faro reaching for the papers as if to snatch them from Georgeann.

She pulled them to her chest playfully to taunt him. "It's a white paper. On something called..." She peeked at the document, "...Bitcoin."

"Bitcoin? What on earth is that?" He finally pulled the document from her clutches and began to read.

He perused the now-famous Satoshi Nakamoto white paper for a spell and then looked up from it at Georgeann. "Ooooh. Babylon's banksters are going to shit bricks if this ever comes about. If this Satoshi Nakamoto is a real guy, I can't believe someone hasn't killed him yet. This could undo central banking and the evil brood that control it completely."

"No high-octane speculation?"

"Looks like it has legs, but it's a few years away yet."

Chapter 42

Anyone who has studied the Apache Wars of the late 1800s knows that the Apache have a unique genius for unconventional warfare. With hospitals in Northern New Mexico and Southern Colorado filled with pink, itchy, wheezing Nazis, Daryl and a small band of his friends took care of the infamous "Dulce Base." Since they were all Indians, none of them got poison ivy.

They made their way down the shaft, broke through the louvers and had their way. The healthy guards that remained were easily overcome in a brief firefight. Once inside they moved daringly and methodically like rats in a maze. From the central work room Greaves, Thorny, and One Flare had discovered, they traced the halls and passages to uncover offices, storage rooms, file cabinets, entrances, and so forth, picking off the occasional opposition with laser precision all along the way.

Their radios crackled back and forth with the Athabaskan tongue of the Windtalkers that had defeated Germany and Japan. Apache and Navajo are similar languages of the Athabaskan group that made it easy for Daryl's mixed team to adapt their own version of the WWII code. Their long black locks swept the air with each turn like the manes of wild stallions while their weapons swept the base of vermin. Once they retrieved some choice booty and exited their escape route, they torched the place.

Most of the men with Daryl had similar professional experience and were handy at improvising things that go BOOM. Everything they needed was right there inside. Outside, some strange but ephemeral puffs of smoke rose over the hills and canyons, and then disappeared.

While Daryl and his team were taking down the Dulce Base, Carrie and her band were on stage in Albuquerque at UNM beating out an Apache medicine song to open their gig.

Chapter 43

Bormann's face turned bright Nazi red. His whole head quivered and seemed about to explode in a bloody mess. His whole body shook with rage. Suddenly, a heavy board leaned precariously against a wall came down with a deafening SLAP that terrified everyone present! Except it wasn't a piece of lumber, it was Bormann's hand on the table. Kammler was more cool-headed, but his eyes seethed with fury.

"How could you let a group of savages," he spit the word savages, "savages, I tell you, get away with this???"

"They're clever, these savages. They know the ways of nature."

"And their Windtalkers kept us stumped for the entire war," added another suck up, almost comically.

"You talk to me of Windtalkers???" bellowed Bormann as the top button on his shirt literally popped.

"We know the ways of Nature!" Kammler rapped the table too. "Our physics is superior to everyone else's!" He continued, "Who's responsible for this?"

"The only man who saw them up close was killed by one of the savages. He was with several others including two young white men. The two guards who came out after the dead man were too late to get a good look. One of the savages was tall with long black hair, and a girl with streaks of blue dyed into her hair."

"Tall? Long black hair?" raged Bormann. "You've just described every fucking Indian on the continent!"

His minions were plussed and cast nervous, anxious glances back and forth.

"Not too many have blue in their hair. Perhaps if we could find her....."

"Yes. Yes. State the obvious." Herr Bormann took a deep breath. "I just know Faro was behind this."

"He was in the Las Vegas at the time," offered Kammler. As far as we know he was never anywhere around Dulce." Kammler rubbed his eyes and wiped his jaw line with both hands, stretching out his lower lip at the end. "Well, what did they get away with?"

"Some technical papers, personnel rosters, schedules, a few financial records, but mostly technical stuff."

"Technical and financial papers.....hmmm....perhaps Faro did have a hand...."

"Which of our Death Star projects were going on there?"

"Almost none. The facility was entirely devoted to newer research and transportation, that sort of thing. There might be a little something in the technical papers. The financial records....? Perhaps a paper trail."

"Phew."

"We must find out what Faro knows of this, if anything, and follow up any leads on these savages and take care of them. Get any information you can and then handle it accordingly."

"We also have to step up our timeline. I don't care how you do it, get more competent technicians and researchers in all the labs and ramp everything up. We just received permission from Dr. Hawass to 'temporarily' restore the casing stones in a demonstration project. Get started on that."

"Jawohl!"

Chapter 44

Meanwhile, back at the ranch, and I do mean ranch, Faro and his intrepid secretary were putting things in order for the Shorleys', er, I mean, Barstows' return. When they were satisfied, they jumped in the old Land Rover, yes, that Land Rover, and headed off to the airport to pick them up, exactly as the Shorleys, er, Barstows, had done for them at the start of our tale.

When Frank saw the old jalopy (more a term of affection than fact) pull up, his eyes burst wide as he stared agape wondering if he could believe his eyes. Faro beamed as if he were behind the wheel of *Chitty Chitty Bang Bang* itself as he steered the car to the curb. Melissa dropped her bag and did a half squat, grabbing Frank's arm for support.

"Could it be?"

"Yes, it could," replied Georgeann gleefully, and she jumped out to embrace Melissa. They both did a happy dance as they beheld each other.

Faro dismounted and stroked the fender as if he were the proud owner himself, and then patted it as if it were a good horse. "Yessir. Rico kept 'er in pretty good shape."

Frank approached the vehicle thoughtfully, like a new car buyer, and stroked his chin. "Huh, new tires. Well, it's the least you could've done."

They betook each other for a beat and then a no longer repressible strong manly laugh erupted with the same glee infecting Georgeann and Melissa. They embraced, then embraced the ladies, then had a big group hug and all was right with the world.

Chapter 45

Over the next couple of years, the Barstows focused on rebuilding what they had in Nevada while Kammler and Bormann played *Pinky and the Brain* back in Bariloche. Hawass was backpedaling on his deal to refurbish the pyramids. That was their second major setback, and they still hadn't tracked down the blue-haired Navajo girl who was hiding out in the high country of the Big Rez. Big blonde blue-eyed types don't blend in well on the reservation, and that makes snooping around difficult. Even bribes weren't accepted when plenty of Native casino money was floating around, and the locals aren't exactly open to a bunch of palefaces asking nosy questions.

So what's better than an agitated, frustrated Nazi overlord? The same Nazi overlord agitated and frustrated again.

"FOOLS!" he berated them. "It's been two years and you've accomplished nothing!" He shook his fists at his waist while convulsing in rage. Once again his head appeared like a giant swollen zit about to explode in a cloud of pus.

"We've been all over the Navajo and the Jicarilla Reservations, but, you know, it's hard to blend in with Indians when you're not one. And they don't just tell a bunch of strangers who come along asking about someone where they are." Opined the lackey, who was the Captain who took over "the hole" after the Colonel's gruesome demise.

"Curse you! Curse them! Now it is Hail Mary time! That Battle of the Bulge all over again!"

"Müller!"

"Hier!"

"Herr Müller, it is time to prove you share your grandfather's greatness again, I'm afraid. Do you feel like the Long Jumper?"

"Always," he grinned.

"Why can't we have more like you who thrive under adversity?"

Müller laughed.

Kammler observed the situation, then looked up and made an announcement to the assembled company. "Gentlemen, let us retire to the council room." He then sneered at the Captain and his lackey, "Dismissed."

Chapter 46

"What I propose is this," began Müller, "a two-pronged attack: Number 1) get rid of Hawass, and number 2) set up a humanitarian or charitable event to flush out the savage squaw."

"Sounds simple enough, but how do you propose it will work?"

"The first prong will be the most difficult. Hawass's philandering is too well-known to blackmail him personally with it. No. What I propose could not only get rid of Hawass, but have potentially huge payoffs as well."

"Go on."

"We use NGOs to stir up unrest, and propel that into an uprising. I'm talking about regime change, and that will include Hawass and all his bootlickers. We of course can profit off the new regime in other ways as well, as Herr Bormann is so skillful at arranging."

"What about Mubarak? He's been such a good stooge for us through the Americans so far."

"The stakes are too high. We must complete the Death Star project before the Americans, or Russians, or Chinese catch up to us."

Most people today, even policy wonks, or perhaps, especially policy wonks, think the Arab Spring was an organic, grassroots movement. In fact, it was all orchestrated from Bariloche. The Germans had a long history of politicized jihad going back at least as far as World War One. It was now time to fully exploit that tradition.

"Better yet!" interjected Edda. "We take down as much of the Middle East as possible. How many countries are ripe for such action? This will surely keep the Americans and their media's attention occupied, like chickens with their heads cut off, and make our reconstruction project look that much better and charitable despite the unrest going on all around!"

"Brilliant, Fraulein! And the Western powers will bankrupt themselves further with various black ops, cover ups, and sanctions and so forth. It will be quite a sideshow for the media as well."

Everyone had a good chuckle.

"So what is the second prong of your attack, Müller?"

"Again, we use the front of 'charity.' We start a foundation for some humanitarian purpose among the savages. Perhaps it is education; perhaps it is medical care or substance abuse treatment. What is important is that we choose a cause that will easily seduce the sentimental do-gooders so that they do not look beneath the surface. Then we hold some event that attracts young people, like a concert. In fact, I think the one thing we did learn about this blue-haired bitch is that she's in a band. Perhaps we can feature local bands alongside some bigger acts. Socially-minded imbeciles love that sort of thing."

"Hahaha!" Kammler and Bormann applauded in unison while the other gray-haired men nodded in approval.

"You are every bit your grandfather, Herr Müller!"

"Your praise is too kind, Herr Kammler."

"Now who shall we get to agitate in the Middle East?"

"I'm sure we have people at CIA who can do that. If they don't bungle it."

"Yes. And you, Müller, you and Edda shall go to 'Indian Country.' Your booming laughter will give every impression of good will. And, er, Edda, ah, well, just go along and smile a lot. I'm sure your unique talents will come in handy. Oh, which reminds me: you better take Mr. Silva along too."

She frowned, and Müller kissed her on the forehead. "It will be like our honeymoon, my dearest."

She looked up and smiled sheepishly at him.

By early 2012, the first casing stones were going up around the pyramid with accolades from the press for the foundations and academicians supporting the project. It seemed like such a good idea, no one thought to question it. Inside the pyramid, engineers were prepping for the repairs. On TV, the propaganda puppets at PBS, National Geographic, and the BBC were touting the project's benefits to science and the increase of human knowledge.

Chapter 47

This left the matter of a certain little troublemaker and her friends. In fact, poor Carrie really came late to the game and was not to blame ultimately. But there was no proof Bormann's arch-enemy (a label he wore proudly) Dr. Giuseppe Faro was behind the shenanigans at Dulce. It could be a purely Apache affair, but in any case, the responsible parties would not go unpunished even if all the damned souls of Nazis in Hell had to be summoned to storm the Pearly Gates of Heaven.

Müller and Edda landed in Albuquerque and made their way to the reservation. He was loud and charming, charismatic and funny. Edda just had to smile a lot, which was hard enough. You see, Müller was the worst kind of Nazi: he was likable. Like George H.W. Bush, he was engaging and humorous, disarming, hard to dislike personally and yet the blackest of hearts throbbed in his icy breast.

He and Edda met with various representatives from the reservations and local governments. They listened intently to their concerns, and Edda's seriousness and officiousness played brilliantly as she recorded all their desires and concerns. Finally they scored a morning TV appearance in Albuquerque.

Mr. Silva pulled the car up to the studio entrance and got deliberately out of the driver's seat. He cheerfully opened the rear door for Müller and Edda to step out, and stood with his chest puffed out and a smile beaming on his face. When they had entered the building, he returned to his seat.

He reached between the seat and console, slipped out an iPad and began flipping through darkly erotic *kinbaku* photos from Japan.

One-by-one he slid his finger across each picture pausing for a second or two with a detached and academic gaze on each before advancing to the next. As he swiped the final pic, an obviously disparate image slid into place, the only supposed photo they had of Carrie Tsosie. It was a few years old, of the only girl at Window Rock High that had blue in her hair. It had been copied from their yearbook. He frowned slightly and placed it face down on the passenger seat.

"So what is it that brings you two wonderful young people to the Four Corners region?" asked the hostess already knowing the answer.

Müller chortled. "Well, we aren't so young, I'm afraid, but thank you for the complement. Yes, we are here to set up 'The Four Corners of Education.' It will have a mission to advance secondary education among Native peoples, as well as provide counseling services to young people in need. We also hope to promote Native culture and artists within the communities—painters, writers, musicians, and so on."

The white man speaks with a forked tongue.

Müller knew how pencil-necked educators, bureaucrats, and sociology types were easily duped by stupidly facile faux-snappy names like "The Four Corners of Education" and cultural Marxist lingo like "Native" as opposed to "American Indian." He was certain they'd fall all over it and drool on their shirts.

"Oh! That's wonderful!" fawned the hostess. The world needs more people like you," she added crinkling her cute little nose and without a shred of irony.

"Well," began Müller, "we would like to announce for the first time on your show a big kick off event in Gallup. It will be attended by all the best people. We're going to hold a New Year's Eve concert to raise awareness and money for the program for the Navajos, Hopis, Apaches, Ute, Zunis and various other tribes around the Four Corners region.

"We want to feature, to play up, the local groups along with one or two celebrity acts we have lined up. We're hoping this will solicit big donations for college scholarships, career training, and counseling services."

Sound familiar?

"Oh! That's simply spectacular. Who are the big names?"

"Welllll, for example, we are in talks with Cher to act as Mistress of Ceremonies. She's part Native, you know."

"Oh! If you can bring Cher out of retirement that would be fabulous!"

"Rihanna and Jay Z have expressed interest in the event, along with Blackfire."

Blackfire, the Navajo punk band. The man had done his homework.

"Oh my God! That would be awesome! Do the young people still say that? 'Awesome?'" She giggled.

"We've also identified a few bands here in Albuquerque at UNM and a couple on the Navajo Reservation we would like to promote. They are still relatively unknown but we think one of them is every bit as good as Blackfire. We're still scouting acts."

"Ohhh. It's so wonderful you're offering young people this chance. I don't know what to say. We'll be right back after this short message with our next guest."

Chapter 48

The air was crisp, clean and clear. It was also thin, like the forest of lodgepole pine that surrounded them. Sheep tracks meandered their way through the trees and meadows. The high country on the Navajo Rez was some of the most beautiful anywhere.

"C'mon," opined Mary. "It'll be fun. We haven't played together for two years."

"It won't be fun if the guys from the bunker are there."

"Do you seriously think they're still looking for you?"

"You never know with some people."

"Look, if there was anything suspicious going on, we wouldn't be here."

"We're also two years out of practice."

"We got plenty of time to tighten our chops."

"Didn't you say the organizer is a big blonde guy?"

"HAHAHA! Yeah. But he's way too funny and charming to be a Nazi."

"Alright. I do miss civilization..."

Mary jumped with glee as the two boys with her high-fived.

"Great. It's settled then. You can stay at my place."

"Hahaha! Excellent. I've stayed out of trouble for long enough now."

Chapter 49

"And here we see what is, perhaps, the most ambitious effort in Egyptology in almost a century. Through generous grants from the Rockefellers, a team of archaeologists and engineers are restoring the Great Pyramid of Khufu to its original state."

The tour guide paused briefly in the King's Chamber, where the bulk of the work was going on, for the tourists to take a gander.

"Working for many years, a team of German engineers working in South America developed a method for making synthetic stone, in this case granite. When it is hard and dry it will be indistinguishable from the native material and have many of the same properties. Compare the restored version of the sarcophagus before you with the way it was found. For those not familiar with it, you can use the photograph to the left."

"Amazing." "Remarkable." "You can't even tell."

"Indeed," the guide agreed. "We expect to have it completed before Christmas 2014, along with the exterior casing stones you saw outside."

All around the tourists, workmen were moving in large bags of synthetic stone mix, others were carefully mixing it, while still others applied the stuff under the careful supervision of the engineers and archaeologists.

One of the tourists raised her hand. "What's in all those crates along the wall?"

The tour guide, slightly surprised, turned to have a look. "Ah. Probably some equipment and supplies they need for the final phase of work." He smiled to pleasantly punctuate his speculation. "In fact, you are all quite lucky to have come when you did. We will actually have to close the entire plateau for 2 weeks to complete the work and set up the re-opening. Unfortunate for those planning trips at that time, but worth it in the long term for the greater benefit to all."

As they exited the Pyramid into the scorching Egyptian sun, the group shielded their eyes and desperately fumbled for sunglasses.

"Now," finished up the guide, "as you can see, we have very ambitious plans here that we believe will greatly advance human knowledge and as such improve the human condition. One final note, I'd like to invite all of you to attend our, how do you say it, "Grand Opening" in two years from now. It will be capped off, so to speak, with what we believe to be an accurate reproduction of the original capstone being set!"

Gasps of profound satisfaction and curiosity erupted from the group. "Oh my!" "Wouldn't that just be perfect!" "They've thought of everything!"

"I bid you good day and hope you enjoy the rest of your stay in Egypt."

"You think he's in on it?" whispered Melissa to Frank. The two had been along "disguised as tourists."

"Does it matter? It looks like their little project's getting along OK anyway."

"I keep thinking of that REM song."

"*It's the End of the World as We Know It?*"

"You got that right, brother."

Chapter 50

"You wanna take down the Pyramid??" asked Greaves incredulously.

"Sound too ambitious?"

Faro, Greaves and Georgeann poured over a detailed map of the Giza plateau and the best architectural drawings of the Great Pyramid they could find.

Greaves scratched his head. "This thing's been standing for 5000 years and survived earthquakes and gunpowder."

"He's exaggerating," Georgeann clarified. "He doesn't really need to take down the pyramid, just the men who are trying to use it for their own nefarious designs."

Greaves nodded half acknowledgingly, half dumbfounded. "Nefarious designs, you say...Well, if this is anything like Dulce, you're gonna need quite a team to get in there. And it ain't exactly a secret place."

"Oh dear me," scoffed Faro. "We thought this was the home of Kelly's Heroes: brave, ingenious, and resourceful men. Don't tell me we've come to the wrong place."

Greaves shook his head while staring at the map. "Well, I didn't say that. But you're gonna need a team better than Delta Force, which theoretically I can provide. But an operation like that ain't cheap. And then there's the time to train."

"The second problem is easy. We have around 2 years before they're ready to go, more or less, according to the Shorleys' report."

"Whose report?" asked Georgeann painfully pinching his ribs.

"The Sho---I mean, the Barstows, the Barstows' report."

"Well, whoever's report it is," began Greaves a bit facetiously, "I take it you trust them?"

"Unconditionally."

Georgeann nodded emphatically in agreement.

"That's probably enough time to get ready. But there's still the matter of transportation, weaponry, lodgings, supplies, etc., much of which we'll have to get to Egypt, er, without, uh, using the ordinary channels."

"Understood. How much?"

"Operation like this'll be a few mil, at least. And that's doing it for cost because I love you so much."

"OK. OK. You don't have to get corny."

"Well, we have to raise around 3 or 4 million dollars in less than two years, Giuseppe. Is that possible? It can't come out of your research grants. People will notice, eventually."

Faro waved his hand, "We'll think of something." He sunk his head thoughtfully. "Why don't we just get that Navajo girl and her friends? They're awfully adept at wreaking havoc on bad guys. On the cheap."

"Carrie or Mary?"

"Yes!"

Greaves threw his head back in laughter. "There's a little more to this op than even she can handle. Anyway, there's some kind of charity thing going on around there now, a concert. Thorny and One Flare are driving out to see it. So she's tied up right now. After she gets away from that we'll see if she wants to help out."

Chapter 51

"Let's have a big hand for No Reservations!" exclaimed Cher as she strolled onto stage clapping her hands. It was dress rehearsal and Carrie's band just finished the three-song set they'd prepared for the concert. Müller and Edda stood up from their seats in the back of the hall and applauded mightily. Mr. Silva and his cohorts joined them.

The Holiday Inn Express in Gallup was the perfect venue for bureaucrats: it was comfortable while being completely uninteresting. It was so inoffensive it was offensive, except to bureaucrats and academics. The conference room had been gaily decorated for the holiday with a mix of Christmas, New Year's, and Native American. The celebrities stayed down the road at the historic El Rancho on historic Route 66, where stars of the great Hollywood westerns had stayed decades before during location shooting.

No Reservations took their bows and left the stage with their instruments as Blackfire made their entrance.

"And now, I'm proud to announce our grand finale for the evening, not just a wonderful local talent, but a band that's ignited places all over the world, Blackfire!"

As Carrie, Mary and the boys who were in the band made their way back to their rooms in the hotel, Mr. Silva and his sinister band quietly exited out the back and moseyed toward Carrie's room behind them. It was just about at that moment that Thorny and One Flare pulled up to the hotel in One Flare's '68 Volkswagen Westfalia.

"You sure this is the right place?"

"You can't hear the music?"

"Yes I can hear the music."

"Gyawd. Alright then."

"Jeezus, what a ride. Why didn't we take the 442?"

"Cuz Westfalias are cooler than 442s, and use way less gas."

"Cooler than a 442," scoffed Thorny.

"Chicks dig Westfalias. What time is it?"

Thorny checked his watch, "almost 10."

The front desk clerk noticed them and immediately thought, "Are you here with the event?"

"We're actually here to meet one of the bands. We'll be in the audience tomorrow night."

"Excellent. Would you like to dial their room?"

"Sure. Thanks. Tsosie. 301."

"I'm afraid there's no answer. Maybe they're still in rehearsal."

"OK, we'll go and watch."

"The bar's open if you like."

"Can't. Driving."

The boys made their way into the rehearsal hall to catch Blackfire. They pulled up chairs next to Müller and Edda and nodded hello.

Thorny leaned over to One Flare and shouted in his ear over the din, "Have you ever seen such a Nazi-lookin' couple in all your life?"

"Dude, we're from DC. You *haven't?*" One Flare shook his head and the boys got into the music.

Chapter 52

The four band members split up and returned to their rooms. Carrie and Mary paused at the doors of their adjoining rooms and smiled broadly at one another. "See you in a few minutes."

As they entered Mr. Silva and crew slunk out of the stairwell and waited for the doors to close. They approached Carrie's room and knocked. Anticipating the "Dynamic Dudes," as our protagonist likes to call them, she incautiously opened the door before she had completely finished changing, in nothing but her bare feet and a long t-shirt beaming with expectation. Four thugs pushed their way in as Mr. Silva stood outside to keep watch.

Carrie looked absolutely terrified for about a millisecond, and then lit into the intruders. She swung with rights and lefts that bloodied their faces and connected with bone-crushing kicks to their knees and groins. The men were flung around the room as if they were small animals tossed by a raging puma. But they were resilient and continued to come.

Hearing the ruckus, Mary rushed in through the adjoining door and joined the fray. Carrie was clinging to the dresser to catch her breath, her chest heaving and her eyes spitting fire from beneath disheveled locks at the men, who now moved more timidly. Mary struck like a rattlesnake, first one hired thug and then another. They were baffled, confounded. They eyed one another as if completely ignorant of what to do next against such fierce vixens. Neither girl had ever studied martial arts, but one grew up Navajo and the other Apache, and that put plenty of kung in their FU.

At that moment, Mr. Silva exhaled an exasperated sigh and burst in to check on the rumpus. He moved quickly and calmly into action. At that moment again, a very annoyed Edda entered the room a few seconds behind Silva rapt in consternation.

Without breaking stride she stated, "Fools! You're lucky I've come to check on affairs."

As she said this, Mary was just turning to meet the threat as Edda leveled a powerful jab to her temple and put her down. Silva moved for Carrie who fought as ferociously as she could in her exhausted state, but she was no match for an internationally renowned professional and well-practiced henchman.

He rolled her over on her stomach and, with a little help from his assistants, got her tightly hogtied limb by limb, wrapping the rope along her legs and cinching each loop like he was tying a Christmas tree, just like in the Japanese pictures he'd been studying. Edda trussed Mary likewise. They stuffed cloths in their mouths and wrapped duct tape around their heads a few times and then finally stood up to brush themselves off and breathe.

The fire hadn't gone out in their spirits though and they writhed and squirmed with such ferocity and with such vengeance in their eyes that even Mr. Silva was shaken, and he wondered if it would ever be prudent to unlash them as long as he or they were alive.

Chapter 53

The four sub-henchmen stood panting with their hands on their hips.

"Idiots. Go find a laundry cart, or something."

"Better make that two," added Mr. Silva. "That other wildcat might prove useful."

Edda gestured commandingly with her hand to shoo the men.

Mr. Silva eyed Edda's handiwork approvingly and looked inquiringly at her.

"Reinhardt taught me," she confessed with breathy embarrassment. "OK?" Silva grinned broadly.

"Haven't you ever heard of chloroform?" she asked recovering herself.

"What? And ruin all the fun?" smiled Silva. He stroked Carrie's leg, causing her to roll away and kick ineffectually against her bonds.

The girls, exhausted, finally lay limp, but conscious. "There. You see?" indicated Silva.

The men came back with a couple of laundry carts full of towels. The towels were taken out and the girls put in, and the towels put back on top of them.

"Now hurry. And be cautious about it."

The elevator doors dinged and Thorny and One Flare stepped out as the men pushed their cargo in. The two parties glared furtively at each other as they changed places.

"That's awfully weird. They don't seem like the kind of guys who go pushing laundry carts around."

"That's for sure. This whole place is weird."

Edda was just disappearing down the stairwell as Thorny and One Flare approached the girls' rooms primed for romance. They knocked and called out. "Mary! It's me!" "Carrie! You there? Open up!"

"Sump'm sketchy goin' on here."

"I'll say."

They looked at each other and their eyes popped. In unison they kicked the doors but they hardly budged.

"The stairs!"

They dashed after the kidnappers, sprinted through the lobby, and sprung through the restaurant.

"Hey, you boys! Stay out of there!"

They danced and dodged their way through the dining room and kitchen and out onto the loading dock. But it was too late. Mr. Silva was speeding away in an ambulance and held out a long, tall middle finger to the boys through the driver side window. The girls struggled against their bonds on the floor while the four lackeys guarded them on every side, every once in a while poking them with a stick.

The boys leapt off the dock and ran to the Westfalia. One Flare started it up and took off in the direction of the ambulance.

"God, I feel like Shaggy and Scooby in the Mystery Machine trying to rescue Josie and the Pussycats," Thorny commented.

"You mean Daphne and Thelma." stated One Flare without breaking his concentration on the road.

"No I don't. They weren't in a band, dumbass! Josie and the Pussycats was a band! Gyawd, didn't you watch those when you were a kid?"

"No. But I saw the movie. Those chicks were hot. And there were three of them, not two. Besides, Josie and the Pussycats lived in Riverdale, like Archie and the gang. And Sabrina. Scooby Doo was somewhere else."

"Whatever."

One Flare slowed the Westfalia and came to a stop on the side of the road. "It's no use. We'll never catch 'em in this."

Thorny jumped out the passenger side and kicked the gravel. "I told you, man! We should've brought the 442! We should've brought the fuckin' 442!"

Chapter 54

The next night at the New Year's Eve fundraiser, the Mistress of Ceremonies made a heartfelt appeal to the audience for any information that might help find the "missing girls." Each band dedicated their set to them, except of course, No Reservations who was unable to perform. In fact, they didn't even show up. They informed the event organizers (that would be Müller and Edda) that they were leaving immediately to jumpstart the search, which meant they were with Thorny and One Flare planning a rescue.

Müller took the stage right before Blackfire's finale.

"Good evening everyone. I'd like to wish you all a Happy New Year, if somewhat prematurely. I'm afraid I'm not very good at making speeches but I will do my best. I am Reinhardt Müller, one of the organizers of this event and I'd like to thank all of you for coming tonight on such an important holiday.

"Before Blackfire lights up our stage with their superb finale, let's remember that not everyone may be having a happy new year. Two of our musicians that were supposed to perform tonight went missing sometime between last night's rehearsal and this morning's sound check.

"We have managed to put together a separate collection for the two girls and their families. My partner, Edda, will be in the back accepting your donations. At the risk of compelling your generosity, please feel free to give as much or as little as you are able."

Edda waved sympathetically from her position near the exit as an enthusiastic murmur spread through the assembly. Some were already reaching for their checkbooks and wallets.

Müller turned the mike over to Cher. "Now, ladies and gentlemen, boys and girls, a very talented group of musicians who have been doing wonderful work for their people and everyone, in all parts of the world.....Blackfire!"

Everyone rung in the New Year, and then departed in

trickles and droves from the facility to return home or to their hotels.

"How much did we get?" asked Müller of the new donations.

"A lot. Thousands, certainly."

"Excellent. Buy yourself some souvenirs and give the rest to Mr. Silva for his hard work."

"I would love to bring some rugs and turquoise back to Bariloche for the house."

"Whatever you want, Schatzen." He kissed her on the top of her head. "I have to dash to you-know-where. They're expecting me."

"Of course, Liebling. See you in a few days."

"I hope so."

Müller spoke into his cell phone as he drove off. "So you have the package?....Ah, two. Perhaps we will double our money.....Hahaha! Is that right? Is that them mmmphing in the background I hear?.... I thought you liked them feisty....No, no. You mustn't use the usual means. Girls like this are worth a fortune right now.....Yes, you'll get your share, as long as they appear unharmed. No scarring, bleeding, broken bones.....Surely you're resourceful enough to figure it out Mr. Silva. You're the best in the business....50,000 apiece....I thought that might be incentive enough....Very well, see you at the rendezvous....Yes, yes. We have an additional bonus lined up for you when you get back to SCB.....Of course, Mr. Silva, good help is so hard to find!"

He finished cheerfully, as if he couldn't help dealing with people any other way. He slipped in a CD of *Die Walküre* and turned the "Magic Fire Music" up loud.

Chapter 55

"A little to the left. Your other left. Little more. Right there!"

Frank hollered instructions to Faro across the scrubby expanse. Faro forced a marker with a green flag into the hard soil, removed his hat and mopped his brow.

Frank peered around his theodolite and hollered again, "Helluva way to spend New Year's, huh, Doc?"

"Well, it's a heckuva lot warmer than Brookings this time of year."

Meanwhile, Kelvin, Georgeann, and Melissa were busy with a tape measure on another patch of ground nearby.

"Are you sure this is all worth the effort?" asked Georgeann.

"If the money comes through we'll be ready to go. This is all stuff we can do on our own to save time," stated Greaves, who always esteemed preparedness and efficiency. "I remember a valuable lesson I learned from Tom: the preparation is the journey."

"Not sure what that means or who this Tom is, but still, a mockup of the Giza Plateau on the property is bound to raise some eyebrows."

"We never told you about Tom?"

"No."

Georgeann made a dismissive gesture. "Don't ask. Books could be written and movies could be made. In fact they have been."

Melissa shook her head. There was always something with Faro, and now was not the time.

"No one'll see it over here. That's why we chose this area. It's not a full mock up anyway. Just the parts we need."

"Well I'm burning up out here. How about a little shade for a while and some nice cold lemonade?"

"Good idea."

Melissa pulled the radio off her belt. "Frank, we're gonna take a break for some lemonade. Why don't you guys join us?"

"Roger that. Doc! C'mon! Let's go get some lemonade with the others."

"Fantastic idea."

The two waved to the trio to acknowledge they were on the way. The group gathered under a tarp set up adjacent to the work site. Melissa opened a cooler and produced a pitcher of lemonade, some watermelon, and banana bread with cream cheese.

"Oh! You made your famous banana bread! And cream cheese! I just may have to hog it all."

"Don't you dare."

"Well, we've almost got site 2 surveyed. Then we can start laying out the construction there as well."

"Now if only we had 4 million dollars."

Suddenly, Greaves set his lemonade down. He cocked his head as if he were listening to something.

"What? What is it?"

"Shh."

"Uh-oh."

They all set down their drinks and food and sat expectantly. Faro reached over and snatched Frank's banana bread to which Frank flashed an angry glare.

"C'mon, Doc. We gotta go."

"What is it?"

"I just got a message from Thorny and One Flare. Trouble in Gallup. Serious trouble."

"What happened?"

"Won't know till we get there."

"Oh my God. Be careful."

"Don't worry, we've got this covered."

"Good Lord! What is *that*?" exclaimed Faro pointing behind Greaves. Greaves turned, and Faro snatched his banana bread as well.

"Hey!"

"This is no time to bicker," indicated the Doc, mouth full of banana bread and cream cheese. "Scramble! Scramble!"

The pair pounced into the Land Rover and raced back to the house. They dashed for their go bags, threw them into Greaves jeep and sped down the long dirt drive onto the road.

"You know we left them stranded out there without a vehicle?"

"They'll figure it out." He paused a moment. "They're very resourceful and ingenious people."

"You don't have to be *that* to walk back to the house a half a mile." Kelvin looked sideways at Farrell as he tried to watch the road. "You owe me a banana bread."

Chapter 56

"Ah, Mr. Silva! You've made me a piñata and it's not even my birthday!"

Müller was just entering the facility where Silva and his assistant henchmen had absconded with their victims. Carrie, still hogtied like she was back at the hotel now hung suspended from steel rafters. Müller approached and spun the piñata slowly.

Silva frowned disapprovingly and gestured to a table.

"Always a man of few words, eh, Mr. Silva?" Müller walked over to the table and ran his hand along the edge as he examined the contents on top. At one end were a couple of compressed air tanks with a respirator mask attached to one.

"Quite some goodies you've arranged for our guests, all perfectly designed to be completely harmless while inducing unspeakable suffering and psychological terror. I knew you could do it."

Müller now approached Carrie. As she spun lazily around, he gently stopped her so they were facing each other. Her face was held up by a rope tied to her hair, pulling it back. Her body was exhausted but her eyes revealed an unbroken fury.

"I see what you mean," observed Müller turning to Mr. Silva.

He fidgeted around her head looking for the end of the duct tape. When he found it, he began to unwrap it. She winced as it pulled her hair. He slowly and gradually tugged the last layer so she could feel every molecule of adhesive pull at her skin. It was as if he enjoyed every second of it. Finally, as it cleared her lips, she spat the spit-soaked rag in his face such that it stuck to his nose and hung there.

He pulled it off with his thumb and forefinger and dropped it on the floor.

"Do you have any idea why you're here?"

166

A slew of oaths and obscenities in Navajo erupted from her that are too ugly to translate here. She shook her whole body as mightily as she could, shrieking at the end of her tirade, but her effort to free herself was fruitless.

"I'm sorry, I didn't catch that."

"Is that what you do? Travel the world producing concerts so you can kidnap the girls you like best like some kind of stinking pervert?"

Müller bellowed with laughter, then abruptly turned serious. "Do you know where you are?"

"I've never seen this place."

"Never seen this place? And yet my men tell me they witnessed you here. You and your friends. The only problem is, we don't know who your friends are. We need you to tell us. Then you can get down, stretch, have a nice cold drink of water, and be on your way."

"Even if I knew what you were talking about I'd never tell you anything."

"Mr. Silva here is very good at making people talk. In fact, he's the best. That's why we pay him so handsomely. Isn't that right, Mr. Silva."

He nodded in agreement.

Müller chuckled. "Ironic isn't it," he gave Carrie another turn. "that Mr. Silva, who is so good at making other people talk, is a man of so few words himself?"

Carrie shook violently again. As she came around to face Müller again, he stopped her.

"Perhaps I have been presumptuous with you. I didn't mean you had been inside here, only that you had been...here." He raised his hands indicatively and rotated his body back and forth.

A glint of understanding appeared in her eyes, but she quickly suppressed it.

"Hahahaha! It seems like we're getting somewhere at last."

"No matter what you do to me, I'd never tell you anything. I'd die first!" She spat the last three words with rage and conviction.

"Yes, you're far too altruistic a person...." He stopped and thought for a second. "Caring. Carrie. Hahaha! They sound almost the same. Caring Carrie. Hahahahaha! Do you like my little pun Mr. Silva?"

Silva grinned.

"Yes you're far too caring to put your own welfare above your friends, and frankly I can't have you dying, or even seriously harmed. Then Mr. Siva wouldn't be getting the commission he's expecting, and I can't have a disgruntled henchman on my hands."

Carrie's eyes bulged with comprehension. "Where's Mary? What did you do with her?" Carrie writhed furiously, but it was all for not.

"Ah, so her name is Mary! We're making progress already. But to be sure, you mean her, don't you?"

Müller dropped a curtain and revealed Mary, secured to a steel pillar as if she'd been stood up and lashed in place. Her head had been stabilized with more duct tape over her forehead and mouth and wrapped around the pole. Carrie stared in some mix of horror and sympathy and tried more violently than ever to free herself.

"Let her go! You let her go! You monster!" Mary glared imploringly out the corner of her eyes at Carrie in turn. She wove another stream of Navajo obscenity.

"Mr. Silva, how about a demonstration?"

Silva affixed the respirator mask to Mary's face and opened the tank. It hissed ominously at first, and then like the hushed taunt of a demon as she convulsed and screamed through the gag. Silva shut the tank and removed the mask. Mary's chest heaved as she hyperventilated through her nose to refresh the air in her lungs as fast as she could. It was a haunting sound.

Carrie shrieked in anguish and helplessness, fully understanding the implications to her friend, and her friends, if she said anything. She shook so ferociously, the steel rafters could be heard clattering above. Something loosened, and she dropped a few inches and grunted in pain. It was not looking good for the good guys.

Chapter 57

Faro and Greaves pulled into the hotel parking lot next to One Flare's Westfalia. They knocked on the doors but no one answered. They stood momentarily at the rear doors looking around when Greaves patted Faro on the chest with the back of his hand. He pointed.

Thorny and One Flare were making gratuitous use of the indoor pool. Faro and Greaves went to meet them. When the two boys noticed the older men, they brought their mirth-making to sudden halt and climbed out of the pool.

"You boys don't seem very agitated considering the urgency of your message."

"Gotta do something to pass the time."

"You think it's safe to talk here?"

"It's New Year's Day and nobody else is here, and I sure don't wanna go outside in a wet bathing suit."

"Well, it's gonna be awfully cold when you go back out to sleep in that heap you drove out here."

"Nah, we're staying in Carrie and Mary's rooms."

"This keeps getting less and less urgent."

"Where are the girls anyway?"

"We don't know. They've been kidnapped."

"What??!!"

"This better not be a joke."

Faro glared at the boys. "I wouldn't put it past them," he added half jokingly.

"Last night right after rehearsal."

"Good God! What are you talking about?"

"A group of five guys. We think they pushed them out in laundry carts. We passed them getting off the elevator. They went down when we came up."

"Is that all you have to go on?"

"Well they sure weren't dressed like housekeeping!"

"Alright, alright. What else?"

"They drove off in an ambulance, lights, sirens, everything."

"We chased them out to the loading dock, and the dude flipped us off as they drove off."

"What did these guys look like?"

"Well, all pretty similar. Hired thug types. The alpha was wide-bodied and kind of bow-legged. Bald."

"Silva!" exclaimed Faro.

"Silva?"

"Yes, Silva, the most qualified, coveted, and dangerous henchman for hire in the world today. And he's currently under the employ of an unknown entity in Argentina, which almost always spells Nazi."

"I've heard the name," commented Greaves. "Never once thought I'd run into him."

"You haven't, yet."

"We tried to chase after them in the bus, but they were too fast."

"Yeah. Why didn't you guys bring the 442 for this trip?"

Thorny made an I-told-you-so gesture, slicing the air with his hand at One Flare.

"That's sort of irrelevant now."

"Well how'd you end up in their rooms?"

"Those two guys in the band with them convinced housekeeping to open up. The keycards were still in the power slots, so we kept them."

Greaves shook his head in amusement. "You guys are shameless opportunists."

"You and Tom trained us well, Kelly."

"Where do you think they took them?"

"We have no idea. The two guys in the band went up to the Rez to rally the forces."

"Well, let's see. These guys are pretty good. Assuming this is related to your little stunt at Archuleta Mesa year before last, they certainly have an agenda other than ransom. They're probably hoping to get the rest of you by interrogating them!"

"Jeezus fucking Christ!"

"Fuck me! What do we do?"

"Taking down the Dulce Base was a huge blow to their operations. It was bad enough you immobilized three fourths of their staff with acute poison ivy for a week, but then going into a firefight with the rest, killing a dozen and half men and then permanently taking down the base, probably caused an unslakable thirst for revenge and a vendetta that would be pursued to the pits of Hell and back."

"Oh, man, did we screw up."

"I wouldn't say that. You've made the world a slightly better place. You just didn't know what you were getting into completely."

"We've got to move fast. The girls could be dead soon."

"Oh no. They won't kill them. They need them alive, first for information, then to sell into sex slavery—a fate far worse than death. A couple of feisty young American Indian girls would fetch a small fortune on the market just for the rarity."

Thorny and One Flare looked visibly ill.

"Here's an idea. What's the last place those guys would expect you to look for them? The very last place you think they'd go."

"Well, we thought about that. We figured it was the Dulce Base, if that's their line of thinking too."

"Bingo."

"There's no time to lose. They'll still be alive, but we can prevent further inhuman suffering and hopefully get there before they give out any names. This Silva is not to be trifled with, nor are his employers. These aren't just bad men, they are evil incarnate."

"Quick, call those guys from the band whose names I can never remember and tell them we're 'OTW'!"

"You guys can dress in the car. Let's go."

As they dashed for the parking lot, Faro added, "Hi

ho, Silver! Away!"

Chapter 58

"What??? Not there? Where is he?"

Greaves screamed into his phone as they raced along I-40 to the Jicarilla reservation.

"Damn!"

"What is it?"

"Our back up is unavailable."

"Daryl?"

"And his team. Bow hunting polar bear in Alaska."

"Bow hunting polar bear! In Alaska. In January! Good Lord." Faro was very impressed.

"That leaves the four of us. And we know there are at least five of them."

"Well, if we go in quietly, we could get four of them before they even have time to reach for their weapons."

"And if we don't go in quietly enough or aren't quick enough, it's lights out. It's the one sure way to make sure the girls are silenced forever before we complete our mission. We have to think about this a little bit more."

"I thought you said they needed them alive."

"Not if we go barging in there to rescue them! The living girls could then spill the beans on their captors and start an international manhunt, if not by government authorities, then by our compatriots at least. No, no. There must be another way."

Chapter 59

As the crew neared the reservation, the old shaman was waiting for them at the side of the road.

"What's he doing here?"

"Can't you guess? That is a decidedly good sign, when the local medicine man unexpectedly expects your arrival."

Greaves stopped the vehicle and the old man climbed into the back seat with Thorny and One Flare.

"How did you know we were coming?"

"Carrie's friends from the band told me. I thought you knew."

"Oh. Yeah."

"Go straight," he indicated laconically.

"Straight? Where?"

"Why do you always have so many questions? I'll tell you when we get there."

They drove for a while when the old man spoke again, "Turn left here, on that dirt road."

Greaves swung the vehicle across the road and headed up the dirt trail.

"Stop here. You boys get out."

They did.

The old man spoke through the open window to them. "Behind those rocks you'll find another entrance. It goes in level, not steep. You'll need that. Wait an hour before you go in."

The SUV drove off. The medicine man directed Greaves and Faro to use the tunnel at the top of the mountain as before. This time they got closer access using a jeep trail, but still had some climbing to do.

Greaves went to the rear of the vehicle and got out a Desert Eagle .45 and CAR-15 for the possible close quarter fighting that lay ahead.

"Need anything?" he asked the Doc.

Faro opened his jacket to reveal the .45. "I believe in going all in," he said.

"Let's go."

They made their way the rest of the way up the mountain. Faro was huffing and puffing a little bit and paused to offer a comment.

"Why'd the old man give us the hard part and the young guys, who are in superb shape by the way, the easy entrance? What was he thinking?"

"He probably knows what he's doing. It'll become clear when we get there."

They entered the tunnel. It was still a little slick from the poison ivy oil deposited from the smoke during that incident. Since no weather got into the shaft, there was nothing to wash it away. They watched their footing carefully, lifting their feet straight up and putting them straight down again to avoid sliding.

Suddenly, Faro lost his footing and started to slide on his seat all the way down the tunnel. Amazingly, he kept his cool. He held his hands out for balance maintaining control of his .45. He also used his hands to control his speed and direction. The opening to the lab grew bigger and bigger as he raced down the slick.

Suddenly he crashed through the remaining louvers, which made a loud CLANG, and into the lab. Carrie and Mary's eyes popped with hopeful surprise.

The Doc steadied his feet, stood up straight, and took a quick look around. "So, Reinhardt, we meet again!"

Chapter 60

Just then, Thorny and One Flare were also arriving on scene, but the tunnel they took put them in another part of the base. They had to make their way through a boiler room, down a hall, and around a corner to enter the central lab. They crept slowly and quietly to the corner. Thorny peeked around first, then pulled back and flattened himself against the wall.

"Holy merit badge, Batman!" Thorny exclaimed in hushed tones.

"What? What'd you see?"

"The girls look like they were trussed up by a Japanese bondage master."

"And you know how Japanese bondage masters work because...?" intimated One Flare jokingly.

Thorny frowned disapprovingly. "It makes perfect sense if you think about it."

"What are you talking about?"

"The Germans and the Japanese?"

One Flare stared puzzlingly.

"The war?"

"So?"

"Well, maybe the Krauts picked something up from them. The Japanese are famous for that."

One Flare sighed in exasperation and shook his head. "Krauts?"

"Just sayin', man."

"Thanks for the history lesson, but we need a plan. How many guys?"

"Same five. And a big blonde dude. Looks like the one from the show."

"We'll have to somehow cut the girls loose and get them out of there."

"Lemme look." One Flare took a peek and then

withdrew.

"Whoa! Dude!"

"What?"

"Faro just popped out of the hole and addressed the big blonde dude. I didn't catch what he said."

One Flare looked again.

"Now they're all six focused on Faro."

"Jeezus that old guy has balls for a college professor."

"I'll say."

"Looks pretty confrontational. Should we help him first or just get Carrie and Mary out of there?"

"How should I know? Hey! Let's move up behind those tables."

"Good idea."

Thorny and One Flare crawled up behind the tables for a closer look.

Thorny mouthed to One Flare, "Where's Kelly?"

One Flare shrugged. He looked again. Then he pointed at Thorny mouthing "you" and pointed emphatically at Carrie. He then pointed at himself and pointed at Mary. Finally, he held up a foot, pointed at it and mouthed, "Shoes off."

Chapter 61

At that moment, Greaves shot through the hole, landed on his feet right next to Faro, CAR-15 locked, loaded and aimed. He swept it side to side pausing on each villain, but they had already drawn too. Faro responded by raising the matte black .45 and pointed it at Müller. It was a Mexican stand-off.

"Giuseppe! How nice of you to join our little munch. And you brought company."

"Is that what it's come to, Reinhardt: damsels in distress to indulge your puerile fantasies?"

"As you can see, this is hardly a fantasy." He became uncommonly stern. "It is all too real, and bears very real, and serious, consequences."

"You can't kill me, Reinhardt. You'll recall that we have an arrangement."

"You've overstepped. This surprise appearance of yours may have just canceled our 'arrangement.'"

This was precisely the chance Thorny and One Flare needed to make their move.

Now, there are three ways to be invisible. The first way is to be invisible, but that is a very difficult trick to learn. The second way is to appear to be something else, which has already been demonstrated. The third way is simply not to be seen. It was this third option they chose to execute, which was easy with everyone else pointing guns at each other and the bad guys with their backs to them.

Leaving their moccasins behind, the boys pranced silently up to their objectives. Thorny positioned himself so his shoulder was directly under the rope hogtying Carrie so it was like a shoulder strap, and began to cut the suspension line with his knife. One Flare stood so Mary and the pole obscured him from the bad guys in case anyone turned around, and sliced through the ropes that lashed her to the pole.

Carrie's full weight sunk on to Thorny's shoulder and they both winced silently in pain. One Flare threw Mary over his shoulder like a sack of potatoes, and they trucked silently off leaving their moccasins behind. All the while Faro and Greaves furtively observed the boys' actions while keeping the miscreants occupied.

The armed palaver continued. "But you see, Giuseppe, I don't have to kill you. I can kill them." He and Mr. Silva turned to indicate their victims but were suddenly overwhelmed with astonishment. They were confounded, stunned, flummoxed, horrified and perplexed.

"Seems like your little party's been crashed, Reinhardt. What will Bariloche say?"

"After them, imbeciles! Silva, see to your men!"

Mr. Silva pushed and beat his men into action, but the culprits were nowhere to be seen, and nobody knew which way they went. Were they really invisible, or had they already achieved the tunnel? Ah, that is a mystery. The men dashed down hallways and kicked open doors, but could find nothing.

"Well, Reinhardt, my work here is done. Exit, stage left."

Greaves had already begun inching his way toward the escape route, weapon still fixed alternately on Müller and Silva. Faro fell in behind him and they increased their pace. Silva raised his pistol to plug Faro, but Müller put out his hand and lowered the weapon.

"He's right. We still can't kill him."

Greaves tracked Thorny and One Flare's bare feet back through the boiler room to the tunnel while the Doc positioned himself so they were back to back and took tail, weapon poised. The hired thugs watched helplessly. There was no one to kill, and no one to pursue, yet. For the first time in a very, very long while, Müller's composure broke. As the two men disappeared from view, he let out an anguished howl.

Chapter 62

The boys emerged from the tunnel panting loudly, Thorny wincing with pain from the shoulder rope, but not half as badly as Carrie from bobbing and swinging.

"Haha! That was intense," exclaimed One Flare.

"The life of a repo man is always intense," Thorny reminded him.

And they high fived still portaging their damsels, who grunted.

They wanted to collapse and drop the girls, but a van was waiting and the medicine man's niece was leaning against the back. She opened the doors and said, "In here."

They noticed a tall Indian from the sweat lodge perched on a horse. He touched the tip of his hat in greeting.

The boys set the girls down as gingerly as they could in the back of the van and looked questioningly at the niece.

"Keys are in it," she answered.

"What are you gonna do?"

"I've got a ride."

The tall Indian hoisted her up and turned the horse to trot away, but stopped.

"Don't stop till you get to the fry bread stand," he told them. And off he went.

"C'mon!"

One Flare jumped in the driver's seat and Thorny took shotgun, where he did indeed find a shotgun. It was a Remington 870 Express tactical. He pumped the action to chamber a round and held it on his lap.

"Talk about riding shotgun. That's a sweet piece ya got there," One Flare commented as he spun out on the dirt road.

"That's what your mom said."

At that moment Mary swung her legs around and started kicking the back of the passenger seat with both feet mmmphing loudly which sounded rather like muffled cussing. Carrie began to berate the boys harshly.

"What the fuck are you doing? Untie us you morons!"

"The guy said not to stop till we hit the fry bread stand."

"It's gonna take more than fry bread for you, mister!" She growled in anger and struggled futilely. The girls exchanged looks of annoyance and frustration with their men.

As they approached the fry bread stand back on the highway, One Flare slowed down and stopped a few yards away. The two climbed back between the seats to free the girls. There was so much damn rope and the knots so complicated, they finally just took out their knives and cut everything.

As they climbed out the back, Carrie and Mary lit into the boys with a barrage of slapping.

"How could you?" "You shoulda let us go right away!" "I can't believe you made us ride all this way like that!" And so on.

The boys didn't fight back because they knew the girls were just blowing off steam, and they just happened to be available. And if they really wanted to hurt them, they wouldn't be slapping. Finally the girls stopped and composed their anger. They fell on the boys' shoulders, embraced them, and cried with relief until composing themselves once again. Gently the boys helped them to sit on the bed of the van, feet hanging over the rear bumper.

Just then Thorny was alerted to the deep whir of an accelerating vehicle. He saw a black SUV speeding toward them that seemed to contain Silva's four assistant henchmen. Gun barrels appeared from the open windows. He dashed to the passenger seat, grabbed the Remington, and then planted himself in the middle of the oncoming lane.

When the SUV was just close enough he blasted three rounds through the windshield. The SUV swerved, rolled over, and stuck in ditch.

The trio behind the van leapt up to see the action. Thorny, resting the shotgun on his shoulder, beheld his handiwork, and then turned to his friends. "It's all in the reflexes."

"Damn Indians call it right every time! How did they know?"

"We better call the Reservation police to come clean that up," suggested Mary with fatigue.

"My guess is they're right behind," quipped Carrie.

A few seconds later the Rez cops pulled over, lights flashing, and addressed the group. "You folks okay?"

"Y'a'reckon."

"You go about your business then. We'll take care of this." The two officers strolled over to the SUV. The senior officer shook his head observing the unconscious occupants. "Kids. Kids did this." His partner nodded.

And so the police went about their business and our exhausted but relieved group of friends went about theirs.

"I just noticed how cold it is," said Mary.

"Dressed like that, I bet you're freezing. Lemme turn that heater up to full blast."

The boys then unfolded some blankets from the back of the van and placed them over the girls' shoulders.

"We'll just go get some fry bread here and some coke."

"God, we're starving."

"And thirsty!"

The girls lay back and felt the rope pieces. "Aaaaarrgh!" They got up and together kicked it all out the back, and then plopped back down in their seats.

The boys came back with fry bread, lamb stew and coke.

"How did you know where we were?"

"We literally guessed."

"Well thank God you guessed right."

"You know my feet are starting to freeze."

"Don't you have any shoes or socks?"

"We left all our shit in Kelly's car."

"Yeah, I can't wait to get home or somewhere and get some warm clothes on."

Carrie started giggling.

"What?" asked Mary, giggling in response.

"I'm so sorry we wailed on you earlier. We were just so frustrated!"

"Don't sweat it. We kinda got that."

"Yeah," said Mary. "Me too."

And they all started to have a good laugh. As the blanket slid off of one of Mary's shoulders, One Flare looked closely at her arm.

"Gyawd, look at that. You can still see the rope marks." He traced them with his finger. "You should get a tat of that, to remember the experience by."

She set down her stew carefully on the bed of the van, grimaced with fierce determination, and slapped him so hard he fell over.

Chapter 63

They arrived at the old shaman's niece's house again to return the van and borrow some clothes. Faro and Greaves had already arrived. The women came out to meet Carrie and Mary such that they were no longer wrapped only in blankets, but loving arms and attention as well.

"Thank God! Are we glad to see you two safe and sound!"

"Safe, at least. Not quite back to sound yet."

"Even so, the new year has come about. It just got a lot better for us, and especially the two of you, and a lot worse for our adversaries."

"Yeah, Happy New Year, sort of," offered the girls.

Faro and Greaves then made their way to the returning heroes.

"Well, well, the dynamic dudes return with our damsels safe and sound!" laughed Faro.

"Why wouldn't we? No real lead got slung."

"Nevertheless, it took so long for you to get back, we were a bit concerned."

"We stopped for a romantic dinner along the way."

Faro gave One Flare's cheeks a turn to compare them. One was red and swollen. "I can see that."

"Where're our bags? Our feet are practically frostbitten by now."

"Pretty hard driving when your feet are numb."

"For God's sake, doesn't the heater work in that thing?"

"Oh sure. But it only does so much good. You know car heat: feels good on the outside but no long lasting penetration."

"Grab your gear and come in by the stove."

After the girls had had hot showers and changed into borrowed clothes, it was the boys' turn. The crew gathered by the stove to sort things out from here.

"Then it's decided. You'll come out to the Barstows' with us where you can not only hide out, but have a very interesting time helping us with the preparations there. The Barstows also have some interesting experiments going on you girls may want to take part in."

"One Flare's got some outstanding carpenter skills I'm sure will come in handy," added Greaves. "Did you know he once built the biggest skateboard ramp on the East Coast entirely out of lumber?"

"And he topped it off with a giant fiberglass gorilla he got from a miniature golf course."

"'Got from a miniature golf course?' Hahaha! I do not want to know!"

Chapter 64

As winter turned into spring, our merry band put their training facility together piece by affordable piece. Thorny and One Flare would take off to Vegas for "romantic getaways" with Carrie and Mary, and somehow always manage to return with a van full of lumber.

"Where the hell are you getting all this lumber?"

"Lucky at craps, I guess."

"Sounds like crap alright!"

Greaves, knowing the boys as he did, would just walk away shaking his head and doing a Sgt. Schulz impression: "I know nothing! I know nothing!"

In the weeks after Easter, the assembly was gathered around the Barstows' lunch table enjoying another delicious meal prepared by Melissa when the phone rang. Farquelle was on the other end with a big shit-eating grin on his face that could be heard through the receiver.

"Hello?"

"Frank?" asked Farquelle slyly.

"Farquelle?"

"Go check your mailbox. Don't hang up."

"Who's that, dear?"

"It's Farquelle, he says to check the mailbox but not hang up."

"All the way down there?"

"It must be important. Here, you hold the phone."

"What's going on?" someone asked from the kitchen.

"We're not sure yet."

Frank grabbed the keys and left. Ten minutes later he burst through the back door.

"HAPPY FRIKKIN' EASTER, EVERYONE!"

"What? What?"

"Easter was two weeks ago."

"Well the goose just laid the golden eggs!" cheered

Frank. "Ah, I mean the Easter Bunny brought them. Oh, whatever, goose, Easter Bunny, who cares about mixing metaphors?"

Jolly laughter was heard coming from Alaska on the other end. "How's that for a day's work?"

Frank handed Melissa a paper. "OH MY GOD!"

"What? What?" "What's going on?" "What happened?"

Melissa's eyes were bulging with astonishment. Her mouth hung open. She was flabbergasted.

Faro went over and turned the paper so he could see it.

"Good Lord, how did that happen?"

That brought the rest of the crowd--Georgeann, Greaves, Carrie, Mary, Thorny and One Flare—all of whom were straining to see the paper.

Carrie and Mary were so stunned, they uttered something in each of their native tongues that no one else understood.

Greaves stated, "I'll call Daryl and have him get started."

Finally Melissa got her mouth to move. "Jacques, where on earth did this 20 million dollars come from? Is it some kind of mistake?"

"Nope. Remember that Bitcoin thing I told you about?"

"Yeeesss....."

"Well, Just for shits and giggles, I bought 200,000 of them at fractions of a penny. Literally fractions of a penny. I just sold half a few days ago for 200 dollars each."

"What???" Melissa's mouth fell open paralyzed again as she just barely stammered the one word she got out.

"Well what is it?" Asked Faro.

Frank looked at him blandly, "We have 20 million dollars, that's all."

The group erupted in cheers and celebration.

"Unbelievable!" exclaimed Faro.

"It was that Bitcoin thing."

"You were right, Giuseppe! It does have legs!" exclaimed Georgeann.

"So wait a minute," began Faro snatching the receiver from Melissa so he could address Farquelle. "Let me understand this. You invested less than 1000 dollars of bankster money in this Bitcoin, and just now you got 20 million dollars of bankster money out of it, and no banksters profited off this deal or got a red cent out of it?"

"That's about the size of it."

"Holy Cow! This is better than Kryptonite. At this rate we can bleed the banksters dry in less than a decade and leave their shriveled corpses to the turkey vultures!"

"Hahahaha! I knew you'd love it, you Dego bastard."

"Farquelle, you magnificent slippery old Frog! Get me some of that too!"

They popped a bottle of some kind of wine they had around the house in lieu of Champagne, which they just weren't pretentious enough to keep around.

"Here's to Bitcoin!"

"And here's to our trip to Egypt!"

"And here's to the death of Babylon's banksters!"

"Now we can really move on getting this mockup done and start training!"

"That reminds me," added Greaves nonchalantly. "You guys can stop with the lumber runs now. We'll just buy what we need."

And they all yucked it up and had a mirthful rest-of-the-day.

Chapter 65

Daryl showed up with a group of men that were not *prima donnas*. They threw themselves into the planning, measuring and construction with everyone else. Not only would it pass the time, it would hasten the success of the team and increase their detailed knowledge of the place.

Obviously, moving 30-ton stones wasn't the most practical way to go about it, nor was their goal to produce an accurate duplicate of the pyramid. Their goal was to reproduce the space they'd be moving in. Wood, plastic, and fiberglass took the place of stone, and in a few instances, concrete.

Faro, Frank and Melissa did their damnedest to guess what the fully reconstructed interior would be like replete with the functioning parts. They also started developing and testing their own scalar technology with the help of Carrie and Mary owing to their experience with electronics and sound. Georgeann acted as administrator of the project. Greaves did quality control along with exercise planning for the paramilitary training with Daryl and his team. Thorny and One Flare took over supply and logistics while Carrie and Mary were utility infielders.

"Check this out," said Frank as Mary and Carrie lifted a .50 caliber onto its mount in the back of the Land Rover and fastened it into place.

They were at the old control center that Frank and Melissa had expanded to contain a workshop for the project at hand.

"Wow, what a beauty. And the gun looks nice too."
Carrie and Mary smiled at the Doc.
"You ladies sure do know your way around firearms."
"Of course, we grew up on the Rez."
"Now we really can play Rat Patrol!" said Faro as he walked around the vehicle admiring its new equipment from

every angle. "But what's it for?"

"Training. And it'll probably come in handy if you know who ever shows up again."

Faro let out a big belly laugh. "You got that right!"

"But look at this baby, here," said Frank sidling over to the workbench. He held up a small black box with some tubes coming out.

"If I'm not mistaken," Faro conjectured, "That bears a certain resemblance to Paul LaViolette's microwave phase conjugate mirror."

"You are not mistaken. I intend to produce our own graser, that is gamma ray laser, a step up from LaViolette's maser, to fire our own electromagnetic oscillation beam into the pyramid to disrupt the resonance the pyramid was based on in order to neutralize it, should it come to that."

"Not the dreaded, hitherto strictly theoretical Mark IV graser!" exclaimed Faro.

"Indeed."

"Looks awfully small," observed one of the girls. "And the pyramid is so big."

"It doesn't matter," countered Frank. "The phase conjugation will amplify the pump graser to enough power to disrupt the pyramid resonance. We don't need to destroy it, or need planet busting power such as the pyramid has, we only need to dampen the resonance to render the pyramid's graser harmless."

"Incredible. But where's the rest of it, the shooting end? And will it be ready in time?"

"It has to be."

Chapter 66

Bormann and Kammler sighed heavily. The year was coming to an end. They were gathered with Müller, Edda, and a man named Dornberger to discuss developments.

"Well, it isn't essential to our operations in Egypt. Nevertheless, they must all still be punished eventually."

"We must also find a way out of this arrangement with Faro. He's clearly assisting these troublemakers somehow."

"Müller, you have done well in the Middle East. The breadth of your success there cannot be overestimated. However, Faro and his associates must be stopped. It's likely the Dulce Base was not their only target."

"What about his dead man's trigger?"

"We'll have to hold off killing him for now, but no more secret hand signs. Why don't you send a courier to inform him?"

"We don't know where he is."

"Send word to the University. I'll have it typed up this afternoon. In the meantime, start investigating the dead man's trigger. Let's see if we can find out what he has and who he's sent it to."

"It could just be automatic. If he doesn't log in on schedule to this or that website or computer, it's automatically distributed."

"Already on the right track, eh, Dornberger? That's exactly what we need you to find out."

"I'll get right on it."

That afternoon, a letter was dispatched by courier on a flight to Brookings. Well, actually I lied. There are no flights from Argentina to Brookings. You have to fly to Chicago, then Rapid City, then finally, Brookings. But you get the point.

The courier made his way across campus to the

Physics Department, where Faro kept his office. It was locked and empty. The courier asked around in the other offices, but most profs hadn't returned from the Christmas break yet, and only a few winter term students were around along with a skeleton crew of secretaries and maintenance crew.

"Excuse me, I'm looking for Professor Faro."

"Ooohh, there's no telling where he is. He takes off to the most unusual places during these breaks. He may be in the middle of the Amazon or ensconced in some obscure private library in Europe, or anything."

"I see. Well, you see, I have this important delivery for him. You wouldn't know how I could get it to him, would you?"

"Like I said, nobody knows what that man is up to. Even his secretary doesn't know until he drags her off with him."

"Maybe if I spoke with an administrator or dean...."

"They won't be around till February. All those privileged higher ups, you know, they just stretch their vacations like rubber bands. Think they're better than the rest of us. They wouldn't know where he is either. He never tells anyone. Brings so much money into this University, no one seems to care as long as the work gets done. Such a nice, down to earth man though. Never goes to his head. Just a little quirky in his ways. Always thoughtful and generous though."

"I see. Yes, that sounds like him," chuckled the courier. "Still, if you can think of anything."

"Best bet is to give it to me, and I'll make sure he gets it."

"Of course. As you can see, it's sealed in wax. Eyes only," warned the courier somewhat jokingly while wagging a finger. "Be sure to sign and print your name here."

"Oh my! That man lives the most interesting life! Wax seals, even."

"Very interesting indeed."

"Well, thank you for taking the trouble to find me.

I'll make sure he gets it."

"And thank you."

"Good day."

The secretary made her way over to Faro's office and slipped the envelope into a locked wooden box hanging outside his office door with the rest of his mail. And there it stayed.

Chapter 67

"I have it! I have it!" shouted Richter as he burst into the conference room.

"What, Herr Richter?"

"The X-ray diffraction! We can finally replicate it!"

"Why would we want to replicate X-ray diffraction?"

"Nein, nein! Not the diffraction. The crystal! We can finally duplicate the crystal."

"What crystal, Herr Doctor?"

"The capstone! As I suspected, it is quartz. But quartz is always a hexagonal prism ending in a hexagonal pyramid. So the mystery was, if quartz crystals always have six sides, how did the ancients build four-sided crystals? Und now ve know!"

"But we have the original capstone."

"Yes. But we are missing 13 of the other crystals we need, according to the texts. None of them are in the inventory, and none of them have been found either. They are probably among those destroyed after the last Cosmic War. But now, with the structure of the artificial quartz revealed by the x-ray crystallography, we have extrapolated the scalar signature of the molecular arrangement. This we can program into *Die Glocke* Mark IV to generate those scalars and engineer a duplicate of the crystal. If that works, we do the same for the missing crystals!" he plopped his hands proudly on the front of his thighs to punctuate his confidence.

"Marvelous, Herr Doctor! But how will you know the scalars needed for the other crystals?"

"They're in texts," he answered smiling and practically squealing with joy.

The entire company stood up and congratulated him.

"Can you have them ready for our *Julfest* opening next year?"

Still beaming and squealing he stated, "Yes."

Excited murmuring broke out among the men.

"Waste no more time, Herr Richter. Get right on it. We have to stay ahead of Faro and his friends, who are probably devoting every spare minute to finding ways to foil us."

"I couldn't be happier to oblige. This will be even greater than my grandfather's accomplishments." He spun on his heel and began to leave, then turned back.

"One more thing. We had the, uh, unfortunate loss of a few of our translators and our X-ray crystallography technician due to an over exposure. I'll submit my requests for replacements at the end of the day. Perhaps, ah, Mr. Silva, can be enlisted for their 'recruitment.'"

"Of course, Herr Doctor. Whatever you need."

"Danke."

Chapter 68

"We have him! We have him now!"

"What's this all about?"

"Faro. We have him now!"

"Where?"

"Nevada."

"Are you sure?"

"One of our cell members up there works in Vegas. Saw him with the Shorleys in a diner."

"Oh really? How very interesting. So the Shorleys never went to Australia?"

"Not sure. Could've been on vacation. I did check out their property. Looks like it was bought up by some trust, so probably not back there. But who's to say? Nothing's ever as it seems in this business."

"What do you propose?"

"How about a flyover?"

"Wouldn't that arouse suspicion?"

"Aw, a small private aircraft out for a little recreation isn't gonna alarm anyone. Happens all the time."

"Excellent. Take care of it."

Chapter 69

"These are just in from our man in Nevada." Kammler tossed a pile of aerial photographs in front of Bormann.

Bormann calmly picked them up and examined them as he placed each successive photo on the bottom of the pile. He sat back in his chair and put his fingertips thoughtfully together on his chest.

"How many people all together?"

"From the photos it looks like 20, 25 at the most. A lot of shooting practice going on."

"What are all those structures they've built? They don't look like your usual outbuildings."

"One of them is. They've expanded the old control center, but we can't see inside. We've carefully studied the rest. Based on the measurements, relative locations, and odd shapes, our best guess is that they've duplicated parts of the Giza Plateau. You know what that means."

"Damn! He's good. I have to give him that. He's a regular Walt Disney."

"Too bad he's not selling tickets."

"You better activate the airborne cell to put a stop to this. Use the Paladins; we don't want any yokels going in there. We can't risk a land assault attracting attention. Our friends at Area 51 can provide the choppers. They'll blend right in with the regular traffic."

"My thinking exactly."

Chapter 70

"My Lord, ladies, the only thing more delicious than your chili and fry bread is your venison."

"Thanks. We try."

The gang was gathered outside under a large mess tent they had erected.

"I need to go to Las Vegas tomorrow to talk to a friend. I was wondering if any of you would like to go along with me."

"What's up?"

"Did any of you notice that flyover the other day?"

"Ah, it's not unusual to see private aircraft out here."

"There was something about the flight path of this one in particular that made me nervous."

"What do you mean?"

"Oh, let's just say it looked like they were trying to get a good look."

"I see. So what's that got to do with Vegas?"

"I have a friend there, who, due to his family name, is able to, shall we say, arrange certain things. We may need to boost our manpower around here, just in case."

"Can you be more specific, Giuseppe?" asked Georgeann. "At least give us your high octane speculation."

"My high octane speculation is we're going to get some unexpected company in the near future."

"We'll go," offered One Flare.

"We're not going on a lumber run."

"I know."

"On second thought, both you boys have some Sicilian in you. That might be just what we need."

"I see where this is going," observed Greaves. He stuffed a morsel of sage hen in his mouth and eyed Daryl.

"Hey, I can work with anybody."

Chapter 71

The trio rolled up to the Luxor and was greeted by Rico Provenzano the same way he had greeted Faro and the Barstows earlier in our tale.

"Cattano and Venditti, huh? I like that."

"Looks like we're all paisans. Now let's sit down."

Rico grabbed Thorny around the neck. "This one likes to get down to business. I like that too. Eat first?"

"Never say no to a free meal."

"Yeah, ya never know which one's your last."

"Your boys understand the world, Doc."

"You have no idea how right you are, Rico. Believe me, they've taught me as much as I've taught them."

Rico took them into a private conference room at the Luxor set for a fabulous lunch. Six friendly but serious looking men stood up from around the table to greet them. They were clearly Italian and everyone clearly knew the proper way to greet each other.

They enjoyed a delicious Italian meal together and talked about life in Italian families, sports, the weather, women, and Thorny and One Flare entertained them with humorous anecdotes of their adventures together, and Faro finally heard the yarn about how a big fiberglass gorilla ended up atop One Flare's skate ramp. He practically choked on his gnocchi he was laughing so hard.

They sat back stuffed for a few minutes staring alternately at each other and the empty plates. The waiter pushed over a desert cart loaded with Italian pastries.

"Oh ho! I might just be able to find enough room left for one of those cannoli."

"Zeppole for me."

"In that case, I'll take the sfogliatella."

Espressos were served all around.

As they finished the deserts, Rico signaled the waiter

who brought over a cigar box loaded with Davidoff cigars.

"Well there's something we don't try too often," commented Thorny reaching for one.

"Nice. Davidoff." said One Flare as he sniffed deeply along the length.

"Dude, what do skaters know about cigars?"

"What do you know about skaters?" he asked affecting an air.

Faro started. "So it's obvious you're the gentlemen we're to do business with."

"That's right."

"Well, let me begin by saying I don't particularly like the line of work you gentlemen are in, but I don't know where else to turn."

"Whattaya mean? Why we here then? We can just leave right now." The men made faux movements of getting up to leave, but Rico and Faro made conciliatory gestures as Faro continued.

"Now, now. We have a common foe that it is in your interest to help us be rid of."

"Who is it?"

Faro sat back in his chair and puffed his cigar. He looked each man in the eye gravely. "Fascisti." He used the Italian.

"Where?" began the group leader excitedly. " They're everywhere these days. You can't get away from them. They're the ones that put the FBI on us so they could bring in their Columbian and their government-run drug operations. It ain't been the same since. You—you think they care about collateral damage when they do business or keepin' neighborhoods safe for kids to play in? The only reason they let us into this country was to be debt slaves in their factories and coal mines. Well we found our way to get a piece o' the pie, we did. Then they tried to take that away from us too!" He was becoming agitated.

"Spare me your indignation. But without saying too much, let's just say we're expecting a visit from these fascisti, a visit intended to thwart our work against them. What they have planned would make things considerably worse for your business, if not mean your certain death."

"What are they up to?"

"The same thing they've always been up to—taking over the world and killing or enslaving everyone they don't like."

"What do you need from us?"

"Two things: manpower and firepower. It would require you to relocate upstate for a while."

"Sounds like dangerous work. Not your normal business."

"We'll pay you $100,000 each."

The men looked at each other in astonishment.

"It's like in 'The Feverman' episode of *Monsters*," whispered Thorny to One Flare. "Charge high, pay high, and you'll die content."

"*Monsters?* You mean that obscure 80s show on right before *Friday the 13th: The Series?*"

"The same."

"Yeah. I think David McCallum was in that episode."

"You boys done with your 'trivial pursuits?' Thank you."

Faro now turned to the boss. "Let me make it perfectly clear, gentlemen. If these people are successful in their current operation, it would mean the destruction of the United States as we know it. No more plea bargaining, no more Constitutional protections, no more equal justice under the law (as if we have much of that left) or attorney-client privilege."

"I see your point. No one fucks with the US of A and gets away with it with us." The men got up and huddled in one corner of the room. They spoke in hushed tones. An odd trait of the Mafia is that their patriotism actually rivals their villainy.

"We want the hundred grand plus cost of weapons, ammo and lodging."

"You'll get free food and lodging. As for weapons and ammo, I have a better idea. How about 100 large and your little skimming operation at the Venetian goes unreported to the authorities?"

"Hey, how you know about that?" They looked at Rico who threw up his hands indicating ignorance.

"I only know the Luxor."

"That's beside the point. And one more thing: this arrangement is purely one of convenience. When it's over, you go your way and we go ours. We don't make friends, we don't have Sunday dinner together, all debts are paid."

Thorny slapped One Flare on the chest with the back of his hand and pointed demonstratively at the remark with his cigar.

The alpha among them eyed Faro furtively. "I can see you're an honest man. I trust you to do business. Plus, you're a Paisan." Then with a suspicious, knowing curiosity, he continued, " What's that jacket you were wearing when you came in, and why'd you take it off?"

"That's a very old jacket. My father gave it to me before he passed away. He was in La Resistenza fighting the fascists. An American pilot he rescued gave it to him as a keepsake in gratitude for his life. I never wear it when I sit down for fear of damaging the collar or the artwork on the chair back."

The men looked admiringly at Faro and nodded approvingly.

"Some of us have similar stories, Doc. Deal."

Chapter 72

Suddenly the chop of helicopters was heard. The groups, scattered around working at the Barstows, looked to the sky and noticed this was not normal. This was the unexpected visit. Only this time it wasn't unexpected. Melissa sprinted to the control room and sounded a loud siren she'd set up for just such an emergency. Daryl and his men moved in rapid order to their defensive positions and the Mafiosi took up theirs. Daryl and Greave's prediction on the assault point were perfect as the Nazi operatives fast roped into a flat just over a hill away from the buildings.

They came charging over the ridge and assaulted the mockups where Daryl's team was ensconced. Brisk fire went back and forth as 30-odd Paladins advanced. They closed on the position and sprayed so much lead Daryl's men couldn't come up to return fire. As the heat intensified and shards of concrete, wood, and stone showered Daryl's men hunched behind cover, the six Italian gentlemen from Las Vegas swept around the "pyramid" and flanked the Paladins with such an enfilading hail of bullets it was they who had to now retreat. The three at the far left of the line bit dust as the lead found its mark. Daryl's men sprang over their barrier and returned what they'd just received—with interest. Paladins dropped like hot dogs in the desert. They withdrew to the ridge and continued to fire from atop. Shit. They had grenades. Daryl's team dove for cover while the Mafia crew disappeared around the end of a knoll.

"Where the hell are Frank and Faro?" Daryl screamed into his radio to Greaves.

"I don't know!"

Meanwhile in the control room workshop Frank was screaming at the girls, "C'mon! C'mon! Get that thing bolted! It's hotter than Hell's frying pan out there!"

"We're trying! The mounting from the conjugator

pushed these slots out of place!"

"C'mon! Yer Rez girls! You can fix anything!"

Frank didn't dare open the door and draw fire into the garage interior, though an occasional ping of a stray bullet could be heard on the steel door. The girls focused intently, as if their very attention was a well-focused laser beam. Coolly, calmly, as if reading comfortably in the garden on a fine spring day, amidst the racket of gunfire, they jiggled and pushed and squeezed until the .50 caliber was in place on its mount and securely fastened.

"Done!"

They dashed to the table and grabbed a couple of AR-15s. Faro jumped in back of the Rover and Frank cranked the ignition.

"Now!"

The girls swung the door open just as Frank gunned the engine and raced through. Carrie and Mary laid down covering fire for the Rover to advance. The Rover bounced as it sped over the rocky landscape. Faro gripped the weapon and spread his legs to steady himself. The paladins launched a grenade from the ridge towards the garage which fell just short before it burst. Melissa meanwhile had picked up another device in the control room and said to herself, "I was prepared for that," and pushed a button.

BOOM! A loud explosion on the ridge near the Paladins drove shrapnel and sand into their position.

Daryl and his team were now advancing on the ridge under hot fire, dodging from structure to structure. Melissa came into the doorway of the control center to get a better look at how her charges were working, gauged the position and pressed another button. BLAM! Two Paladins flew in opposite directions in a plume of sand and gravel.

The Captain of the mercenaries directed a squad to take the control room and neutralize Melissa and any remaining charges. Four men got up guns blazing and, in crouched runs, charged the control room. Carrie and Mary spotted them from the garage door and charged the men without regard for life or limb, shrieking wild and terrible things that only they and the wondrous spirits of war understood.

Melissa handed the box to Georgeann as she swung her weapon into place on its sling and shouted, "Push the buttons!"

"Which buttons?"

"All the buttons!"

"Oh dear!" Georgeann closed her eyes and grimaced. One by one her fingers found the buttons. Explosions rocked and shattered the ridge above the mercenaries. Daryl's teams exploited the chaos to take the position. With chilling war whoops that rent the mighty and impenetrable veil that guards the Other World, they rushed up the ridge emptying their magazines with righteous fury. And some of those there that day said they witnessed with newly opened eyes, Geronimo and Cochise burst through that fractured veil with a supernal band of warriors and fall upon the Paladins. At that moment, our Italian friends from Las Vegas emerged from around the knoll and again rained enfilading fire on the Paladins.

Melissa kicked open the control room door and added to Carrie and Mary's fire. Soon the four Paladins charging the control room lay wounded. Carrie and Mary's suppressed rage from the personal violation of their kidnapping exploded to the surface and they pounced mercilessly on the helpless men with their knives and finished them off, up close and personal.

Now it was a race. The Paladins had lost the element of surprise and were beaten. They conducted an orderly retreat toward the choppers protected by a competent and professional rear guard action. The mafia crew kept on their flank to harass them. Healthy men jogged along helping the wounded ahead of the skirmishers, and towards the choppers where pilots awaited with rotors turning for a speedy exfiltration.

But Frank and Faro blazed in from their right at the head of a cloud of dust. Faro gritted his teeth, braced his feet against the walls of the truck bed, lowered the muzzle, and squeezed the trigger.

Back in the control room, Georgeann gnawed her nails as she beheld her employer in both amazement and fear. "Ohhh dear, this isn't what I had in mind when I mentioned playing *Rat Patrol.*"

A fiery stream of armor piercing projectiles found their marks. The choppers were sitting ducks. First one, and then another burst into flames where they sat. The Rover continued to close, audibly spraying gravel behind it, seeking point blank range to torch the other two whirlybirds which were somewhat occulted by smoke and flame and wreckage. The good doctor managed to deliver a healthy dose of lead, but return fire caused frank to duck and veer as he dodged the incoming projectiles. It threw Faro's aim off.

The remnant of the Paladins boarded their choppers and took off over a nearby ridge that shielded them from further ground fire. It was all over in less than 10 minutes. Indians 3, Brewers nothing.

Chapter 73

As the choppers disappeared, cheers erupted from our merry band of castaways. They rallied on Daryl's position since that was the biggest single group. Some limped or held wounds, but only a few injuries were serious, and men from Greaves' and Daryl's teams began tending to them.

Georgeann was breathless but relieved. "Oh, Giuseppe! You finally got to play Rat Patrol!"

"And it was exhilarating!"

"Well, we have got some serious clean up to do here," observed Greaves.

"Don't worry, it's a big desert out here," responded the Mafia Capo with a wink.

"All debts are paid," Faro reminded them.

"Not yet, Doc. It goes with the service."

Faro glared at him suspiciously.

"I gotta protect my guys."

"Fair enough."

"What about those two choppers?"

"Oh, I'm sure somebody will come up with an explanation for them. Can you say 'training accident?' We'll see it on tonight's news."

"Didn't we tell ya, Doc?" proffered the Capo. "We also have a waste removal business."

Faro chuckled. "Why am I not surprised?"

Chapter 74

I'll spare the reader yet another ugly scene in Bariloche. Suffice it to say the group of gray-haired old men had lost patience with Faro and his merry band, but hadn't yet figured out what to do about them.

After the ugliness had subsided though, there was the usual Nazi mischief to get up to. In early 2014 it was a coup in Ukraine. The reader might well ask, "If they were about to take over the world with the Giza Death Star, why would they bother with the expense and danger of a coup?"

Let's peer into their secret Andean lair and find out.

"How much of the central bank bullion did we get?"

"All of it, 330 tons."

"Excellent."

"Flown out of the country on a pair of CIA C-130s."

"So we have a friendly neo-Nazi regime in place in Ukraine, and we have their gold. That gold will go far funding operations."

"Yes, and Azov Battalion will be spearheading the invasion of eastern Ukraine to eliminate any political opposition. The battle plans were drawn up even before the coup."

"We even have plans for a Stepan Bandera celebration lined up to celebrate Ukrainian Nazism, er, excuse me, nationalism."

"This is all too good to be true."

"And we have the full backing of Victoria Nuland and the US State Department!"

"HAHAHAHA! Imagine that: A black President fully backing a neo-Nazi coup!"

"Not only that, they paid for it! Even for the training and equipment for Azov!"

"There is no end to the idiocy of these people."

Chapter 75

"This is magnificent!" exclaimed Kammler. "To think after all these decades our fathers' and grandfathers' work has come to fruition!"

Kammler, Bormann, Müller, Edda, and the gray-haired old men were getting a VIP tour of the Pyramid from Richter.

Making their way through the grand gallery, they were overcome by an ironically soothing hum and bathed in psychedelic light from the various crystals Herr Richter's team of scientists and technicians had fabricated or unearthed based on secrets revealed in ancient tablets.

"The crystals," began Richter, "are constructed with the scalar fabrication technique of the Mark IV Bell. They gather energy from the very ether and store it in their crystalline structure. Excess energy is emitted as visible light and radiation. Thus, the need for our protective suits.

"These were among the most interesting components we uncovered," Richter stated indicating the white, almost weightless spheres recovered from the Baghdad Museum. "These are resonator arrays that will enable us to amplify and tune the electro-acoustic resonances that will wreak death and destruction if our demands aren't met. They are made of a precise combination of orbitally re-arranged monatomic elements dominated by the platinum series metals."

"Brilliant!"

"It is an ancient technology, but we have our loyal brother Walter Gerlach to thank for rediscovering it. Note how the spheres fit perfectly into the niches carved by the pyramid's ancient builders millions of years ago. And to think Egyptologists think they were carved for statues! Stolen by tomb raiders! In fact every niche in the pyramid Egyptologists told us was for accommodating statuary or figurines is tailor-made for the crystal or other piece of technology designed for it."

"What are these large stone slabs resting in these slots?"

"Those are baffles, also for tuning the resonance. By raising or lowering them, we can dampen or amplify the acoustic-like longitudinal waves that pass through the grand gallery. In fact, it's not a 'gallery' at all but a tuning chamber."

"Extraordinary!"

"How can you be sure all of this will work?"

"In fact, we are not 100% certain. To be that certain, we would need the so-called Tablets of Destinies, which have never been found. They were secreted away by Ninurta, also known as Nimrod in The Bible, after the second pyramid war, and were never found again. These Tablets of Destinies, to the best of our knowledge, contained the keys to operating this marvelous device with resonance tunings and settings for vast expanses of the very cosmos, from our own planet, planets within our own solar system, the galaxy, even far distant realms of space..."

He was cut off my Müller. "A long, long time ago, in a Galaxy far, far away..."

"Your little joke has more truth than you might suspect Herr Müller. But to continue, we did discover a partial transcription with relevant resonance tunings to a few places on earth that will enable us to cause horrific regional catastrophes. We, of course, will call these catastrophes with precision in advance to show that we do indeed have the power to cause and direct them. In fact, some State powers like the US, China, Japan, Russia, France, are already experimenting with such technology. This will put us a century ahead of all of them."

"Herr Richter, I must confess, this is a bit unnerving. Are these flimsy suits enough to protect us from such a redoubtable weapon?"

"Do not worry. It is not at full strength. While the visible light emissions are impressive, there is very little other radiation to be concerned about. Just some low level UV and

X-ray emanations. Once the capstone is in place and we initiate the weaponized resonance, the interior will be drenched with devastating gamma ray emissions that will kill any living thing that is unprotected. And that soothing hum that has you all so calm will crescendo into the most paralyzing and awesome shriek ever heard on Earth. Well, perhaps it is more of a roar, well, no, something like a shriek and roar combination, or blare, maybe it's more like a blare. In any case it will be a most unique and terrifying blast."

"We understand, Herr Richter. It's beyond words. The device's operators?"

"We have just enough suits for them; in fact they are more like capsules. But getting back to my earlier point, once the world is held hostage, we will continue the search for the Tablets of Destinies, which will also enable us to direct the creative power of this giant machine as well and create or re-create the world as we like." He took a good-natured, half-comic bow.

"Astounding, Herr Richter! Truly astounding!"

"It is not quite operational. I have a short video presentation on how it will work for you back at the hotel. We have some finishing touches to put on, and, of course, the capstone will be the final essential element. That will be in place as of midnight, just before the winter solstice for *Julfest*. Not only is it an auspicious holiday, the torsion alignments with Earth, the Sun, and the other planets will be just right.

"Ah, and, of course, barring any mishaps," he went on. "My team depends on you gentlemen to keep any White Hat operations at bay that are trying to prevent us."

"Indeed, but I remind you that from our perspective we are the white hats. Why do you mention this?"

"It has come to my attention that someone is secretly moving arms into the area. They aren't using any of our agents nor purchasing from any of our sources. Therefore it must be a group of White Hats, pardon me, vicious meddlers."

"Interesting. Thank you for the information. We will

continue along those lines immediately after the tour."

"Yes, let us now continue to the so-called King's Chamber so you can see what we did there. It is in fact a phase conjugation mirror in which the destructive beam is cohered and then pumped to its target through the capstone. What you are about to see, gentlemen, you will not see on the National Geographic Channel..."

Chapter 76

"OK, well, here goes nothing." Frank sat in the driver's seat of the Land Rover flipping switches and adjusting adjustments for the miniature graser he had created to stifle the Giza Death Star should it be deployed. Beside him was a Plexiglas above-ground swimming pool full of sloshing water.

"So wait a minute," piped up one of the assembly. "What exactly are we witnessing here?"

"This is a graser," joked Frank doing a Doctor Evil from *Austin Powers* impersonation.

"That is, a Gamma-ray laser. It's based on the same principle as optical phase conjugation.

"In optical phase conjugation, a laser beam is directed at a target and light rays reflected back from it, but scattered due to passing through the gases of the atmosphere, enter the phase conjugator, a chamber containing a nonlinear medium. In this nonlinear medium, such as a plasma, the scattered rays interact with two opposed laser beams of similar wavelength to form a hologram-like pattern called a 'grating.'" This last word he did his Doctor Evil for again.

"The grating pattern essentially enables the system to lock onto its target. A powerful laser is then discharged into this grating pattern, whereupon the cohered laser reflects in such a way as to produce a powerful outgoing laser beam that retraces the path it originally took when being reflected off the target, thus destroying it with devastating accuracy and precision. Even decoying or spoofing attempts are fruitless since the grating pattern only corresponds to the original target. As soon as the device is fired, the whole thing occurs at faster than the speed of light."

"That's impossible!"

"Not so. It is essentially a time reverse process, and provided the 'barrel' of the weapon is a reduced wave guide, it accelerates the destructive beam to many times faster than the speed of light. Dr. Faro's research shows that this has been done successfully both in the laboratory and field testing. Furthermore, he has shown how, in the dim, lost past of humanity, such weapons existed on a galactic scale. The so-called air shafts in the King's Chamber of the Great Pyramid, are in fact, reduced wave guides.

"There is one drawback to this system as I've designed it. It must be operated by its creator or it will not work. This has to do with the subtle scalar signatures of the maker being embedded in the weapon's encoding system."

"Why didn't you make it so that anyone could operate it?"

"Good question. First of all, that could be catastrophic if it fell into the wrong hands. Secondly, I don't know how to, yet, anyway. It is theoretically possible, but I haven't figured it out yet. I guess you can say I'm too attached to my work." He paused for chuckles.

"Now, instead of using only the visible spectrum of electromagnetic waves, we will add X-ray and gamma-ray components as well, and this mixed beam of electromagnetism will carry acoustic waves as well, tuned to a tone that is disharmonic to the pyramid's natural frequency. We have to have this device in place and operating before the Death Star is switched on to prevent its destructive harmonic resonance from forming, and keep it on until Daryl's and Greaves' teams can take down the operators."

"Can't the frikkin' Nazis just re-tune the thing?"

"Yes, for example if they changed targets, but there are basic parameters to the resonance they must operate within. Having thoroughly studied the thing, we know what they are and what the basic resonance is they have to tune to for any target. We only need to disrupt that. It's 440 hertz, in case you're interested."

"Holy cow, Frank! But if these sorts of weapons can be made in someone's garage, why don't we have them?"

"Who says we don't?"

"Well take it from us, we worked at the highest level

of training and special operations, and I can tell you there is nothing like this in our arsenal."

"Fair enough. But I can tell you that there is. The problem is that deploying such weapons can be devastating on a colossal scale. The slightest mistake can lead to planetary catastrophe. Just look at the asteroid belt. That used to be a planet. Even worse would be for a deployment of such a weapon to lead to an escalation with other powers that have them, terrifying beyond imagination even for the sociopaths who run our governments."

Everyone frowned thoughtfully and whispered awestruck murmurs to one another.

"Are we ready?"

"You haven't told us what the wave pool is for. We goin' for a swim to cool off after the demonstration?"

"You'd hardly cool off. The water in that pool is boiling.

"Now I want you to look over there. You see that big concrete construction? It's a resonance chamber. It has similar dimensions to the so-called King's Chamber in the pyramid. Right now it is emitting a subsonic resonance tuned to the pyramid itself. It is also emitting powerful microwave and x-ray radiation that if we don't turn off soon, will cook us on the spot like it is the water in that pool. Just joking. The reason the pool is boiling and sloshing is that the resonance chamber is precisely tuned to its structure, contents and location. It took me three days to get everything set up right. When I switch on this machine, it'll fire a bright optical laser that you can plainly see along with everything else I explained. Instantaneously, the pool should stop sloshing and begin to cool."

Frank scanned the crowd.

The crew nodded.

Frank moved back to the controls in the vehicle. "Girls, you'd better hold onto your boyfriends," he half-joked, this time quoting Daffy Duck from *Show Biz Bugs*.

He flipped the final switch. A bright red laser touched

the concrete and the water in the pool was suddenly still as astonished gasps arose from the assembly, who were unsure of what happened first, the laser hitting the building, or the water going still. Even the most battle-hardened among them were struck silent, and the masters of weirdness, Thorny, One Flare, and Greaves, stammered in awe at what they'd just witnessed. And then:

KA-BLAM!

The concrete resonance chamber disappeared in a powdery puff as if vaporized in an instant. Everybody's eyes, including Frank's, practically popped their eye sockets. The powder wafted gently away downwind, leaving a fine film of debris where once stood the structure.

Frank turned sheepishly to his friends and laughed nervously. "Hehehe, ah, that, uh, was just my, ah, 9-11 demonstration. I'll have to fiddle with the adjustments."

Melissa rushed to his side and put an arm around his waist.

Georgeann turned to Dr. Faro, still stunned by what she'd witnessed. "Maybe that should be in your next book."

Chapter 77

Faro unlocked the door to his office. "It's good to be home again, isn't it, Georgeann?"

"You got that right, brother. I'll be in in a minute. Let me just grab the mail." Georgeann unlocked the wooden box outside the Doctor's office and extracted a jumbled bundle of letters.

"Ooooh. Look at this one, Giuseppe. It's got a wax seal on the back."

"Let me see that. Hmmm. Oh, I'd recognize this seal anywhere! The Black Sun! This most assuredly is from our friends in San Carlos de Bariloche!"

"Open it! Open it! What does it say?"

Faro carefully scraped the seal intact from the envelope and set it on Georgeann's desk in the front office. "Let's keep that as a sample," He indicated.

Georgeann rummaged in one of her desk drawers and pulled out an Air-Tite, a plastic round that's used for keeping coins, and put the seal in it for safekeeping.

Faro then extracted the letter:

"Dear Herr Doctor,

It has come to our attention that you are meddling in areas you were specifically warned off of. Whether you were 'merely' helping friends or not is of no concern to us. Our arrangement is concluded.

Signed,

Bruno Kammler
Bruno Kammler

A. Bormann
Adolf Bormann"

"Well, I must say, this is disconcerting news."

"Let me see," She said as the Doctor tilted the paper towards her.

"Weellll," Georgeann added hopefully, "they still can't kill you—your dead man's trigger."

"Oh I'm sure they're looking for it."

Chapter 78

"We don't have time to dwell on this now. We have to pack for Egypt. Remember, we're going as tourists. Just pack touristy things. Most of what else we need will be provided."

"Well how are we going to get Frank and Melissa's thing-a-ma-jig there?"

"Greaves is arranging that. He 'knows a guy.' Remember? I just hope it's waiting for us when we get there. It doesn't take any high octane speculation to guess they plan on testing the Death Star before the solstice to make sure it works."

"Well, if we're gonna play tourist, be sure to pack that Desert Rats outfit. I want a picture of you by the pyramids in that."

"Very funny. We're preparing for the most serious and dangerous moments of our lives, and you're worried about a fashion shoot!"

Georgeann giggled, composed herself, and then broke out into full on laughter. "I'm sorry Giuseppe. I just can't help myself. That picture would be one for the history books! Literally!"

He started chuckling himself. "I'll grant you that, as long as you mean hidden history books. The kind of history we're involved with doesn't make the textbooks."

"That's for sure."

"OK, let's finish going through the correspondence. Fortunately the Christmas break is upon us so we don't need any excuses to not be here." He started chortling again, "Isn't that just everybody's idea of the ideal Christmas—Fighting the Nazis in Egypt!"

"It's 1942 all over again!"

Chapter 79

As the Advent season was getting under way, mischief was not just afoot, it was stampeding. If the Death Star was to hold the world hostage, then it must be proven to work. A test was needed.

CLOSED UNTIL DECEMBER 21ST FOR FINAL RESTORATION

The sign was posted at intervals outside a cordon that surrounded the Great Pyramid. Tourists ogled the blinding white casing stones that now covered the exterior all the way to the peak. They watched with fascination as Richter supervised the finishing touches to get his machine operational.

The Germans are rightfully renowned for their engineering, and it was on full display at Giza. The convex design of the four faces was clearly visible to anyone with eyes to see. It was placed with such precision that even the mainstream press was openly ridiculing Egyptologists who claimed it was due to a random collapse of the structure at some time in the past. Some even tried to claim it wasn't there at all, and they were hailed as complete idiots in newspapers and on TV all over the world.

"Easy! Easy! That's it."

Richter had engineered a contraption that would position the capstone precisely into place. Since it was practically weightless, it wasn't that difficult but the crowd watching and the old school archaeologists had no idea. They marveled at Richter's contraption that lifted the capstone, swung it over the sloped sides and suspended it directly over the tip. While the lay public marveled, conventional archaeologists responded as they usually do, by making stuff up to explain what they cannot explain.

"Wunderbar!"

The crowd was seized by a loud, sub-bass hum as the

capstone settled into place, almost as if it were a Lego block. Enthusiastic oohs and ahhhs arose from the onlookers, who were getting their final glimpse of the powerful behemoth before them before a great wall of sandbags around the exterior was completed. The purpose of these sandbags will be revealed to the unsuspecting reader in a later chapter.

Richter conferred with Kammler, Bormann, and some of the gray-haired old men below the entrance. The traditional tourist entrance through the Robbers' Tunnel that had been dug by Caliph Al Ma'mun had been restored to its original state by the Nazis, so they were using the original 'entrance', several courses above the Robbers' tunnel.

Richter produced a small stone tablet for the old men to see.

"This is very ancient. Modern archaeologists would probably date it to Sumer, but in fact, it is millennia older. It is over 3.2 *million* years old! You see the writing here, and a geometric design. The writing refers to some place in Central America. It's hard to translate exactly, but the late scholar who accomplished it for us, God rest his soul, thinks it may be the Isthmus of Panama. The geometric design is the grating pattern we need to create in the King's chamber before pulsing the graser through it. I'll need you gentlemen to return to the safety of your hotel and watch the news for breaking stories on earthquakes in that region. The infrasonic harmonic resonances here will undoubtedly cause local tremors, but there's no need to worry. They won't be serious."

The gray-haired old men murmured excitedly, wished Herr Doctor Richter success, and then departed.

Chapter 80

The plan, indeed, was to have the Land Rover and its phase conjugator waiting at the port for their arrival. Frank and Melissa had driven it to Houston to get it on a fast ship to Alexandria rather than lose time navigating the Pacific and the Panama Canal. Greaves and Frank were there to make the pickup.

"I'm terribly sorry, Mr. Greaves and, ah..... "

"Barstow. Frank Barstow."

"Ah, yes, I see you here, Dr. Barstow," the official said indicating some papers. "Your cargo has been held up by the Port Authority. We will release it to you as soon they clear it."

"When will that be?"

"It's hard to tell with these things. Inspections, paperwork, customs fees.....Maybe a few days, perhaps a week or two."

"A week or two?" Greaves was flabbergasted. "Let me talk to Abu Samra."

"I'm afraid Abu Samra is not here at the moment."

Frank slapped his copy of the paperwork on the custom officer's desk. "It's very clear we need that equipment for urgent archaeological work which has been approved by the Department of Antiquities. Our grant will expire by that time!"

"I'm very sorry. These delays aren't uncommon. I'm sure you will find a way to work around it in the meantime. Er, what institution did you say you were with?"

"South Dakota State University. See? Here are all the permits. Again."

Faro had been sure to supply the legitimate paperwork Greaves' 'guy' needed at the port. It was just a portion of it, but all of it had been done and cleared by the relevant authorities.

"Look, Mr. Greaves and Dr. Barstow, I know the Department of Antiquities has approved your permits. I know the cargo matches your manifest. I know you have done everything correctly. So, I have no doubt that the Port Authority will also soon comply. I'm terribly sorry. Again. Now please, I have too much work to do in Mr. Abu Samra's absence. Check back tomorrow."

Greaves and Frank left grumbling. When they were clear of the office, Müller emerged from a back room. "Well done, Al Busiri," he said placing an envelope obviously loaded with cash on the table. "You can have your family back now."

Al Busiri leapt from his chair and raced into the backroom where his family sat bound and gagged in the presence of Mr. Silva, and freed them. They embraced as Müller and Silva made their surreptitious exit.

Frank and Greaves found a hotel and checked themselves into a room. Then they made a call to Faro.

"Hello?"

"Doc? Frank."

"Well, well, well. What's going on at your end?"

"Let's just say this wharf is full of rats."

"I see. What about Greaves' guy?"

"Not here for some reason. That's probably the fishiest thing about this."

"Hmmm. I can smell those rats from here. The bratwurst and sauerkraut farts give 'em away."

"That's one way to put it. They did just orchestrate a coup to get their people in for the Death S...." He stopped himself. "You know what I mean."

"So what's the plan there? Georgeann wants to do a fashion shoot here, with me in my Desert Rats outfit."

"Huh. Wharf rats and desert rats. Sounds like a regular rat row brewing. Plan here is to snoop around and see what wharf rats come out of their holes."

"Well you better hurry. It's very obvious now they're preparing to test the thing. We need the kill switch on that

224

vehicle. And watch your backs. Those are the biggest, craftiest rats you'll ever run into."

"Watch yours. You don't wanna be out shutterbugging and making a scene with Major Strasser and all his Nazis in Cairo expecting you."

"Thanks. Major Strasser was in Casablanca, not Cairo, but I know what you mean."

Chapter 81

It gets cold out on those wharfs at night. Frank and Greaves were there poking around with their manifest. They knew which container the Rover was in, they just had to find it. Wharves are not as romantic as they used to be, chock full of shacks and crates and old warehouses. Today they are mostly container yards with endless mind-numbing rows of stacked containers and concrete tarmacs.

"Jesus, there's thousands of containers here. I'll bet ours is hidden good."

"Yeah, my guess is someone figured out who we were and what we had. Maybe they swiped it altogether."

"Cripes, I hope not."

"Well this says it came in at Berth 62," stated Greaves flashing his "scout light" at the manifest. A scout light is basically a single red LED bulb and a squeezable switch in a waterproof housing about the size of a locket. It's worn around the neck and only illuminated when necessary. "They usually park the containers nearby so they can unload faster."

"Where are we now?"

"There. Looks like berth 15."

"Sounds like we're a long ways away. Better get hoofing and watch the numbers."

"Nah. Screw that. It's probably already at container and cargo near the port office. They can hide it better in there with all the other containers."

"OK, let's do it your way."

"The men crept carefully but quickly to the container yard, slipped silently into the water, and inched their way along the sea wall to bypass security. When they got to a raft of coal barges, they hoisted themselves up on the tire fenders draped along the sides. They made their way across the barges until they attained the container yard.

"What are you doing?"

"These clothes are wet and heavy. I'm taking some of them off. I suggest you at least remove your shoes. They'll squeak."

"Good idea."

"Let's stash 'em over here."

"Damn, it's cold."

"Ya might wanna take yours off likewise. You'll dry off faster."

"Oh how did I get into this?" Frank stripped down to his boxers like Greaves had done.

"Bet you can move a lot easier now. Can't you?"

"Let's just get started."

"Looks like we have just enough light to read the numbers. Whoever finds it, remember the location and come get the other one."

"Roger that."

The men split up and made their way in opposite directions along the long rows of containers keeping a sharp eye out for security and ducking around corners when necessary. Frank found it first and made his way systematically through Greave's end till he found him.

"Found it."

"Where?"

"Few rows back that way. They stashed it good. It's three containers up and has two more on top, making it impossible to move without a derrick."

"Damn!" Greaves thought for a moment. "Well show me. Maybe we'll get an idea."

They returned to the container's location.

"Hmmm. Well, at least it's on an end row."

"What's that mean?"

"I'm thinking we can get up there, pick the lock, then set up a ramp to drive down, and then bust out of here."

"And have the police or the army chase us all the way to Cairo, if we even make it that far."

"Is the .50 caliber in there?"

"Now don't start. That might get us further, but only

227

before we die."

"You have a better idea?"

"Yeah! Find your friend Abu Samra, and have him clear it for us."

"OK, OK. But let's climb up and have a look first. I bet I can just get a toe hold between them and pull myself up on the locking bars. You keep an eye out."

Greaves pulled himself up till he reached their container.

"Well?"

"It hurts my feet. Why'd we take our shoes off again?"

"Besides that."

"Padlocked. Four locks to pick."

Just then, inside the container, Abu Samra was coming to and heard the door jiggling as Greaves shifted his weight back and forth. He sprang to his feet, went to the door, and tapped cautiously a signal he and Greaves both knew.

"Wait! I hear something! There's someone inside."

"Who?"

"It must be Abu Samra." Greaves tapped back to acknowledge.

"Kelly?" Abu Samra shout-whispered through the door.

"Yes. Hold on, buddy. I'll be back."

"Where are you going?"

"Back to my clothes. Lock picks are in the pocket. You stay here and keep an eye out."

Greaves returned after what seemed like an eternity to Frank and climbed back up to the container. He strained to pick the locks unable to stabilize to keep tension on the tension wrench, but finally worked his way through all four. Before unlatching the doors he issued a warning.

"This is where it starts to get really dicey. These doors will be wide open and fairly noticeable to passersby. We're also gonna make some noise. Be ready for anything."

Abu Samra hung his feet over the end of the

container, inched forward and dropped down with a loud thump. He winced as he stood up and hobbled with the momentary pain of a sprained ankle.

"You OK? Nice to meet you. Frank Barstow."

"A pleasure, I'm sure. Ehab Abu Samra."

The doors squealed as Greaves swung them closed as gingerly as he could and relatched and relocked them. He then climbed down again.

"I'm terribly sorry about this, Kelly. As I was personally supervising the transportation of your container from the pier, someone knocked me out. We can infer what happened next."

Just then a pair of security guards approached with weapons pointed at the men. They were shouting something in Arabic.

"I'll handle this," stated Abu Samra.

"You there! You laggards! Dogs! Do you even know what you are doing?"

"Ehab Abu Samra?"

"Yes, of course, you idiots."

"But what are you doing here?"

"I work here, remember? Do you also remember that I am your boss?"

"Yes, yes, but---"

"Never mind. Escort these men to my office. If anyone tries to stop you, you are to shoot them. Understand? There is something very wrong going on here."

"Yes, Sir. Yes, Sir."

Abu Samra whispered to the two men, "Go with them. I'll retrieve your things and give you a dry change of clothes. Just play along for now."

The two men nodded in agreement and pointed to the location of their belongings before departing at the business end of a couple of MP5s.

Chapter 82

Frank and Greaves sat shivering in their boxer shorts on a cheap vinyl sofa in Abu Samra's office with the aforementioned MP5s pointed directly at them.

"Well they can't put 22 feet between them and us. That means we can take them."

"Whoa there, big fella. Samra said to just play along. Let's just hold our horses."

Abu Samra pushed open his office door with one hand, cradling the wet bundle of clothes with the other. He paused momentarily to notice the imposition his friends were in and made a lowering gesture with his free hand to his guards. They responded by lowering their weapons.

"You can go. I'll take it from here. Stand watch at the door and shoot whoever tries to enter."

He plopped the clothes on an empty chair and went to a locker. "Here are a couple of fire blankets. It's all I have until your clothes arrive."

Samra maneuvered behind his desk, sat, and then put his head down in pain, clutching the back. "Aagh! What a headache!"

Greaves got up and tenderly lifted Samra's hands. "That's quite a knot you got on your noggin."

"It's making it exceedingly difficult to maintain my composure."

"You keep any aspirin or ibuprofen?"

Samra sat back wearily and waved dismissively. "Let us first conclude this little matter. I'll unleash on the villains who did this soon enough."

Their conversation was interrupted by a soft rap on the door. One of the guards opened it and said something in Arabic.

"Yes, yes! Let him in." A gentleman appearing like a local merchant entered the room with a bundle wrapped in brown paper.

"Gentlemen, your clothes. I'm afraid it's not what you're used to, but it will keep you warm until you get back to your hotel."

"What about our truck?"

"I'm afraid that will have to wait until morning, at the soonest. I can almost certainly have it for you some time tomorrow. I haven't the staff to do it now, and I don't know what the risks involved are at the moment. You understand, of course."

"Of course."

"Let me arrange a car for you." Samra picked up his phone and talked to someone again in Arabic. "It will be here shortly. We have a couple of drivers on call for the port facility which of course is a 24-hour operation."

"Thanks."

"Come. We'll meet him outside." He gestured for the guards to accompany them. "One can't be too careful," he winked.

The men exited into the cool damp seaside air, shared a smoke, and saw the car pulling up. Frank went for the door but Greaves stopped him.

"Abu Samra, if you please." He turned to Frank, "You can't be too careful," he winked.

Samra peered through the passenger side window and was suddenly facing down the muzzle of a CZ-75. He immediately dropped flat on the pavement before the driver had a chance to react. The two guards opened up, concentrating their fire on the driver seat and the man fell over limp.

Greaves went around to the driver's side, opened the door and yanked the bullet-ridden corpse upright.

"Looks familiar. Didn't we meet him at Dulce?"

"As a matter of fact, yes. One of Silva's men."

Abu Samra got up and dusted himself off. "I guess I'll be driving you myself." He spoke Arabic to the two guards who dragged the body out of the car and onto the curb.

Samra poked around in the glove box and found a rag. He wiped the blood from the seat and slid cheerily under the steering wheel.

"Well? Aren't you getting in?"

Greaves and Frank looked puzzled and pointed to Silva's late assistant henchman on the sidewalk.

"Don't bother about that. My men know how to handle it."

Frank and Greaves got in and off they drove.

Chapter 83

Faro and Georgeann could not resist their morbid curiosity. They called their other companions and caught a bus down to the Plateau with the other tourists. They watched with grave consternation as the earth under their feet trembled softly, like the faint vibrations of an organ pipe.

With the capstone in place along with all the crystal arrays, the Helmholtz resonators in the grand gallery, the coffer in the King's Chamber restored to its central position, all the damaged granite and limestone repaired, all the plugs removed and the operating baffles restored, the wall of sandbags complete, and repairs to the subterranean chamber, the Giza Death Star was now fully operational, or at least close to its paleo-ancient tenebrous splendor.

Faro beheld the monster, resurrected from time itself by monsters of another sort, in utter horror. He was a man not easily spooked, as we have seen. But now, he was quaking in his boots, the hair stood up on the back of his neck, and goosebumps covered his flesh.

"We have got to get in contact with Frank and Kelly. We need that phase conjugator here immediately."

Thorny and One Flare stared in awe and muttered, "The wall."

"What's that?"

"The Wall. It's now inside 'The Wall.'"

"I'm afraid I'm not following you."

"It's just something we learned from Tom. Evil lives behind the wall. We've been there and seen it."

"Well these developments are always multi-layered, aren't they? While you boys are probably seeing this hastily erected symbol correctly, it also has a more mundane purpose. If I'm correct, they're going to fill the space between the pyramid and the sandbags with water to power the pyramid's ignition system."

"Do tell."

"The water, and there it is, they've started. You hear those pumps going? They must be pumping it up directly from the Nile. Anyway, I might as well explain this to all of you so you know what's going on. Gather around.

"So that water, when it gets high enough, is going to flow into the pyramid through the original entrance. It will flow down the descending passage to the subterranean chamber where it will activate a hydraulic ram pump slash pulse generator that will switch the thing on!"

"What? We know what a ram pump is," replied One Flare, "but how does that power a pyramid?"

"Well, for those of you who don't know, a ram pump is a kind of pump that works on gravity, which is exactly what you'd expect with the pyramid since it has so many resonances, including important physical constants and the logarithmic value 'e', that powering it with the Earth's own gravity makes perfect sense. According to my calculations, assuming the subterranean chamber is the compression chamber for this pump, the check valve will blow open with a pressure of 3,360 pounds per square inch, another perfect resonance for the Death Star.

"These sorts of pumps have only two moving parts: a waste valve and a check valve. The waste valve for this is most likely somewhere under the subterranean chamber, if it is indeed the compression chamber, and I think it is, according to the work of John Cadman, Chris Dunn, and Edward Kunkel. The check valve is at the end of the so-called 'dead end passage,' which isn't a dead end at all, it's just that the back side of a big stone check valve appears to be a dead end. The well shaft is actually the standing pipe and the grotto, which even Egyptologists admit is man-made, dampens the shock wave so it doesn't blow out the entrance and empty the makeshift moat. In ancient times there actually was a retaining wall around the pyramid for this purpose. It was removed after the Second Pyramid War so that it couldn't be used again, at least not easily."

"Holy cow! This is unreal! And it's all done with the power of nature? No electricity? No coal? No steam?"

"In ancient times, yes to the power of nature and no to the artificial power source. They'd have used a reservoir at a higher elevation than the pyramid base. And there was one, we know that. Nowadays that reservoir is gone, so they're using gas-powered pumps to take water from the Nile.

"Now since you boys are familiar with ram pumps, you probably know that they pulse. This giant ram pump creates huge pulses that induce a sonic wave of 440 hertz that resonates perfectly with the so-called King's Chamber which is also tuned to 440 hertz. This resonance turns everything else on and creates all kinds of terrifying acoustic effects from the infrasonic to the audible. These acoustic effects will resonate with microwave, X-ray and gamma-ray effects. The electromagnetic waves will contain a carrier wave for the acoustics delivering them not at the speed of sound but at many times the speed of light, and those acoustics, if they are strong enough and powerful enough can blow apart whole planets. Witness the asteroid belt, once a planet.

"The whole 'death ray,' if you will, will be shaped inside the King's Chamber by a grating pattern induced by the tuning, and that grating pattern will match one and only one target in the entire universe. It will be instantly destroyed, or at least damaged, depending on how much force these Nazi bastards can deliver. If their target is Earth, which I'm sure it is, it will most likely be a devastating local catastrophe."

The crew stood speechless staring at Dr. Faro.

"We need Frank's phase conjugator to disrupt that resonance and neutralize it."

Now the crew stood speechless and nodding agreement.

Chapter 84

Just after lunch on December 6, 2014, people in Punta de Burica, Panama, were rattled by a magnitude 6.0 earthquake. Roads buckled, dwellings shook, and landslides slid. Although the economic damage was slight and casualties minimal, the lives of half a million people in two countries—Panama and Costa Rica—were seriously disrupted.

Back in their hotel, when the news broke, the gray-haired men and Edda rejoiced at their success and the misfortune of others. It was a grim and unholy day for planet Earth. Dr. Faro, after doing so much to reveal the nature of the threat at Giza and warn humanity, after having invested so much toil and treasure, now faced the very destruction of civilization that was worse than the worst nightmares of mortal men.

The New Agers had won, and handed the Nazis *their* victory. Every rainbow clad, unicorn hugging hippy that just couldn't stand to even think about the pyramid as a Death Star had pushed the Nazi International's agenda perfectly. Ancient Egypt was a land of peace and love and consciousness and anyone who thinks otherwise must be mad, if not evil themselves.

Yes, it's true. The New Age movement shares its roots deeply with those of the Nazi Party, all the way back to Blavatsky, who taught us to worship this ancient horror and wrap it up in love and light. And it goes deeper still, to the first moment Yahweh, the usurper, instructed the ancients to kill their neighbors just because they were different.

Ever since then, the various tribes of Mankind have been on an endless quest to conquer their fellowmen through a simple formula: convert or kill to establish Utopia. The masters will come, and in their enlightenment rescue you from your enemies (who must be bad) and relegate them to damnation and sweep you (who must be good) to paradise.

Less than a generation after WWII had ended, the Nazi-infested CIA was down in Laurel Canyon, and their Communist counterparts in the universities, sowing the seeds of the New Age movement, all dressed up in flowers, paisley and rainbows so no one would notice. But that is the subject of other books.

A column of police and military vehicles approached the plateau and surrounded the restored Death Star. Ostensibly, this was just a precaution to protect a culturally and historically invaluable project from vandals. But Faro and his team knew it was much more than that. Now that the Nazis had succeeded, they meant to protect their pet monster at any cost, even human.

Chapter 85

Meanwhile things were not going well in Alexandria. As good as Ehab Abu Samra was at protecting the world from evil and lending a clandestine hand to the forces of good, he had been trumped. The forces of evil held all the aces in Egypt at the moment. It was by their very design the country had just undergone its recent turmoil and changed government. He, Kelvin Greaves, and Frank Barstow who several hours ago held the fate of humanity in their hands, had lost their grip.

The port was suddenly on lockdown. No one was to go in or out. Abu Samra had lost his pull and couldn't overturn or overrule the recent decisions.

"My God, my friends, did you see the news today?"

"About the earthquake in Panama?"

"Yes, that. And now the port is closed. It's still receiving cargo, but nothing can leave, and no personnel is allowed in or out until the shift change."

"This doesn't bode well. And I can still feel the earth trembling from the Death Star all the way from Cairo."

"The news is saying it's just a prolonged tremor. Earthquakes are not uncommon here."

"Here's a hint: they're lying."

"Indeed. But I have a plan. We will drive down the coast to El Alamein. There we will meet a friend of mine who has a fishing boat. He will take us back to Alexandria by sea where we will enter the port with a cargo of fish. We will unload the fish at the pier as usual, then we will get your vehicle."

"But how will we exit the port?"

"Again by sea. We will drive the Land Rover onto the fishing boat. It will just fit. Then we will sail back to El Alamein and drive to Giza."

"Brilliant, Ehab! Simply Brilliant!"

"El Alamein. I like it. Like history repeating itself. 'Rommel, you magnificent bastard! I read your book!'"

"Will your friend's boat hold the weight of the Rover?"

"Do we have another choice?"

The men got into Ehab's car and drove off along the coast.

"By the way, Frank" began Ehab, "Patton was not at El Alamein. He was at El Guettar. In Tunisia."

"Minor detail."

Chapter 86

Frank and Greaves left the TVs on in their rooms loud enough to annoy the neighbors and so anyone in the hallway would hear. After making sure the coast was clear, they made their way down the stairs and out a loading dock to rendezvous with Abu Samra.

They drove west along the coast to El Alamein where Ehab's friend was waiting with a trawler full of the day's catch. They boarded his ship and sailed for Alexandria. After receiving the routine permissions, the fish were unloaded and the boat docked. Almost a full day had now been lost.

The Giza Death Star remained tuned and ready. Richter had the capstone lifted with his contraption to turn it off and water pumped out to below the level of the entrance. The Death Star sat there, in a kind of neutral, waiting to be engaged again. Men in protective suits entered to do inspection and maintenance.

Amidst the commotion of unloading, Frank, Greaves and Ehab nonchalantly left the vessel and began to execute their plan. They "requisitioned" a long ramp from a repair shop and brought it to the end of the row where their container sat, three levels up.

Greaves climbed up to the doors of the container and picked the locks as he had the night before. Then the three men heaved the ramp into position and walked up into the container. Frank checked the vehicle, which seemed to be unharmed. The phase conjugator was still mounted on its stand.

"What's this wooden crate?"

".50 caliber."

"You brought that?"

"You never know. Just throw it in the bed."

Greaves and Abu Samra strained to lift the crate into the bed.

"My God, this is heavy!"

"Packed lots of ammo."

"What made you think you could get this thing in here?" asked Greaves.

"You said your guy was good. And he's proven such." Frank smiled and nodded at Ehab.

"Thank you."

"Let's get this thing out of here."

Frank fired up the Rover and guided it down the ramp where he stopped.

"Toss that ramp in here so we can skee-daddle."

Greaves and Abu Samra placed the ramp in the bed. Samra sat on one end so it wouldn't flip out. Greaves climbed back up to the container and re-locked the doors so the open container wouldn't raise suspicion, then climbed down to join his friend holding down their end of the ramp.

When they got back to the trawler, Ehab's friend swung open a gate in the bulwarks where they laid the ramp to make a gangplank. Frank drove gingerly over the gangplank, adjusting the speed and balance as if the Rover were a part of his own body. It just barely fit.

Quickly, quietly and unceremoniously, Ehab Abu Samra's friend and his crew cast off and headed out of port not mentioning their new cargo to the harbor master. When they reached the open sea, they opened the throttle and cruised back to El Alamein. It had taken a full day and night. They parked the vehicle at Abu Samra's friend's house.

They were exhausted from their adventure and opted for a few hours' sleep before setting off to Cairo. It was a decision they lived to regret.

Chapter 87

The maneuver with the repair shop ramp had broken a ball joint in the Rover which had to be repaired before the drive to Cairo. It would take hours, if not the whole day. Series IIA Land Rover parts aren't available at your local parts store. You have to order them from a Series dealer, which is not the same as your regular Land Rover dealer nowadays. In fact, now that Land Rovers have become a luxury item, modern dealers don't even like to touch the old jalopies. Fortunately there are a few old Series Rovers floating around Egypt owing to the former British presence and the dry desert air keeping them well preserved.

"Hey, look here, on this Land Rover forum. There's a guy with a Series IIA back in Alexandria. He's posted pics."

"Looks pretty sharp. You think he's got any parts lying around?"

"Worth a try. Series owners usually do."

"Frank DMed the guy to see if he could help, and sent Ehab's cell number to him. While they waited they continued to search the loosely knit but ever friendly international network of Series Land Rover owners."

A few hours later, Ehab's phone rang. They spoke Arabic.

"I have good news. Our friend in Alexandria has the parts you need. But he wants us to pay first. I'll contact my wife and have her take the money over. Then he will send them here by courier."

"Oh, God! Wonderful!"

"Ehab, once again, you're brilliant!"

Chapter 88

"Herr Richter, my compliments! You have realized our vision at last!"

"Thank you so much, Herr Kammler. But your father was critical to keeping our research programs alive after the war. And you have succeeded him magnificently. I'm honored to be a part of it."

"Always so humble, eh, Richter?"

"How can one be otherwise before such great men?"

"HAHAHA! You flatter us. But there is still another test."

"Yes?"

"We want you to repeat your performance. To make sure your system works properly, we need replicability. Make another earthquake in exactly the same place. Then we will know for certain that the texts, the grating patterns, the locations, and the Death Star, are exactly as you say."

"Well, the full moon was of great help. You recall that the torsion fields in the solar system greatly influence the effect. But perhaps if we strike quickly......It will be a pleasure to prove it so!"

"Good! Get down to the plateau and perform it immediately. The security force we sent will ensure your safety."

Just then, Kammler's cell phone rang.

"Yes?.....Yes, I see......Yes. By all and any means. Thank you. I'll inform the others."

"What is it?"

"That was Herr Müller. He says that a special cargo had come in that was headed to Cairo. It had been cleared by the authorities but he was able to intercept and impound it. It's an old Land Rover with some kind of device mounted on it. The recipients appear to be associates of Faro."

"Curses! Curse that man to Hell!"

"You didn't really think he'd stand by and let us deploy the Death Star, did you? Even a gentleman such as Faro knows when to stop playing fairly."

"Yes, yes. But do we have to like that he plays unfairly as well as us?"

"Indeed not. But he's not playing as well as us right now. We have his whatever-it-is in Alexandria and he doesn't."

"If only we could spare Herr Dr. Richter to look at it. Perhaps after today's test."

"Yes, let us make sure we are ready to, er, ring in the *Julfest*, as it were."

They looked at each other and laughed.

Chapter 89

Edda was back in action in the desert. This is what she loved best. Being a member of the council had its comforts and benefits, and that was all well and good for gray-haired old men. She was still in her prime and lusted for the smoke and blood and action. She always thought it superior to do the killing herself than to send others to do it.

She personally met Richter at the hotel entrance to escort him to Giza. When they had arrived, she immediately barked orders at the security force to tighten their positions and be more alert. The pyramidion was lowered into place, the earth trembled as before, and water was pumped into the moat. All of this occurred while Frank, Greaves, and Ehab helplessly and anxiously awaited a Series IIA ball joint from Alexandria.

On the second shot, the Nazis struck gold, if you're a Nazi that is, and on December 8th, an even more powerful M6.6 earthquake struck Punta de Burica, tormenting the same half a million people a second time, and before they could even catch their breath from the last earthquake just two days ago. Weakened and unstable structures that were still standing, this time collapsed. Utilities that were still functioning went dark. The crisis was barely manageable.

A sinister joy filled our villains, and that night they celebrated their success.

"Haha!" Kammler laughed as he put his arm around Richter. "You're a real Egyptian magus, eh, Richter?"

"Herr Kammler, you flatter me now. I merely ride on the shoulders of giants."

"Which puts you above them all."

"Herr Bormann, please. Come here and share with Herr Doctor your magnificent plans for the holidays."

Bormann broke away from the men he was mingling with and came over. He was beaming with satisfaction and confidence.

"Well, Herr Doctor, it was quite simple in principle, but difficult to pull off. What we will do on the 20th is contact the major world powers and announce our plans, telling them that if they don't comply, we will strike with an earthquake at such and such a place at such and such a time. To make sure we reach them, we will use above top secret codes, as we did with the Americans on September 11. We fully expect that they do not comply, at which time you will perform your magic."

"And who are the powers you will be contacting?"

"America, Russia, China, Japan, and England. Which of them do you have grating patterns for?"

"Only China, I'm afraid. But I like this grating pattern here for the Maluku Islands in Indonesia. It's placement on the globe is better for the torsion fields that will be in play that day and easier to pull off."

"Well we only need one to make our point, don't we?"

"I suppose so. Being able to call and cause earthquakes accurately anywhere in the world will certainly send a strong message."

"Oh, you know how these big boys work: They'll only listen if it hits close to home."

"Let us start with Indonesia, and then hit China next if they fail to comply. It is better to get China, as with the other powers, with the infrastructure intact."

"Why don't we just crank the thing up and let her rip?"

"No! No! Far too dangerous! You could destroy the entire planet and us with it! These forces are far too dangerous to go mucking about with!"

"And yet, Herr Doctor, that is exactly what you are doing," observed Kammler slyly.

Chapter 90

Back in El Alamein our three heroes wailed in anguish at their failure to prevent the tests.

"Gentlemen, I understand your pain. Believe me. Our enemy, Mankind's enemy, has won this round. But let us bear in mind that at least no one has died as a result, at least not yet."

"You're right. We can't lose focus. Let's get the Rover repaired and down to Giza as quick as humanly possible so we can prevent the next one."

"The courier has already left Alexandria. We should have the parts we need soon."

"Well at least that's going our way."

Meanwhile, at Giza, Daryl and his team, along with Thorny, One Flare, Carrie and Mary, were already scoping out the set up to see what they could do if their clean-up batter couldn't get off deck.

"Well, the most straightforward way is to just put some charges on that wall of sandbags so they can't fill it up."

"It would be hard to get up that close with all the security. Damn. We didn't plan for that in our designs."

"These guys could get up there," said Daryl indicating Thorny and One Flare.'

"Except we don't know squat about setting charges," stated One Flare.

"Unless there's trip lines and Pyrodex involved," added Thorny.

"This isn't really a trip line situation."

"How about the water pumps or the hose lines? How well guarded are they?"

"Guard teams on each pump and about every 10 yards on the water lines."

"These guys seem to have thought of everything."

"Do we have enough firepower to just shoot the hell

out of those sandbags until they break?"

"Well, that's a good way to attract a lot of attention."

"You know," One Flare spoke up, "we spotted a work shed with some atmospheric diving suits in it, or something like that anyway. They must be for going inside there, otherwise why would they have them? What if we used those to get inside?"

"How you gonna get over the wall?"

"Use the same step ladder they do. They won't know who's in the suits."

"Speaking of getting over the wall, why don't we sabotage that crane they built so they can't put the capstone back on?"

"Good idea, but it's also pretty closely guarded."

"Damn! These frikkin' Nazis think of everything!"

Mary slapped One Flare on the chest with the back of her hand. "So much for low tech beating high tech every time."

Chapter 91

Kammler's cell phone rang again. "Yes?"

"It's me."

"Müller! What's the good news from Alexandria?"

"None. The container their vehicle was in is now empty!"

"What? You fool! How did this happen?"

"I have no idea. It was still in there last night and still locked up. No vehicles were allowed in or out without our man's explicit approval. They must have picked the locks on the container and somehow gotten the vehicle on a boat. And the agent who was assisting them has gotten away as well."

Bormann interrupted Kammler. "What is it?"

"It seems Faro and his associates have gotten away with their vehicle and the device that was on it."

"Damn! Damn them to Hell!" Bormann recovered his senses after this outburst. "Find out every boat that was in and out of that port in the last two days and where it went."

"Did you hear that, Herr Müller?"

"I did. We are already looking into it."

"Good. Call me—"

"Wait. We already have something. A large trawler out of El Alamein. That looks like our best bet for now."

"Excellent. Track them down."

Chapter 92

But it was already too late. Frank had replaced the ball joint, mounted the .50 caliber, loaded the Rover with supplies, and they were headed across the desert towards Cairo. Ehab hitched a ride back to Alexandria with the courier.

"Ah, I love desert camping," sighed Greaves cheerfully.

"Even when Nazis are hunting you?"

"Especially when Nazis are hunting me."

"You're not normal. No wonder Faro likes you so much."

"You don't know much about Geronimo or the Apache scouts, do you?"

"Obviously not as much as you."

"So you don't know how Geronimo and just 27 warriors were able to evade the 5000 US cavalry troops that were hunting them in the desert?"

"I do not."

"Well, they didn't have motorized vehicles of course, or aircraft back then, but the same principles still apply."

"I'm glad you're up on that, because I still have no freaking idea why we aren't racing to Cairo on a modern highway."

"Look at this way: they've already done two tests on the pyramid to make sure their system works as advertised. It's unlikely they'll test it again owing to the immense difficulty and expense that must be involved in operating that thing. So there's no point in hurrying. Secondly, if they got drift of our plan—"

"Now how would they get drift of our plan, exactly?"

"Well, I doubt they'd ignore the container the Rover was in. They obviously have some idea what's going on, and they're bound to want to check out the phase conjugator. My guess is they'd be back at that container by now to get the vehicle and find out it's gone. So they'll be looking for us on the highway."

"Well, I think you're wrong. I think they'd be trying to figure out how we got out of port and where we went."

"That could be too. But it's irrelevant. Even if they track down Ehab's friend's boat, trace it back to El Alamein, and find us gone, they're next step would be to patrol all the roads to Cairo looking for us. They may just do it as a safety precaution before they even get to El Alamein."

"Always two steps ahead, eh?"

"Actually we're three steps ahead. Getting off road is the third step. Geronimo never used trails. Except to deceive."

"This trip is going to be 'educational' isn't it?"

"Probably."

Chapter 93

Müller and his men burst into the boat yard just as Ehab's friend and his family were about to scram. They held the family at gunpoint while they searched for any out-of-place people and the Rover. They found nothing.

"Where did they go?"

"They didn't tell us anything. Why should they?"

"So you could live a little longer. I shan't ask you again."

He waited a second studying their terrified faces. While the family cowered at the business end of their weapons, Müller mercilessly executed them for sport.

Chapter 94

That afternoon, Frank and Greaves caught the sound of choppers in the air.

"Look over there."

"Choppers over the highway. You think they'll spot us out here?"

"I doubt they'll be airborne much longer," observed Greaves. "Sandstorm rolling in."

"How do you know that?"

Greaves started chuckling. "Let's pull up over in that ravine to make camp. It'll be safe in there."

Frank steered as directed. They got out of the vehicle, jogged back to the entrance of the ravine, and peered back over towards the highway to see if there was any change in the movement of the helicopters.

"Holy shit!" exclaimed Frank. "Where did that come from?"

A high wall of billowing sand appeared out of nowhere stretching from horizon to horizon. It was barreling down on the highway like a ravenous monster.

"You were right! How did you know that was coming?"

Greaves just laughed as he busily set up the poles and tarp that would protect them from the driving sand. "You never heard the story of how Geronimo was once trapped on a mesa, surrounded by the cavalry, and was suddenly saved by an unexpected sandstorm?" he quipped.

The two men were now protected on two sides by stone walls and a tarp strung between them with parachute cord overhead and propped up by two poles. At either end of the ravine the wind howled as it kicked up heralding the imminent arrival of a thick comforting blanket of sand.

What's that? Thick and comforting? It's all in the perspective, you see. The sandstorm was to Frank and

Greaves as the blanket of leaves is to the vole. It concealed them from aerial predators.

Frank removed the grill from the Land Rover and gave it a stiff once over with a steel brush while Greaves lit a fire with tightly bundled reeds they'd brought along.

Up in the lead chopper, the pilot shouted into his headset. "That's it! This sand will kill the engines. We have to head back."

Müller was visibly upset, but he knew the dangers. He flipped a hand signal to the pilot who turned the chopper as the other followed. They flew just ahead of the line of the storm back to safety.

The grill was set. Frank plopped a couple of steaks on it.

"So did Geronimo have steak?"

"Better. He had venison," Greaves said rubbing his hands together and licking his chops, as it were. "But don't get me wrong. This is a great setup! I may get me one of these when I get home," he added indicating the Rover. "It has a built in barbecue grill!"

Chapter 95

The quietness jarred the men awake.

"You hear that?"

"No."

"Me neither. Let's roll."

The men packed up their camp, concealed the remains of their fire, and were off in a flash.

"Can we navigate this desert at night?"

"We have a GPS heading."

"Well, yeah, but what about unforeseen obstacles, like mushy sand or the Marshes of the Nile?"

"We'll deal with it. Anyway, the marshes will all be way east of us. We're going to swing wide west towards Moghara Lake and then turn east to the airport. C'mon. We gotta get a jump on those choppers."

"Good thing we have these."

The men slipped on night vision goggles and headed across the desert with the firmament of stars dominated by Orion blazing over their heads. In the blackness and blankness of the Western Desert, the expanse of stars stretched around them and receded into the terrible height and unfathomable depth of infinity like a matrix of illuminated crystals.

Chapter 96

Next morning Frank and Kelly pulled into the airport, made their way to private aviation and pulled into a hangar where they parked the Rover. While hefting his duffel from the back of the Rover, Greaves indicated a '68 Mercedes 250S, also parked in the hangar.

Frank put his hands on hips. "You don't say!"

"Oh, I do say."

"I'm only riding if it has the real wood trim."

Greaves paused and turned to Frank. "Would I disappoint?"

"Call Faro and see where he's at."

Frank made the call and ascertained they were having a powwow at Daryl's hotel.

They made their way in style down the highway into Cairo, arriving in style at Faro's hotel.

As they approached the entrance on foot, three sinister men made their way towards them. They crossed paths in the very doorway. As if in slow motion and by some hidden design, they caught one another's attention and eyed each other defiantly, like rival gangs.

Chapter 97

"Has anyone at all seen Thorny and One Flare and the girls?"

"Not for a few days, what's up?"

"Exactly that," explained Faro. "No one's seen them for days."

"I'm sure they can take care of themselves."

"Yes. And so can Carrie and Mary. And look what happened to them in Gallup."

"C'mon, the four of them together? The Devil himself wouldn't mess with them."

"You underestimate the Devil. But I know what you mean. Kelly?"

"Why ask me?"

"You have a unique relationship with the Dynamic Dudes."

"And that's why I know those clowns come and go." He paused. "It's their way."

"Aren't you afraid they might endanger their girlfriends."

Greaves threw his head back in laughter. "Rezzed out chicks like that?" He shook his head in disbelief. "If anyone can hold their own with the 'Dynamic Dudes' (he made air quotes as he said it), it's those two girls."

"Kelly is right, Georgeann." It was Daryl's turn. "You saw how Carrie slit that Nazi bastard's throat at the ranch. She's the last person we need to worry about."

Just then the foursome surprised them all at the breakfast table. They were covered in dust, and holding food trays piled high with starchy, syrupy delights and fatty meats. "Mind if we join you guys?" Thorny was wearing a bright, crisp white polo shirt.

As the seated group began sidling chairs to make room, Faro questioned them. "Good Lord, don't you have the decency to shower first?"

"What?" wondered Thorny with mischievous delight. "I put on a clean shirt."

Greaves and Daryl sat shaking their heads trying mightily to conceal their laughter.

"OK, I'll bite," offered Frank. "What have you been up to for the past, what is it, four, five, days?"

"It's like the great Yogi Berra once said, 'You can observe a lot by watching, 'with all due respect to Grandfather."

"And prithee, sirrah, what have you been observing?"

"Foxes."

"That is to say, rodents and birds. "

"Well which is it? You're saying foxes, and she's saying rodents and birds."

"Yes!"

"It's easy. This was our gateway animal."

"Gateway animal? What?"

"Alright kids. Stop, stop, stop. No one knows what you're talking about or why you're talking about it."

"I do," said Kelvin Greaves, "but let them explain."

"Well, this one time at Tracker School, One Flare and I were talking to Tom about concentric rings...."

"Finally!" interrupted Faro. "A clue to who this Tom character is. Please." He motioned for them to continue.

"We were talking to Tom about concentric rings when he brought up a very interesting point: 'If you can recreate the concentric rings of a fox, wouldn't you then be perceived as a fox? Thus you stand at the threshold of shapeshifting.'"

"And? What? You're going to turn yourselves into foxes?"

"Well, we had to learn the local concentric rings first. Waves on a pond. Get it?"

"Oh I get it. And what's this supposed to accomplish?"

"It'll get us into that work shed. Just a couple of

mischievous vermin roaming around."

Faro bellowed with laughter. "HAHAHAHA! That's an accurate description of you two alright."

"And we're comfortable with that," declared One Flare who shoved a load of syrupy pancakes into his mouth and chewed to punctuate the remark.

Chapter 98

After breakfast the crew hopped a bus to Giza. Thorny and One Flare opted to go on foot in order to "get into it." Soon a couple of foxes were prancing along the road to Giza, and it wasn't long before they were sniffing around the ruins.

The rest of the crew had taken up positions where they could observe the shed. It wasn't long before a pair of indolent young foxes showed up sniffing around the base of the shed and occasionally nipping playfully at each other.

"Shoo! Shoo!" shouted the guard at the two critters, but it was to no avail. They scampered right by him as he kicked and into the shed, sniffing around the compressed air tanks and suits and crates and equipment that were stored within. The guard pursued.

Fearful of discharging his weapon, he swung a boot at one and connected with the rib cage that sent it flying as it yelped. As he turned to deal with the other, he found himself face to face with a punkass bike messenger with a Mohawk and an attitude who clocked him squarely in the nose, shattering the bridge and knocking him out cold.

One Flare stood up rubbing his side. "Damn! That hurt!"

"Y'alright?"

"I'll survive. Man, you really put that guy out."

"I could hear his nose breaking."

"Yeah ya could." They high fived.

"Check out what's in here man."

"Look at this. These tanks are full of hydrogen."

"Wonder what that's for."

"This hose connects to a bunch of them and runs out the shed to the water line. Look. They hook up right before the wall."

"We'll have to ask Frank or Doc about that. They

obviously need a lot of hydrogen for something."

"And they sure ain't usin' it for the Hindenburg."

"Here are the suits. Let's get 'em on."

"Hold on. Don't you think it might look a little suspicious if two guys just appear in atmospheric diving suits going into the pyramid? We don't even know how they work."

"Unscheduled maintenance. Just make sure y'all bring a clipboard."

"A clipboard?" One Flare was incredulous.

"Yeah. The best way to look like you belong somewhere it to carry either a cup o' coffee or a clipboard. We don't have any coffee, so...."

"Tsshhh. Aiight. Don't suppose coffee would look right with these suits on anyway."

Chapter 99

A comical scene ensued in the storage shed. Thorny and One Flare bungled about as the robotics in the suit whirred and sent them tumbling into the air tanks and smashing into crates.

"How do you work these things?" The shouted questioned was muffled through the visor.

"I'm tryin' to figure that out!"

Whirrrr. Smash! Whirrr. Clank!

Finally, One Flare was getting the hang of it. "Just move naturally."

Thorny swung around to respond and smashed into One Flare, sending him into the wall causing a rain of tools to come down on him.

"What?"

"Ya freakin' clod! Just move naturally! Don't use any extra force."

Thorny started off slowly and weakly. He realized that the suit, though being bulky and weighing hundreds of pounds, responded precisely to his movements. The force that seemed intuitively necessary to throw the suit around was completely superfluous.

He reached over to give One Flare a hand getting up. "Here," he reached out a hand.

One Flare gripped the robotic hand and Thorny hoisted him across the shed smashing a crate on the other side.

"Dude! What the fuck?"

"Sorry. Whoa! Look behind you."

"Whoa!"

Lustrous, dreamlike beams emanated from the cracks in the broken crate.

"What is that?"

"Looks like, like, I dunno, pure light!"

"Some kind of stones, or crystals, in there."

"Spare parts?"

"Maybe."

"Well throw something over it so they don't see it."

They looked around and found a tarp they threw over the escaping luminescence.

"What's in that one? Looks like it has a door and hinges but it's padlocked."

One Flare clutched the edge of the crate and pried the door off.

"Wow! Look at that. It's like a bell."

"What's that for?"

"Damned if I know."

"Get the clipboards and let's go. **Carefully.**"

They made their way over to the step ladder that had been erected to span the sandbag wall and the moat and descend to the entrance. At the entrance they waved their clipboards at the guards and shouted through their face screens, "Unscheduled maintenance!"

The guards stepped aside allowing them to enter.

They made their way up the ramp to the tuning chamber, which is also known as the Grand Gallery. The bright white orbs of the Helmholtz resonators glowed eerily in the light cast by the crystal arrays.

"I'll bet if we smash these things it won't work anymore." One Flare cocked a fist and thrust it with all his might into one of the orbs.

"Ow! Goddammit!"

"Geez, that didn't work," observed Thorny.

"I know it didn't work."

"I've got an idea." Thorny grabbed One Flare's wrist, swung him mightily around a couple of times and released him into the orbs. A loud resonant hum filled the gallery and then slowly dissipated. The guards outside looked quizzically at each other, peered into the darkness, and then shrugged. One Flare fell on his haunches as his head bounced off the orbs.

263

"Wuttayou doing, dumbass?"

"I guess those orbs are among the artifacts that couldn't be destroyed. I thought you in the full weight of the suit might shatter them."

"Well, you were wrong," he instructed as he got up." C'mere, now I've got an idea," he added sardonically.

"Wait. Some of this stuff has to be breakable." Thorny randomly chose a crystal and smashed it with his robot fist. It cracked. "See?"

The two of them went to town gleefully punching at every crystal they could reach. Some broke and some didn't, but the light in the tuning chamber grew slightly dimmer, and they knew they had some success. They removed the ones they could and tossed them, broken and unbroken alike, in the center of the chamber, and left them there.

"Better leave them here. It'll probably look suspicious if we try to carry any out."

"Probably."

The boys made their way back to the entrance and gave a couple of manly nods and thumbs up to the guards as they passed. Back in the shed they shed the suits and returned them to their racks. Two foxes cocked a leg each and peed on the man on the floor, then scampered off into the desert.

All the while Faro & Co. watched with anticipation and awe as the boys pulled off their maneuver.

Chapter 100

Edda sniffed the air like the She-Wolf of the SS she was. She addressed the man next to her. "Something's not right. Go get Herr Richter and bring him to the shed." She dashed off to the work shed where she discovered the collapsed party, bleeding from his nose and eyes starting to blacken. She felt his pulse, then stood up and looked around at the damage and disarray.

The man trotted over to a tent where Herr Richter was nervously examining some displays. "Herr Richter, Fraulein Siebrecht requests your presence at the work shed. Something's not right."

"I know something isn't right!" He grabbed a small handheld device from the table and walked briskly with the guard to the work shed. As he entered, he spied the carnage and was momentarily speechless.

"W- W-What happened?" He stammered while tapping his device.

"We must find out."

Edda turned to a laptop that was discreetly placed on a high shelf and took it down.

"Let's check the security footage."

They played the video scrutinizing every second. They were baffled. They glanced bewilderedly at each other.

"Rewind it."

They watched again.

"Rewind it again."

They watched it a third time.

"Who are these two men? They come out in shield suits, but they never come in beforehand. And here they are returning from the pyramid but they never come out again. Unless...."

"Don't be ridiculous. That's impossible. Throw some water on this man."

The guard looked around and saw a half of a bucket of water near the door. He threw it over the man's face, who slowly revived.

"What happened here?"

The man slowly rose to his feet, supporting his weight first on a crate, then on a steel drum, and lastly pulling himself up on a pulley rope hanging from the ceiling.

"I...I...don't know."

"You were here weren't you?"

"It seems so strange now."

"Well?"

"Well...no... it's too strange. It can't be." He was still stunned from the flattening of his nose. "I must have been dreaming while I was out...."

"Out with it!"

"Well, I ran after these two foxes in here thinking they might cause some damage. I kicked one to chase it out, and when I turned to kick the other, a man was standing there and punched me in the nose."

"Ridiculous. Where did the man come from?"

"I...I...don't know. It happened so suddenly, he was just.....there."

"And what did this man look like?"

"Oh, every bit of six feet, youngish, and a fist that got bigger and bigger. That's all I got in a flash." (Author's note: In fact, the man used the metric '1.8 meters or more', but our principle audience is English speaking and familiar with the British system, which I dare say is more precisely and accurately attuned to the measurement of the earth, having been based on the Pyramid inch and ancient rod.)

Edda stamped her foot in anger. Being so baffled herself she had a moment of clarity and chose not to kill the man.

"See to that nose." The man left.

Herr Richter had busied himself inspecting the damage. "We must check inside the pyramid immediately." He held up the device for Edda to see, though its readings were meaningless to her.

"You stay here," Edda instructed the guard who had come with them.

Chapter 101

Edda and Richter marched across the bridge to the pyramid entrance. The guards saluted and turned in order to permit their entrance, but the guard on Edda's side was ill-rewarded for his etiquette. She thrust her palm forcefully into his chest and sent him tumbling into the moat with a splash.

"Gott im Himmel!" exclaimed Richter when he saw the tatters of his magnus opus piled in the chamber.

He knelt reverently over the debris and began examining and sorting it.

"Well?" inquired Edda.

"It will take days to repair. Some of them are unbroken and can simply be replaced, but others, we must rebuild from the ether."

"Fortunately, we have days. But only days. You must get to work immediately."

"Of course. Unquestionably. And I don't need you to tell me! Thank goodness I had the foresight to bring the Bell for just such a contingency."

"Wise move, Herr Richter," she said somewhat apologetically. "I must contact the council and inform them."

"Indeed. Have them send the rest of my staff. I will need every technician to keep production going 24 hours a day."

As they exited the pyramid, the sopping wet guard Edda had pushed into the moat was just reclaiming his position at the entrance when she pushed him again, sending him tumbling a second time.

Chapter 102

Thorny and One Flare emerged from the Western Cemetery and strolled nonchalantly over to their group who were all craning their necks and scanning the landscape for the pair. One Flare tapped Mary on the shoulder. She turned around and erupted with glee, then threw her arms around him, her eyes beaming. Carrie, who was next to her, then did the same with Thorny.

Faro chuckled admiringly. "I have to admit, I seriously doubted it could be done, but here you are."

"Yeah getting in there wasn't easy."

"Not that part. That looked easy enough: the ole slip on a uniform and carry a clipboard trick. The part I doubted is that you could literally shapeshift."

"Why couldn't we?"

"Not that you personally couldn't do it, boys, but that shapeshifting *at all* were possible."

"It's OK. We don't believe half the shit you tell us either, so I reckon we're even."

"Hahaha! So we are."

"Concentric rings, Doc. Waves in the medium."

"Indeed!" the Doc laughed. "I'm just used to it being done with technology."

"We better retire somewhere safe where Thorny and One Flare can debrief us," mentioned Kelvin. "We'll need to know what we're up against."

They hopped a bus back to Cairo, lunched, and then headed out to Greaves' secure hangar at the airport. Whoever could fit in the Benz went with Kelvin; the rest took a couple of rented vans.

Chapter 103

"Nice place ya got here," commented Daryl as they strolled into the hangar. "But aren't these things usually used to park airplanes?"

"Usually. But then we're unusual people."

"Ya got that right."

They gathered around a number of large folding tables Greaves had set up with the usual white board and A/V facilities for such meetings. Some large documents, probably maps, were rolled up and neatly placed.

"So what you boys see in there?"

"Y'all want the shed first or the pyramid?"

"I wanna know what happened to the dude guarding the shed," someone quipped.

"Yeah," laughed one of Daryl's Apache friends. "What happened to that guy?"

"Thorny laid him out cold," explained One Flare. "Broke his beak with one shot."

"You didn't waste him? He's sure to report to his superiors."

"Who's gonna believe him?"

"All part of the psyop, the freak out," someone else pointed out.

"Good point."

"Well what else happened in there?"

"We saw a bunch o' stuff."

"OK, well?"

"There was at least one crate that was full of rocks or crystals that glowed a lot."

"Spare parts, most likely," said Faro. "They'll probably use them if any of the crystal components they fabricated go on the fritz."

"We'll get to that directly. We also saw a whole lot of hydrogen tanks. Some of them were hooked up to an array of intake valves that led to a hose that connected to the water line. Like they were pumping it into the water."

"Ingenious."

"What's that, Doc?"

"It's simple. They need a plasma to form the grating pattern in the interferometer, which as you know is the King's Chamber. When they pump water into the subterranean chamber, they apparently are pumping in Hydrogen gas along with it. The gas will bubble off and rise through the passageways into the chamber. As the power builds up inside, that hydrogen gas will eventually form a plasma, from which they can form a grating pattern for targeting. The paleo-ancients used a chemical reaction, but Richter's taken a shortcut."

"Very interesting. But all that hydrogen can be highly inflammable."

"Indeed."

"What else?"

"In one crate we saw something that looked like a bell."

"So they've brought it along then."

"Brought what along, Doc?"

"That latest incarnation of the old Nazi Bell they were working on during the war. I always suspected they kept that project going."

"What do you think it's for?"

"I really don't know. It's designed to access the ether. It could be for harnessing unlimited amounts of power, a propulsion device, or perhaps for even manipulating the ether itself to form new types of matter. No one really knows how far the research has come except those working on it, but the theoretical implications were clear enough as soon as it was discovered."

"Anything else of interest?"

"Not in the shed. But we did have some fun in the pyramid."

"Do tell."

271

"Well, all along both walls in the Grand Gallery are these stacks of spheres that get smaller as you get to the top. They fit perfectly in the niches that are there."

"So Dunn was right! Helmholtz resonators!"

"We tried to bust 'em, but they seemed to be indestructible."

"Of course. Could you tell what they were made of?"

"Not with those suits on. We couldn't feel them to get an idea."

"What else?"

"We had a lot of fun trashing the place. Not all of the crystals would break, but we removed all of them that we could and tossed them all on the floor. It should slow them down for a while."

"But for how long?"

"There's no telling. I wonder if, since they brought the Bell, they could re-fabricate any of them and how long it would take..."

"When do they plan on making their move anyway? I mean, do something more than just cause an idle earthquake the whole world thinks is a natural event?"

"Well, these Nazis do love important anniversaries and calendar dates. The next big one is *Julfest*, which is December 21st."

"Julfest?"

"Yes. Nazi Christmas."

"That's less than a week away."

"Can they repair and replace everything Thorny and One Flare trashed in time?"

"Damned Nazis are very resourceful."

Chapter 104

Richter carefully sorted the crystals in the crates and selected the ones he needed to replace in the resonance chamber. This provided him with some of what he needed, but Thorny and One Flare's little thrash session in the pyramid inflicted significant damage. His men worked feverishly day and night at the Bell recreating from out of the ether the others they needed. Men donned shield suits to enter the Death Star and restore the seemingly magical devices to their assigned positions.

Edda patrolled the guard positions and conducted inspections herself. Every minor infraction was punished. The guards were reprimanded and even physically abused, a task she took great delight in. Additional surveillance equipment was brought in and set up.

She contacted the council on a secure phone from Richter's tent.

"It is a most unfortunate setback. Will Herr Doctor Richter be ready for the appointed date?"

"He believes so. He has authorized me to inform you that you should go ahead according to plan."

"We have good news for you, Fraulein. Herr Müller has arrived. Why don't you take a break and come see your husband?"

"I'm afraid that will not be possible. There is too much to do here."

"There is also much to do here. We need you and Mr. Silva to track down the troublemakers. You did such an excellent job of it in Gallup."

"I see."

"It may seem a strange coincidence, but we think they might be staying in the same hotel."

"What gives you that idea?"

"Oh just a feeling, a strange occurrence a few days

ago that Herr Kammler and one of our colleagues and I had with a couple of men coming in."

"Who were they?"

"We really don't know, but it was the way we betook each other. There was something, I don't know, too coincidental, about it."

"I shall proceed immediately."

Chapter 105

Edda entered Bormann's suite where the council gathered each day to plan and monitor their mischief. Müller met her beaming with pleasure.

"Liebling!" he sang and pecked her on the lips.

"Schatzen." Her body armor discouraged too much intimacy.

Silva just clicked his heels and bowed slightly.

"While you have been busy, we have been busy too. We have important information for you."

"Go on."

"We think we have identified some of the opposition. They have rooms in this very hotel: two young men, the two angry squaws from Gallup, and a half dozen of their friends. They should have known better then to set up a convention of savages in the same hotel in Egypt. Unfortunately, Faro's intrepid colleague who accompanied him to Dulce does not seem to be among them."

"What about Faro and his secretary?"

"They seem to be staying elsewhere. We need you to find them, along with the two gentlemen we crossed paths with the other day. Herr Müller thinks they were the ones disrupting his operation in Alexandria, but it's difficult to know."

"Anyone else?"

"A female we spotted with the others. Attractive but nerdy."

"I see."

"And let's use more official channels this time."

Chapter 106

Mr. Silva handily determined which rooms were registered to the people in question in his inimitable way. Müller contacted his stooges in the Egyptian police and set up the raid. They rendezvoused in the lobby. The police were in full SWAT gear, Müller, Edda and Mr. Silva looked like ordinary business people. The manager was ready with key cards for each room.

The SWAT crew was so big the group had to take two elevators to the floor where our friends had all checked in. The raid commenced with a loud knock and the SWAT team shouting to the occupants in Arabic and English while the three Nazi comrades looked on. When there was no response at this first room, the SWAT leader gestured to the manager who inserted the key card.

The SWAT team burst in, weapons mounted, to take down the subjects, but the room was empty. The trio of Nazis looked slightly embarrassed, but they continued to the next room.

The second time they didn't knock first. The manager gave the SWAT leader the key card and they entered the room directly with their weapons drawn. Same result. Each time the trio of Nazis became increasingly embarrassed and more desperate.

Thus they continued. In the next to last room they found a famous photo of Geronimo with three of his warriors posing with rifles in the desert. On the back of the photo was written "We don't need no hotels."

Then they went to the last room in the same fashion. Inside they found a Navajo medicine wheel dangling from the dresser mirror with a swastika in the center. A note was taped next to it. Müller took the medicine wheel by the string in one hand, held it up, and studied it briefly. It had a swastika in the colors of the four directions. Then he removed the note with the other hand, holding it up next to the medicine wheel, and read it: "We've been at this a lot longer than you have."

He dropped them to his side and quietly crumpled the note in his hand. He turned his back to the assembled company and stepped out onto the balcony to stare out into the desert.

Chapter 107

"You know we're going to owe a lot of money on those rooms. We never checked out," explained Georgeann.

"I'm sure they've taken care of that for us. Our sudden exodus must have come as a big surprise."

"I'm sure the 'check out' got taken care of. It's the bill paying I'm not so sure about."

"OK, you're right. Call the finance guy and have him take care of it. We can't be leaving hotel bills all over the world," Faro laughed. "It would greatly impede our work if we got banned from hotels all over the world."

"How do you suppose Daryl knew they were coming?" asked Melissa.

"I'm gonna guess it has something to do with 'concentric rings,'" offered the Doc.

"What's the plan from here?"

"Melissa and I are going to rig up the phase conjugator here, keeping the Rover free for the .50 cal so we can deliver it to the plateau."

"The Doc and I will drive the Rover down to the plateau and move in when we see Daryl make his move," added Greaves.

He went on, "Thorny, One Flare, Carrie, and Mary will move the hydrogen tanks from the shed to the sandbag wall. They'll be used as explosives to blow the wall and drain the water that powers the pyramid. What's inside will drain out through the waste valve. Although if our interference is sufficient, we could create enough of a shock wave to blow it all out the entrance before we get there."

"I don't get it," complained Georgeann. "Why don't we just crank up the conjugator now and have Daryl's team take the damn thing down?"

"Good question. First of all, the conjugator isn't ready yet. I have to play with the settings to get it tuned to the new location—here as opposed to the ranch. Secondly, if we turn it on too early, they'll know, could come looking for us, or have time to take counter measures with the Death Star. Also, Daryl needs a couple of days to get into position and do what he needs to do. He wouldn't tell us exactly, but he said we'd know when we see it—old Apache war trick of glorious proportions, he says."

"Well all this sounds like a lot of fun, but what do I get to do?" asked Georgeann.

"You get to be our spotter."

"What's that mean?"

"You go out to the plateau and watch the pyramid. As soon as that capstone comes down, we need to know about it so we can make any necessary adjustments to the phase conjugator here. When it's properly tuned, there should be visible changes you can report back in real time. Just don't get spotted yourself."

Chapter 108

"You there! Get these tablets into the resonance chamber and install them. You, how many more do we need?"

Richter barked at his crew as they worked feverishly to fabricate the damaged crystals from the ether. It was an almost magical process. The suspended Bell would buzz and hum twisting the ether, and then the crystal tablet would drop out of the bottom. Then Richter would make his adjustments, enter his settings, and set it off again.

"How much longer?" snapped Edda to Richter.

"It's hard to tell exactly. While the obvious damage inflicted by the vandals was significant, it can be easily overcome. The real delay is in inspecting the rest of the Death Star to make sure they didn't get anything else."

"A very clever move. They knew if they could cause some quick destruction, we'd be forced to thoroughly recheck everything."

"True enough. But I feel certain we will be ready just in time."

"Excellent, Herr Richter. I will be off now to check the comms with Bariloche."

Chapter 109

On December 19th, the gray-haired old men debarked their private jet in San Carlos de Bariloche having no idea that Faro's crew was holed up in a hangar at the very same airport in Cairo where they had boarded it.

They made their way to their subterranean lair to prepare for their nefarious work. The information they needed was kept securely at HQ and was far too sensitive to risk carrying across the world to Cairo. They would have to watch their triumph on television.

Carefully they collected the information supplied by their moles all over the world, deeply ensconced in the intelligence agencies of various governments and Deep State organs that secretly pull the puppet strings.

On December 20th, at the appointed moment, they called heads of states around the world simultaneously. They used each government's secret codes and call signs, just as they had done on 9-11 in the US, to make sure their message was received.

They concluded their message, "To show you we can be merciful, our first demonstration will be a fairly harmless earthquake in the Maluku islands of Indonesia at 11:34 a.m. Greenwich Mean Time. If our demands are not met, we will wreak havoc closer to your homes."

From Downing Street to Beijing, the alarm sounded.

"Call Washington! See if they've received the same message." The President, however, was not in Washington, he was in Hawaii, and proceeded to Marine Corps Base Hawaii in Kaneohe Bay to handle the situation.

"Call London! See if they got the same message!"

"Call Beijing!"

"Call the Kremlin!"

And so it went, all afraid to give too much detail, all afraid the details would be the same for each other.

"Is that possible? Could they cause an earthquake anywhere they wanted? Get me the USGS on the horn!"

"Is there such a thing as such a weapon?"

"A global government under the UN led by Nazis? Preposterous!"

"Surrender our military bases and nuclear arsenals? Are they joking?"

All this panic went on behind the scenes. The leaders knew that if word got out to the public that they'd ALL been so compromised, public chaos would ensue. It would be *War of the Worlds* times a million!

Chapter 110

That morning, friendly news hosts and hostesses presented a charming story accompanied by footage of the final construction of the pyramid, capstone dangling over the peak of the shining white edifice.

"Today brings the culmination of one of the greatest projects ever undertaken in modern archaeology. The conservators of the Great Pyramid at Giza will conduct their final inspection before its scheduled New Year's Eve grand opening. The capstone, replacing the familiar ball from Times Square, will come down precisely at midnight Cairo time while the Cairo Symphony Orchestra performs live. The chief test today will be the timing of the capstone's descent...."

And so it went, on this cheerful strain, all merely a cover story for the sinister machinations about to ensue.

"Final check is complete. We're ready," Edda told the gray-haired old men.

"Excellent. Müller and Richter will be operating the Death Star?"

"With the technicians, of course."

"Yes, of course."

"They're going into the Pyramid now." Georgeann spoke into her mobile to Melissa in the hangar with Frank. She switched between her binoculars for close ups and naked eye observations for the big picture.

"She says they're going in," the message was relayed to Frank.

"Who's going in exactly?" asked Faro.

Melissa relayed the message, then answered, "She doesn't know. They're in big protective suits but there are six of them."

"Well, I'm sure Richter is one of them. After all it's his baby," speculated Faro. "He's not a guy you want to survive this thing or his evil genius will surely rise again."

"Agreed."

"Wait," Melissa broke in. "She says the big blonde Nazi bitch is outside. Looks like she's shouting orders at people."

"How about Müller? Can she spot Müller?"

"She says she can't."

"He could've returned to Bariloche with the others...."

"Possibly, but he is a man of action. A hands on kind of menace-maker."

"I'm going in for a closer look," said Georgeann.

"Not a good idea..." began Melissa, but it was already too late. Georgeann was creeping up on their position.

Georgeann made her way delicately along the far side of the work tent. As she approached the shed, Edda spotted her from the catwalk over the moat. She descended and came around the other side of the building. As Georgeann turned to peer into the door, Edda clocked her with the butt of her rifle, and she was out.

"Quickly," she said summoning Silva with a gesture. "Tie her up in the shed. We'll interrogate her later."

Silva performed his handiwork and emerged from the shed. "That's the second time."

"I understand, Mr. Silva. Expect anything. Now see to your men!"

"How we going to get down the highway to Giza with that big .50 caliber protruding above our heads?" asked Faro.

"Watch," answered Greaves. He pressed a button Frank had installed and the .50 Cal folded neatly onto the bed.

Faro chuckled in his jolly way, "You boys think of everything."

Greaves and Faro were off to take up their position, off road and near enough to Giza to crash the party.

Chapter 111

"Georgeann? Georgeann? Georgeann!" Melissa called frantically into her phone. "Hey! I think something happened to Georgeann!"

"Holy smokes! What's wrong?" asked Frank, the only other one left in the hangar.

"I don't know. She's not answering."

"Hang up and call back."

Melissa did so. This time Edda felt a vibration in her pocket. She reached in and pulled out Georgeann's phone. "Hallo?"

Melissa held the phone out in front of her and made a strange face. Then she put the phone back to her ear. "Who is this?"

"I'm afraid your friend is a little tied up right now." She promptly hung up and powered off the phone. Then she smiled to herself. Surely Müller would have liked her accidental joke. Why couldn't he be here to hear it? She is usually so serious. But Edda's musings never last very long and she was back in action.

"Quick! Call Faro!"

Melissa did so. "Are you guys in position yet?"

"Just now."

"One of you has to get to the plateau! Something's happened to Georgeann!"

"What a time for a rescue mission," observed Faro.

"I think she's alright for the time being. We need you or Kelly to spot."

"How do you know she's OK?"

"Don't ask now. Just get down there! And make sure you bring your phone!"

Faro turned somewhat heroically to Greaves, "Georgeann is MIA. I'm off to play spotter. Pick me up when the action starts."

"How will I know where you are?"

"The concentric rings!" Faro shouted as he trundled off.

"Of course! I should've thought of that."

Chapter 112

Faro jogged up to a spot where he had a clear view of the pyramid. He could just hear the pumps chugging away as the water level in the makeshift moat began to rise. The capstone hovered ominously over the apex.

Faro hunched over breathlessly and recalled his and Greaves trek up the mountain at Dulce. "Where are the young guys when you need them?" He panted to himself.

He heaved a few deep breaths to where he was at least conversational and dialed Melissa. "OK, I'm in position," he paused to catch his breath.

"You really should keep in better shape if you're going off on these adventures all the time," quipped Melissa.

"Thanks for the advice."

"Well, what do you see?"

"I see Egyptian police herding tourists into buses. I guess they want to clear the plateau. The big blonde she-wolf of the SS is having an animated conversation with one of the police. I can't make out much without binoculars."

"Well that's good news."

"I also hear the pumps working and see the water level rising rapidly in the moat. Some guys in protective gear like atmospheric diving suits are entering the pyramid."

"Damn! It sounds like we're close to Zero Hour."

"Closer than you think. The capstone has started to lower."

"The capstone is coming down!" Melissa informed Frank.

"Right. Let me know when it touches."

"Wait," said Faro, "If I'm seeing things correctly, it seems like the fill rate and the lowering of the capstone are in sync. It looks like, from here, that the capstone is going to touch just as the water rushes into the entrance to power up the Death Star. Get ready."

Chapter 113

"Now! Now!" Shouted Faro.

At precisely 6:34 p.m. Jakarta time, a 6.3 earthquake struck west northwest of Tobelo, Indonesia in the Maluku Islands. Rumblings under the plateau and across the desert indicated the Death Star was operative.

Melissa pointed and nodded at Frank. He switched on the phase conjugator.

"My feet are still tremblingggg..." sang Faro.

Melissa spoke into the phone, "We're working on it!"

Suddenly everything stopped. The Nazis, of a sudden confounded by this unexpected turn of events, stood dumbfounded staring quizzically at each other.

Around the globe, world leaders were in a rarely harmonious conference call. They had put their best and most secret scientists and resources to work.

Secret scientists you ask? Yes. There is public consumption science, the dead-end science of relativity and Darwinism, and then there is the closely held secret science of torsion physics, neuron microtubule quantum consciousness, and the plasma Universe. They had all confirmed the horrifying truth—earthquake causing technology did exist, and it seemed to be coming from Egypt! Putting two and two together, they concluded it must be the Giza Death Star! It had caught them off guard.

China, Russia, the United States, Great Britain, and Japan, all agreed to immediately dispatch rapid response forces.

"Shouldn't we clear it with the UN first?"

"There's no time. Anyway, these perpetrators are not a sovereign state. They're an extraterritorial entity."

"Still, we're sending forces into a sovereign state."

"Alert the relevant parties in Egypt to the operation a few minutes before contact. Tell them it's not an attack on them but only on the fiends who are perpetrating this horror."

"We need codes so that our forces don't interfere with each other. This is a superb opportunity for international cooperation."

"Agreed. Let's immediately notify the generals in charge to contrive the codes that will enable cooperation, en route if necessary." The Leaders were gesturing frantically to their aides to initiate contact with the generals.

Troops were mobilized and rushed dutifully to their transports, already live and being loaded with gear.

Chapter 114

"Dammit! Try harder!" Müller shouted at Richter. He'd pressed a com button on the side of his helmet that Thorny and One Flare hadn't noticed during their escapade.

"It's not a matter of trying harder. Someone is dampening our resonance! And we can't change the resonance of the Death Star itself! It must operate off 440 Hertz!"

"Who could do such a thing?"

"Anyone who can build a phase conjugator to cancel it out," Richter shrugged.

"Faro!"

Müller pressed the button again but this time addressed Edda, "Edda, someone is dampening the frequency with another conjugator. They must be nearby. Find them!"

"Jawohl! I know just where to look!"

Edda sprinted to the storage shed where Georgeann was squirming against her bonds. Georgeann's eyes widened with alarm when she saw Edda come in. Edda shot daggers back. She pulled a knife from its scabbard and hovered over her hostage. She hoisted her up on her feet by the collar and was about to carelessly cut the tape from her mouth when a bone-chilling howl on the plateau stopped her. She dropped Georgeann back to the floor.

And there it was, just when the Nazis were at peak confusion, a wall of sand 1000 feet high roared in on a wrathful wind that froze the Nazis' blood solid in their veins and seared their icy hearts with agonizing fire.

And charging out of the front of this wall of sand, sporting scarlet headbands and their fierce black mains blown around their faces by the wind were Daryl and his warriors, driven by the spirits of their fearless ancestors!

They pounced on their blind, unwitting foe, slashing wildly with their knives, silently claiming the souls of the damned. The dust soon enveloped the entire company and their foe fired aimlessly into the dust unable to see their phantom attackers, hitting each other with their own bullets more often than not.

Just behind them, Thorny, One Flare, Carrie and Mary, made their way to the shed to set up the tanks of hydrogen. They paused momentarily in the doorway as they spotted Georgeann and rushed to free her.

Georgeann spit the rag out of her mouth. "Blecch! What was on that rag? Anyone got a mint?" She panted, "You got here just in time!" She adjusted her position so Carrie could better access the ropes with her knife. "I think that big blonde Nazi bitch was just about to kill me, or something. Thanks for the help," She continued as her limbs were freed.

One Flare produced a hotel mint from his pocket and held it out.

"Thanks!"

"Always be prepared. You learn that in Scouts."

"We wouldn't mind your help either," stated Thorny.

"Yeah," added Carrie. "You up to moving these tanks?"

"I'm up to anything that'll bring these monsters down."

"Good. Get in line."

The five of them formed a chain from the shed to the sandbag wall and passed the tanks along Thorny to One Flare to Georgeann to Mary to Carrie who placed them strategically in a mass against it. Occasionally, they dodged bullets.

"Quick, now let's get these crates against the tanks."

"What's that for?" asked Georgeann.

"Tamping. You have to tamp the explosion if it's going to work."

"Well then how did Timothy McVeigh's truck blow up the Murrah Build....Ohhh!"

The five of them struggled with the heaviest of the crates and stacked them against the tanks as the battle raged around them.

Just then Greaves pulled up next to Faro. "How'd you find me?"

"Concentric rings."

Frank pressed the button and the machinegun rose into position. Faro took his place and braced himself. Frank floored the accelerator and the Rover lurched forward spraying sand and a cloud of dust behind it.

The storm Daryl and his men had created started to clear. Bodies littered the plateau, and the crooked Egyptian police who had assisted the Nazis were beginning to flee the scene.

Edda shouted at them, "Come back here you cowards! Dogs! Schweinhunds!"

Daryl and his men closed in on the hardcores who remained and who kept up a brisk fire.

"To the catwalk!" Ordered Edda, as cool as ever. "Move into the pyramid!"

Mr. Silva was the first on the bridge and laid down covering fire for the others to get up the stairs. It was at that moment that Faro and Greaves roared in on the Rover. The .50 Caliber sprayed incendiary rounds at the combatants as well as at the sandbags, weakening the structure. Water trickled through the leaks and soon became large sprays dousing everyone within a few feet of the wall.

As Greaves maneuvered the Rover, Faro spotted the tanks between the crates and the wall.

"Stop here!"

Greaves hit the brakes as Faro practically endoed into the front seat.

"Easy, Big Fella!"

"What?"

"Watch this."

Faro took careful aim. Up on the catwalk, Silva saw what was going on. He dashed and then dove for the pyramid entrance. The Doc blasted a stream of incendiaries into the mass of hydrogen tanks and in a few seconds "KA-BLAM!"

Debris, sand, cloth, tools, bits of steel flew

everywhere. Thorny, One Flare, Georgeann, Carrie and Mary were seen diving behind the shed. A great ball of fire erupted and water gushed out of the breach in the sandbags which were then plowed away by the immense current. Edda and her gang were caught up and carried along like rafters upended in a rapid.

The water rushed out of the drain valve below the pyramid creating a powerful suction that swept along the technicians in their protective suits, through the valve, along the tunnel and into the Nile.

Without the water powering it now, the Giza Death Star was overwhelmed by Frank's conjugator and began to rumble unsteadily. Inside the interferometer, that is the King's Chamber, the ceiling stones began to crack and drop debris on Richter and Müller. They dove for cover into the resonance chamber, known to most people as the sarcophagus. They were just in time as a large slab of granite came down on top of it.

Mr. Silva was stuck in the ascending passage, clinging to the floor for dear life as crystals shook loose from their nooks and the Helmholtz resonators separated and rolled towards him. Reflexively, he rolled to one side and effectively dodged them.

Faro took out his phone, "Turn it off!" He yelled at Melissa. "You'll bring the whole thing down!"

"Isn't that what we want?"

"No! It's a cultural treasure and important link to our dim past! We'll never get the answers we want if it's completely destroyed! WHY AM I HAVING TO EXPLAIN THIS???"

"Turn it off! Turn it off!" Melissa repeated to Frank who switched off his device.

The rumbling stopped and Faro heaved a sigh of relief. The five behind the shed stood up and dusted themselves off. They stared in awe at the wreckage and bodies around them. Thorny put a hand on One Flare's shoulder and looked him squarely in the eyes.

"We really shook the pillars of Heaven, didn't we Wang?"

One Flare let out a deep belly laugh and answered, "No horseshit, Jack. No horseshit."

Mary came up to One Flare and put her arm around his waist. Indicating the pyramid with her lips she quipped, "Yep. Low tech does beat high tech."

"Every time."

The group embraced each other, then the two couples stood with their arms around each other's waists taking in all that was around them. Faro and Greaves drove up.

"We best skee-daddle," commented Faro. "Best to let someone else take the credit for this." He gestured to Daryl who gestured in kind to his men, and they melted into the desert.

Chapter 115

An Egyptian navy boat on the Nile was scooping up the technicians, still in their diving suits, to the distant chop of helicopters descending on the plateau from all directions. US, British, Japanese, Chinese, and Russian rapid deployment forces were arriving just in time to take the credit. They scooped up any Nazis nearby their landing positions as other forces closed in on the pyramid.

Edda hung her head as she was taken into custody, then glanced longingly at the megalith. The leaders of the forces met peacefully and professionally for a palaver and manly pointing. After a brief inspection and the bodies were bagged, the all-clear was given. They departed as they had come, leaving the clean up for local authorities.

Chapter 116

They rendezvoused at the airport. A C-130 was thundering on the runway.

"How'd you manage this?" hollered Faro.

"I know everyone," shouted Greaves and steered the Rover up the ramp into the cargo bay. Everyone else followed as they arrived.

Twenty-four hours later they emerged to a soft gentle snowfall. They scrambled for warmer clothes in their baggage.

Daryl and his men stood there shaking their heads and pointing with ironic derision.

"You white guys were always such pussies," he chuckled.

Thorny gave One Flare the movie line gesture. "A brave man likes the feel of nature on his face."

"Yeah, and a wise man has enough sense to protect himself from the cold and snow," responded One Flare. It wasn't exactly what Egg Shen said in the movie, but it fit the situation.

"Next lesson for you guys is body control," added Greaves good-naturedly. "But right now I am way too bushed myself to pull it off." And he pulled on a coat.

A little while later they found themselves at Dr. Faro's favorite steak and buffet.

"It's all on me folks! Still some of that Bitcoin left! Just don't fill up on the bread. That's how they getchya."

They gathered their steaks and sides. They piled their plates precariously with salads, potatoes, cooked vegetables, dinner rolls, sliced baguettes, golden kernels of corn, and everything else they found.

"Well, Giuseppe, after that adventure I can't wait for a nice vacation back at the University working!"

Faro laughed, "Home just in time for Christmas too."

"I think I'll make it a quiet holiday this year."

"What'll you boys do?"

"Heading back East," One Flare said smiling at Mary.

"Gotta introduce the family," Thorny added with a glint at Carrie.

Frank raised a glass. "Here's to the defeat of the forces of evil."

They all raised their glasses in turn as Faro added ominously, "You can never defeat evil, folks, not completely."

Thorny gestured to One Flare that he was about to give another line from a movie but Melissa interrupted.

"I've got this one. 'God bless us, everyone!'"

Cheerful laughter rang about the group.

Chapter 117

That night, Müller recovered consciousness. Using the additional strength of the suit, he heaved the chunk of granite that trapped him in the sarcophagus aside. Richter wasn't stirring. He hoisted him out, removed the helmet, and tried to revive him, but to no avail.

He removed his own suit and made his way to the descending passage. He was just in time to see Mr. Silva emerge from behind a large white ball, one of the Helmholtz resonator components. Together they limped out of the pyramid and quietly made their way off the plateau.

They managed to find a car parked a few miles away. Müller hotwired it.

"Well, Mr. Silva, our transportation."

They drove on in silence for a few minutes when Müller remarked cheerfully, "Good to be alive, eh, Mr. Silva?"

"Feliz Navidad."

"Feliz Navidad, Mr. Silva. Feliz Navidad."

Afterword

Nonfiction Works by Dr. Joseph P. Farrell in suggested reading order:

- *The Giza Death Star* *

- *The Giza Death Star Deployed* *

- *Reich of the Black Sun* *

- *The Giza Death Star Destroyed* *

- *The SS Brotherhood of the Bell* *

- *The Cosmic War* *

- *Secrets of the Unified Field* *

- *The Philosophers' Stone*

- *The Nazi International* *

- *Babylon's Banksters*

- *Roswell and the Reich*

- *LBJ and the Conspiracy to Kill Kennedy*

- *Genes, Giants, Monsters and Men*

- *The Grid of the Gods*, with Dr. Scott D. de Hart

- *Saucers Swastikas and Psyops*

- *Yahweh the Two-Faced God: Theology, Terrorism, and Topology*, with Dr. Scott D. de Hart (Amazon Kindle e-book)

- *Transhumanism: A Grimoire of Alchemical Altars and Agendas for the Transformation of Man* (with Dr. Scott D de Hart, 2012)

- *Yahweh the Two-Faced God: Theology, Terrorism, and Topology* (Lulu Print-on-demand book, 2012)

- *Covert Wars and Breakaway Civilizations: The Secret Space Program, Celestial Psyops, and Hidden Conflicts* (2012)

- *The Financial Vipers of Venice: Alchemical Money, Magical Physics, and Banking in the Middle Ages and Renaissance (2013)*

- *Covert Wars and the Clash of Civilizations: UFOs, Oligarchs, and Space Secrecy* (2013)

- *Talk Radio for the Eyes: Transhumanism in Dialogue;* with Dr. Scott D. de Hart (2013)

- *Thrice Great Hermetica and the Janus Age: Hermetic Cosmology, Finance, Politics and Culture in the Middle Ages through the Late Renaissance*(2014)

- *The Third Way: The Nazi International, The European Union, and Corporate Fascism* (2015)*

- *Rotten to the (Common) Core: Public Schooling, Standardized Tests, and the Surveillance State* (2016)

- *Hidden Finance, Rogue Networks, and Secret Sorcery: the Fascist International, 9/11, and Penetrated Operations* *

- *Hess and the Penguins: The Holocaust, Antarctica, and the Strange Case of Rudolf Hess*

Dr. Farrell's Website: https://gizadeathstar.com/

Indicates books that directly inspired The Giza Death Star Restored.

CPSIA information can be obtained
at www.ICGtesting.com
Printed in the USA
FFHW010740180319
51130110-56568FF

9 781797 497976